DEDICATION

*This one is for Samantha and Krystle,
for always believing in me.*

CONTENTS

ACKNOWLEDGMENTS

I'd like to thank my husband for knowing when to give me space and quiet time to pace, mutter, and hammer furiously at the keyboard. This kind of support is one of the most important when the muse comes to town.

I would like to thank my experts: John Spencer, Amanda Whitwell, Marsha VanHoutte, and James E. Warner, III, for their willingness to inform me on methodology and legalities without asking for details as to why I want to know. Stay close, ladies and gentlemen. I will be calling on you again. Muahaha.

A few other people who have cheered me on and supported me every step of the way deserve a special thanks, as well. In no particular order: Cheryl Hall, Stephanie Heskew, Amy Burch, Gina Leeds, Erin Rychalsky, Kathy Lapeyre, and Kelli Smith, along with the zens, rejects and fancrushers of my world. Ladies and gentlemen, each and every one of you rock. Seriously.

I would also like to thank each and every one of my readers – YOU – for giving me the drive to continue on. Seeing your emails and your comments on my Facebook page, asking when the next book will be out or expressing how much you enjoyed reading my stories, that means the world to me. So thank you for continuing to read my writings. I started this journey alone, for me, but I continue it now, with you.

At the end there is a short excerpt from *The Boomerang Effect*. If you've read it already, refresh your memory; if you haven't read it yet, I invite you to pick up a copy and get ready for the sequel. I anticipate bringing that to you in 2014!

A couple of the stories contained herein can also be found in compilation anthologies produced with other authors:

"The Watcher" can be found in an anthology called "Stalkers," produced by Cynthia Shepp and Rene Folsom.

"The End – Or Is It?" can be found in "Horrors of History – an Anthology by Fey Publishing" as well as "Anything Goes," an anthology put together by the Anything Goes Authors Group.

As a final note, I'd like to remind everyone that these stories are fictional. One story is based on a true life event, the tornado that ripped through the heart of Oklahoma in May of 2013. The similarity in my story stops there. Everything contained within is a fabrication of how events might have gone; I was not there, I do not know. What I know is what I have seen of the damage in person as well as over and over on the television, as we watched the clips of the horrific event for days afterward. My heart goes out to those affected by every tornado that terrorizes and takes from people in the Midwest every year. As for the rest of these stories, the characters and situations are all figments of my imagination. If you think I modeled one of them after you, take a look in the mirror. Do you see it there, too? Do you like what you see? Food for thought.

GARDEN OF EDEN

The sound of the chain saw pierced my brain, drilling tiny little holes in it that once again I'd have to try to fill with Excedrin. The new neighbor, only known as Mr. X to me, had moved in several weeks ago and had been quiet up until last weekend.

I didn't realize the noise had quit until he pulled the handle again and fired that thing back to life. Gripping the arm of my chair for control, I held on until my sudden rush of hatred for him subsided and I could be reasonably sure I'd head for the kitchen instead of the gun safe.

Grabbing a glass from the cabinet, I filled it with water from the tap. I'd bought this house partly because it was away from the busier sections of town, and partly because it had a well. Well water was the best.

Reaching into the drawer, I shoved the menagerie of miscellaneous items aside: pens, paper clips, rubber band ball, reading glasses, spare keys to long-forgotten locks, a screwdriver, and something fuzzy though not warm, until I found the bottle. Quickly I shook two pills into my hand and tossed them back, drowning them with water.

Once again the noise climbed inside my head through my ears, invading my brain. Leaning back against the counter I pinched the bridge of my nose between forefinger and thumb, trying to relieve the pressure.

Writing a novel was hard enough without the incessant interruptions foisted on a person by everyday life. Moving to the edge of town, at the end of a long dirt road, should have negated the need for noise-canceling headphones. Apparently that was not the case.

While I waited for the promise on the back label of the bottle to be fulfilled I looked out the window toward Mr. X's house. I couldn't see him or any activity at all from where I stood. All I could see was the side of his house, one window covered by what appeared to be a lacy curtain, and part of the backyard. The way the houses had been built afforded a modicum of privacy. Part of the charm when the realtor had shown me this one came from knowing the neighbors would not be able to look in my windows while standing in their own homes. Some of the housing additions being built these days had that against them, and I wanted no part of it. The older I get, the more reclusive I become, and the fewer people I want to see. I wondered idly if everyone felt the same way as they aged. *Apparently not*, I decided, *the way people throw parties and actually invite other people to their houses. Maybe it's just me.*

The chain saw fired to life again, and the fluttering of the curtain in his window caught my attention. I rubbed my eyes and looked again. No, the noise was definitely coming from inside his house. Once again the noise quit, and when it started again the curtain waved at me. Mr. X was using a chain saw *inside* his house, in what I imagined was his kitchen, or dining room. I didn't know if the floor plan was the same as mine, reversed, or something else entirely.

What in the world would someone be doing that required the use of a chain saw in the house? My brain couldn't quite wrap around the concept. *If I could only see better, maybe I could find out,* I thought, the irony of the situation not lost on me. I moved out here for privacy, yet here I was contemplating which box hadn't been unpacked yet that would most likely contain my binoculars.

Torn with indecision, I stayed where I was. If I hadn't, I wouldn't have seen Mr. X pull the curtain back and look directly at me as if he were reading my thoughts. I jerked back from the window, my hand flying to my chest as if to hold in my heart. It was pounding hard enough to jump out, that's for sure. *You're an idiot, and this is ridiculous,* I chastised myself. *He was kinda freaky, though, yanking that curtain back and popping into view the way he did;* I thought in my own defense. *Great, now you're having conversations with yourself, in addition to the ones with your mom. If anyone could hear you, they'd have you committed.*

My internal conversation continued as it so often does, while I went on to other things like edging back toward the window. The curtain was closed again, and this time the window was too.

An unexpected knock on the front door echoed through the almost-empty living room and scared the beejeebers out of me when I heard it. I jumped back from the window a second time in as many minutes. My hand was still on my heart, and I felt it skip a beat. *For the love of Pete, I can't take much more of this,* I told myself.

The knock came again, a little more forcefully this time as if the person on the other side of the door knew I was in here. But how could that be, unless... I swallowed audibly. Unless it was HIM.

Stop being a baby and answer the door. I didn't mind my mother's voice being stuck in my head, but she didn't have to be mean to me. A baby, indeed. I'm a full grown woman who can make her own decisions.

I marched myself over to the door and managed to grasp the doorknob on the first try. Before I could talk myself out of it, I opened the door and stood face to face with Mr. X.

He grinned sheepishly and shuffled back a step. "I'm sorry to bother you. I thought I was the only one home on this end of the block." Was this his way of apologizing for scaring ten years off of my life? He could use a refresher course. His dark brown hair was short, reminiscent of the military buzz cut I'd seen my dad wear for so many years, his brown eyes a shade darker than his hair. He stood about even with me, and I was five foot four flat-footed. Being that I was currently standing up one step from him, I guessed his height to be around six feet even or so.

I must have been looking at him with my "what are you doing on my porch" look because he shuffled his feet again, his loafers making a whispering noise across the wood deck. "I just wanted to apologize. I saw you in the window, and I thought... well, I thought I was alone down here. I'm sorry for the noise." The dimple flashed in his cheek when he smiled. "Well, okay then, I'll just be going..."

My mother's voice inside my head chimed in. *Invite him in, don't be rude. If he were over there cutting up body parts with a chain saw in his kitchen he wouldn't have come over here to apologize for the noise, and he'd be covered in blood. Child, I taught you better.*

I mentally rolled my eyes at her and reached for the latch on the screen door. "Would you like to come in? I have iced tea."

He stopped and turned back to face me. "Um, if it isn't too much trouble, that would be nice. Thank you." As he reached for the screen door handle I caught sight of a band-aid on his left hand. Blood had seeped through the padding and darkened it to a deep brown color.

As I backed away to let him in, I looked around my living room and sighed internally. "I'm sorry for the mess." It was true; the place was a disaster area. I'd been working on a new storyline for the past week, and all of the notes I'd jotted on pages that had taken me wrong directions had been crumpled up and thrown at the miniature basketball net hanging over the trash can. Let's just say I could play for the Chicago Bulls most days. Potato chip bags and cookie wrappers were strewn around my chair and couch, scattered in among to-go containers from various fast food places. The pizza box from last night's dinner was still open and on the floor. I didn't look back at him to see if he was appalled; I'm pretty sure I would be if it were me looking at this pigsty for the first time.

"Do you take your tea sweet or un-sweet?" I asked over my shoulder as I led the way to the kitchen.

"Un-sweet." He replied, his voice directly behind me. For the third time today, I jumped.

"Oh! I'm a little jumpy today. You'll have to excuse that, too. I'm working on a new novel, and when I immerse myself in my writing I tend to bring it with me in my head when I come back out of it." *That's a lame excuse.* I knew it was thin, but it's all I had on short notice.

"I'm sorry, too."

What an odd thing for him to say. I was almost afraid to turn around. I was sure he brought a kitchen knife and was going to kill me here in my own house before dragging me back to his, to cut me up and stuff me in the freezer or down the garbage disposal. "Have a seat, I'll get the tea. What brings you to this little corner of heaven? The realtor that sold me this house said your house had been for sale for over a year without even a looker. I had no idea it sold. Guess if I'd have paid attention I would have noticed the sign was gone."

He perched half on, half off the barstool closest to the end of the counter. "I didn't buy it, the management company leased it to me on an open-end contract while I'm in town. I can't imagine why it hasn't sold, there doesn't seem to be anything wrong with it." He took the glass I passed to him.

I leaned against the counter and made a mental note that he hadn't answered my first question. I tried again. "Are you in town on business, then?" *What kind of business could someone who used a chain saw in their kitchen be on, Miss Smarty Pants?* I tried not to let expressions show on my face in response to my mother's quips.

"Yes, business." Looking down into his glass, he swirled the ice around and around, a frown crossing his face. He still hadn't answered my question. I didn't want to let it go, but I did anyway.

I stuck my hand out. "My name is Sara. What's yours?"

After wiping the glass sweat from his hand, he grasped mine. "Bill." His grip was firm, almost too firm. He held on too tightly for a beat too long before releasing. I looked him in the eye and smiled what I hoped was a carefree smile. His eyes were flat, and his own smile wasn't reaching them at all. My heart stuttered in my chest while adrenaline poured into my system. Red flags shot up all over the place. These weren't good feelings. All of a sudden my kitchen was entirely too small.

"It's a great day outside, want to sit on the porch?" I had to get some air or I was afraid I was going to pass out. Funny, I've never been the "Nervous Nellie" type. I didn't wait for him to agree, just grabbed my tea and made a beeline for the door.

I pushed through the screen door. When it should have crashed back against the door jamb, it didn't. I turned to sit in one of the two padded deck chairs and saw him standing in the opening, an unsure look on his face.

"Join me?" I motioned toward the other chair. I took a slow, deep breath. The suffocation I felt moments ago in my own kitchen dissipated with the breeze.

It's all in your head.

Hush, Mom.

Bill took several hesitant steps and perched stiffly on the edge of the remaining chair. "I feel as though I should explain," he began. "I don't often meet new people or get to know strangers at all. That was my wife's lot in life. She was the social butterfly. Any time we moved or anyone else moved in or out of the neighborhood, she was the one who went over and introduced herself, told them about us, found out everything there was to know about the new neighbors, arranged the pool parties, card games... I'm not like that." He stared off into the distance. "When she... during the last few weeks of her life she was in and out of the present, sometimes living in her childhood, sometimes with me. During one of her last lucid periods, she made me promise..."

Way to make a guy uncomfortable. I reached across and put my hand on his arm. "I'm sorry for your loss." It's not the phrase we're supposed to say, mostly because it doesn't help, but what else can be said when it's two strangers and the revelation is out of the blue?

He jerked his arm away as if I'd burned him and shot up off of the chair. "No, I'm sorry. This isn't how it's supposed to go. I wish she were here. She was the one who knew how to do this. I shouldn't have come." He stood, swaying. "I promised, but I'm not... not ready… to do this, to meet people." He took off down the steps and power walked across the yard, not slowing until he reached his own front door.

My heart was too busy breaking for him to call out or stop him. My mother had passed away just over two years ago, and I still missed her every day; I couldn't imagine what it would be like to lose a spouse. I picked up both of our glasses and took them back inside.

As I loaded the dishwasher, my mind turned to the story I had been working on and the scene that would need to take place next. I'd been unsure how to get where I'd been going when, as it usually happened, the wall crumbled and the storyline was clear in my brain. I rushed to my chair and my laptop, typing as fast as I could to keep up with what my brain was churning out.

~~*~*~*

The pain in my back forced me to stop writing. I leaned back and relaxed, the pain radiating from my lower back all the way up to my neck and down into my legs.

The clock said 9:40. No wonder my back hurts. I'd been writing non-stop for hours.

A groan escaped my lips as I stood. Sitting in one position for any length of time had been hard for me since the car accident; lucky to be alive, yet paying for it every day. I rolled my head from side to side, my neck crackling with each movement.

My stomach reminded me that it had been hours since I'd eaten. Saving my work, I picked up the empty wrappers and cups that were within reach as I worked my way to the kitchen. No way could I bend over right now to get the rest off the coffee table or the floor, those would have to wait.

Dumping the empties in the trash, I looked out the window and saw a light. The curtains were open. He passed by the window carrying... something. A leg? Surely not.

That's your writer's brain making things sinister, you know it is.

It's not always my brain, mom.

Really? What are you writing in there? You just blew up an oil refinery and had body parts flying through the air... tell me that's not your writer's brain landing a leg in his kitchen.

I harumphed out loud. She was probably right. I did just kill about eighty people. On paper, though. *They don't normally fly out of my computer in 3D.*

Don't you sass me young lady.

He walked back past the window, then again carrying a glass and a bottle of wine.

See there, people carrying body parts don't go back for wine.

Okay, alright, mom.

I threw a sandwich together and took it into the living room. My back gave a twinge when I looked at the computer chair. *Not a chance*, it said. I opted for the couch and picked up the remote. Channel surfing and I were old friends; we'd spent many a night together, waiting for my subconscious to come up with the solution to whatever situation I was writing at the time.

As I watched a rerun of... whatever this show was called... my eyes grew heavy. The bedroom seemed like a long way away, so I snuggled down on the couch instead. *Just a little nap and then I'll write some more.*

When I opened my eyes the sun was just coming up, the light filtered through my opaque curtains chasing the shadows into the corners. *Coming up? I slept through the night?*
You slept through the night. You needed it.
Hi mom.
I sat up and stretched, testing my back. Sometimes a good night's sleep helped, sometimes sleeping on the couch didn't. This morning it felt pretty good. With a sigh of relief, I got up and headed for the shower.

After I'd cleaned up and thrown some clothes on, I headed back toward the kitchen to get the coffee pot going. As the machine gurgled and the water trickled through, I looked out the window. Bill's house looked like it, and everything in it, was still asleep. I found myself hoping he was enjoying as restful a night as I'd had.

Not much to do while the coffee brewed, I wandered around picking up the trash I hadn't last night and straightened the rest of the living room.

When the coffee was ready I poured a cup and savored the first sip while leaning against the kitchen counter; the first was always the best. I carried my cup with me to the computer and got ready for another day of either writing or banging my head on the desk, I didn't know which yet.

As was my habit, I read back through the last couple of pages to get the flow of where I'd gone and where I was going. The story sparked again, though not as strong or as fast, but it was going so I picked up where I'd left off and wrote.

A knock on the door brought me out of the world I'd created and back into the real one. I saved my work and got up to answer it. Pulling the small curtain back along the side panel window I saw it was Bill.

I opened the door. "Hi, Sara."

"Hi, Bill."

"Listen, I wanted to apologize for yesterday..."

"It's okay, really, you don't have to."

"Yes, I do."

Invite him in, honey.

I'm trying to write, mom. You know how hard it is to get the muse back once she's gone.

She'll be back. Live life in the moment and write about it later.

I looked at him for a second. "Would you like to come in?"

He smiled. "That would be nice."

Pushing the screen door open, I motioned toward the kitchen. "Would you like some coffee? I was about to get another cup myself."

"Sure."

He followed me into the kitchen and perched on the same stool as yesterday.

"Cream? Sugar?"

"Just black is fine. Thank you."

I handed him his cup and leaned back against the counter, blowing across the top of my own.

He wrapped his hands around the cup and looked down into his coffee as if he were reading tea leaves. "I want... I *need* to apologize for yesterday. I don't want to get off on the wrong foot, and I'm pretty sure I came off as a whacko. As I said, I'm not used to being the one to meet new people first; my wife, Eden, died this past year, and the promise I made to her is important for me to keep. She was worried that I would turn into a hermit, a recluse, and pull away from society altogether. She's right. If she hadn't made me promise, that's exactly what I would have done. But she did, and I did, so..."

I wasn't sure if he was thinking or if he wanted me to fill the silence, so I let it go on.

"So, I was wondering, could we start over?" He looked up, unsure.

Reaching my hand out, I said, "Hi, my name is Sara. What's yours?"

The tension drained from his face and he stood, reaching his hand out. "Hi, Sara, I'm Bill, your new neighbor."

"Hi, Bill."

The silence returned. At this point, I knew it was up to me to keep the conversation going. "So what brings you to Aspen Grove, Bill?"

"Work."

The conversation was back to pulling teeth. "What do you do for work?"

"I'm a district manager. I oversee the company's branches for the entire western half of the United States. Sometimes I travel a lot, sometimes I end up staying in one place for months at a time. I'm never sure until I arrive on location and have a chance to see what's going on at a particular site how long I'll be in any one place."

He relaxed a little as he talked. "What do you do, Sara?"

"I'm a writer."

"Really. What do you write?"

"Novels, short stories, that sort of thing. Occasionally, I write a piece for a magazine or newspaper, but not often. That sort of writing is pressure-based and not really my cup of tea. I prefer to take my time and bang my head on the keyboard until the thoughts pour out." I smiled, though it was more truth than fiction, the banging of the head.

He smiled back. "Do you hold down a daytime job or is your writing lucrative enough to allow you the freedom to bang your head on the keyboard whenever you like?"

I almost choked on my coffee. Humor, I hadn't expected. "I'll never be rich, but writing keeps me in groceries. I don't work a regular job anymore. I can't. I was in a car accident a few years back. The other driver ran the red light and t-boned me, breaking my back in several places. I spent a long time in the hospital and in a body cast, and haven't been able to sit comfortably for any length of time ever since."

He frowned. "I'm sorry to hear that."

"Thanks. I'm okay most of the time. The jury went in my favor, and because of that I don't have to hold down a day job. I write to keep from going crazy. Once I started, I found I liked it, so I've kept on."

"That's good, then. Nice to have a hobby that keeps you out of the nuthouse." Bill emptied his cup.

I picked up the pot. "More?"

Holding up his hands, he said, "No, thank you. I should be getting back. I should prepare for tomorrow. Long day coming up, for me and for the employees who may have to be let go. Have a few more things to read over before I can go in."

He stood and made his way toward the front door. "Thank you for the coffee and for giving me a chance to apologize."

"You're welcome." I followed him and stood in the doorway as he stepped out. "See you later."

"Would you like to have dinner sometime?" He turned to face me, putting his hands up, palms out. "Neighborly."

Well, don't just stand there, let the poor guy off the hook. Look at that face, he's expecting you to say "no."

Mo-om....

"That would be nice. Sure."

"Okay, um, tomorrow night?"

"Tomorrow night it is. What time?"

"Could you come over around seven o'clock? I make a mean steak, and I'd love to break in the new grill out back."

Oh, right... he wasn't comfortable in a social setting. His place made sense. "Okay, seven o'clock, your place. I'll bring dessert." *Oh, jeez, that sounded like a come on.* "Do you like chocolate cake?" *Nice save.*

"Who doesn't?"

He did have a nice smile, with another flash of dimple.

"Great, see you then." I stood by the door until he was off the porch. He turned and raised a hand. I waved back, closing the door and leaning against it.

Do you have everything you need to bake a cake?

I'll just go buy one.

You'll do no such thing, young lady. You've got the best chocolate cake recipe in the state in that book I left you, and you'll use it.

Alright, okay.

That's better.

The rest of the day was a blur of words. They flowed smoothly, and I was happy with my progress. Any time the muse wrote like this it was best to let her. She didn't visit nearly often enough.

A pot of coffee and two hours later I stopped for a break, grabbed a bagel, piled it high with cream cheese and ate it over the sink. My back wasn't excited about the prospect of going back to the chair, so I picked up a pad of paper and a couple of pens and headed out to the porch for a different chair, different angle, different view.

Instead of writing, I spent more time watching a hawk circle lazily above the copse of trees across the road and several hummingbirds dip and dance, chasing each other away from the feeder. My mind wandered back to last night's encounter with Bill and then this morning's visit. He'd seemed like two different people. Maybe that was from doing something outside of his comfort zone, though something just felt a little bit off. I couldn't quite put my finger on it.

Regardless, it was time to get up and move around again. It seemed that my muse had gone on her way and left me with time to review what we'd written. Hopefully it would make sense and I'd be able to work with what was there. For now, though, I needed to finish the housework and get a load of laundry or two done, as well.

I finished frosting the cake and carefully set the cover in place. It looked really tasty. *If the cake tastes half as good as the frosting, I'll be in business,* I thought as I swiped my finger around the edge of the frosting bowl, scooping up a blob and popped it into my mouth, humming over the deliciousness.

I still needed to shower and dress before dinner. The clock confirmed I had plenty of time.

When I'd finished blow drying my hair, I combed it out and thought about leaving it loose. If this were a real date, I would, but since he'd said it was a 'neighborly' dinner I felt more casual about it. Grabbing a ponytail holder, I scooped my long hair back and up. These days I pretty much preferred to keep it pulled back away from my face while I was trying to write. It also gave me less chance of pulling it out from frustration.

I spent a couple minutes on eye shadow, mascara and lip gloss. My face didn't get make-up very often since I lived alone and had no need to work. I didn't bother keeping much of it around at all.

Slipping on my favorite pair of jeans and a pale blue button-down shirt, I called it good and went in search of my sandals. I found one under the couch. Fifteen minutes of searching did nothing to bring the other one to light; I gave up and put on my comfy old deck shoes.

Picking up the cake, I locked the door behind me, pocketed my keys and made my way carefully across the yards, carrying the cake with both hands. It wouldn't do to step in a gopher hole now and drop all of my hard work onto the lawn.

I climbed the couple of stairs to his porch and knocked. I could hear him inside and apparently he hadn't seen me coming; I heard a door slam, a crash, a muffled swear word and then, "Just a minute!"

Turning my back to the door gave me the opportunity not only to enjoy the view from his porch, but also hide my face until I could get the smile under control. Seemed it was my turn to startle him. It was more amusing from this side of the fence.

The door opened as I turned back. He was a bit disheveled; his hair sticking out in different directions, his face red and sweaty, and his clothes were rumpled. "Hi, come on in, I'll be right back," he said as he turned and headed down the hallway. "Please, make yourself comfortable!" he shouted from the back of the house.

The front door opened into the living room, as did mine, only his didn't have any pictures on the walls, and the only furniture was what appeared to be a thrift store couch and a matching end table/coffee table set across from a flat screen television that had been mounted to the opposite wall. From what I could see, the floor plan looked to be the reverse of how mine was set up, so I wandered through the doorway and into what should be the dining room. It was. The window with white curtains was there, as was a tree trunk being crudely carved into a statue. It stood on an upside down wooden crate and looked to be in the beginning stages of being turned into what might or might not be a bear. Or so I imagined. The migraine-inducing chain saw was sitting on the floor next to the crate, along with goggles, ear protectors, and work gloves.

Continuing on, I turned to the right and found his kitchen. It was as sparse as the rest of the house had been, with only the necessary stove and refrigerator. The counters held nothing at all, not even a dish drainer. If I were a gambler I'd have laid money on the cabinets being almost empty. I set the cake down on the counter and went back into the dining room, looking out the sliding glass door into the backyard. On the back porch stood a shiny gas grill and a small patio set overlooking pretty much the same view my house had—trees and more trees.

Bill was already apologizing as he came back down the hall and rounded the corner, straightening his clean shirt before running his hands over his still-wet hair. He must have taken the fastest shower on the planet. "I'm sorry I got sidetracked and didn't get back in time to have everything started before you arrived. I didn't even get my shower in until just a minute ago. I hope you don't mind."

He cleans up real nice, doesn't he?

Yes, mom, he does.

"I don't mind at all. I thought I wasn't going to make it on time. I got sidetracked with editing until about an hour ago myself, then had to frost the cake before I could get ready to come over."

Slipping an oven mitt on his hand, he opened the oven door and reached in, pressed down on two foil-wrapped potatoes and closed the door. Tossing the mitt on the counter, his gaze landed on the cake and I thought he was going to start drooling right then and there. "That looks really good. You know…" he stopped, raising one eyebrow as he looked at her. "My grandfather used to eat dessert first every night so that he was always sure he wouldn't get too full and run out of room. What do you think about following his lead?"

Your grandfather also liked his dessert first. I hadn't thought of that in years.

You never told me that. What a fun memory.

I laughed. "Your grandfather sounds like he was a smart man, and apparently had the same thought process as mine. I'm all for learning from our elders."

"Great! I'll get the plates if you'll get some forks and a knife out of that drawer right there," he said, pointing at the extra-wide drawer closest to me.

Pulling the drawer open I expected to see two forks and maybe a spoon. Much to my surprise, the drawer was not only filled with silverware in their own slotted tray. It also held a sectioned tray with larger utensils; spatulas, spoons, hand mixer, a hard-boiled egg slicer, melon baller, orange juicer, meat mallet and several other items that I had no idea of their intended use.

He caught me staring and explained. "Eden did the people meetings, and I was in charge of cooking for our dinner parties. I enjoy cooking, always did. It lets me feel like I'm still close to her, somehow." Reaching around me he pulled open the refrigerator, flipped over a marinade container and closed the door. "When I finally settle down somewhere I'll go for the appliances I want; for now, these will have to do. As long as I have my utensils I can make anywhere work."

He's single; he has a job, a hobby that keeps him at home, and he likes to cook. This just keeps getting better and better.

Hush, mom.

He held out the plates for me to take. "Okay, ready?"

I nodded and automatically reached for them. He picked up the cake holder and motioned toward the living room.

"I haven't bothered with a dining room table, so we'll be eating in the living room. Hope that doesn't bother you."

"Not at all." As we passed back through the dining room I asked about the wooden statue.

"That's a hobby of mine. There was a shop in Red River, New Mexico, that sold some like this when Eden and I took a vacation there a few years back. She thought they were cute and would have liked to bring one home, but there wasn't a way to get it home on the airplane and the cost of shipping something of this size and weight would have been outrageous, so we didn't buy one. I wanted to surprise her, so I took a class and figured out how to apply the techniques they taught to this, and eventually was able to make one for her. She was so thrilled I made her a whole family of them: papa bear, mama bear, and baby bear. I've still got the set I made for her. They're out back next to the porch where I can see them when I'm out there. Normally, I work on these outside, but the weatherman said there was a chance of rain and until I finish a piece and get the sealant on, I don't like for them to get wet, so I brought it inside."

I told you there was a good reason he was using a chain saw inside the house.

I still think it's weird, mom. A little bit, anyway. But he lives alone, so whatever.

I cut the cake and passed a plate to him. "That's very sweet."

"*This* is very sweet," he remarked as he forked a second bite into his mouth. "Actually, it's a slice of heaven."

"Thank you." I took another bite myself. Mom was right; this was definitely the best chocolate cake. I'd forgotten just how good it was. "It's my mom's recipe. She shared it with me before she passed away."

When we had finished our before-dinner dessert, Bill took the plates to the kitchen. "I'm going to step outside and start the grill. Be right back." The sliding glass door opened and closed.

I wandered back into the dining room for a better look at the bear. There was something a little bit off, a niggling in my brain, but once again I couldn't put my finger on it.

The door slid open again. "Would you mind taking the steaks out of the fridge and setting the container on the counter? They should have a little bit of time to lose some of their cold before I put them on the grill."

"Sure." I did as he asked and then stepped out through the back door.

"So what do you think of Aspen Grove so far?" I wandered toward the edge of the deck to look for his bear family.

"First impression, it's quiet. The people I've met so far have been polite, if not outwardly welcoming. Is this a close-knit town?"

"It was started by two families, and their bloodlines still live here, so in that sense it is though there are plenty of other people who have moved in and out since it was established around the time of the Land Run. I'm a transplant myself, so I only know what I've been told about the town history. There's a library in town if you like, though it's more of a bookmobile than a real brick and mortar building. The library in Oklahoma City may have more information on the history, but I haven't gone to look. The people here do keep their eyes open and especially with new arrivals. Once they're convinced you're not evil they'll move on to watching someone else. Of course that could take ten or twenty years."

He looked at me, his eyes flat, distant. "Small towns are so much different than big cities. I spent two years in Los Angeles and not one person looked twice at me."

I nodded. "Small towns are definitely different. It grows on you."

Bill slipped back inside the house and came back out with the steaks. His demeanor had been different again for just a minute there. He'd gone somewhere in his mind. I wondered what he'd been thinking.

"Are you ready to watch the master at work?" He grinned and with a flourish laid the steaks on the grate.

"*Yes* I am." I pulled out one of the patio chairs and made myself comfortable.

~~*~*~*

By the time dinner was ready the mosquitoes were coming out and looking at us like we'd be their dinner, so we ate in the living room.

When I'd finished, I laid the napkin down next to my plate and tried to contain an un-ladylike burp. I was successful, mostly. "That was a wonderful dinner, thank you Bill."

"I'm glad you enjoyed it. It's been a while since I've cooked a meal for someone else. I enjoyed it, too. Would you like a glass of wine?"

"Sounds good."

"Red or white?"

"Surprise me."

"I'll be right back."

While Bill was getting the wine, I cleaned up the coffee table, stacked plates and gathered napkins and silverware. I picked it all up and took the pile to the kitchen, intent on setting it in the sink. Bill had his back to me and was uncorking the bottle. I put the plates in the sink and wandered back toward the dining room.

At the same moment I heard the cork pop, the thing that was wrong hit me like a freight train and my heart sank like a rock. He'd been using the chain saw when I saw him through the window; he said he was working on the bear, yet *there was no sawdust.* Not even one tiny little piece, nothing. If he wasn't using the chain saw on the bear, *what was he using it on?*

By the edge of the crate was one tiny drop of darkness on the otherwise clean, tan carpet. Is that wine, or... *his thumb had a band-aid and there was blood soaking through...*

I remembered him walking past the window carrying what looked like a leg. All of a sudden I had a really bad feeling.

I'm sure there's an explanation.

I'm sure there is, too. I'm just not sure I want to know what it is.

I walked over to the window and pulled the curtain back, for all appearances looking out at the view and my own house, while in reality looking hard from the corner of my eye at the spot on the carpet.

"Here you go. I hope you like it."

I jumped and turned around, having not heard him come up directly behind me. I bumped the glass in his left hand and he bobbled it.

"Whoa, almost lost it. Are you okay?" The look on his face said he knew I'd put something together, though he wasn't sure what. Next move was mine.

Oh, Lordy. Keep cool, Sara, there's definitely something not quite right here. I've got the bad juju.

"Yes, you startled me. I didn't hear you walk up." I tried to paste an innocent look on my face. I couldn't tell if he was buying it or not.

"I tend to do that. Sorry." He held out a glass. "Try this. It's one of my favorites."

I took the glass, careful not to touch his hand. Raising it to my lips, I sipped. The flavor was wonderful. "This is really good, what is it?"

"Keenan Cabernet Sauvignon. The winery is near Napa Valley, and I tried this particular blend when…. back when I lived in California. I spent some time touring different wineries and kept coming back to this one."

I took another drink, rolling it around in my mouth. "I really do like this."

He smiled over his own glass then took a leisurely sip. The smile didn't reach his eyes. "I'm glad." He seemed to be waiting for something.

My vision blurred. *Oh crap.*

"Careful, there. You don't want to fall. This wine can make you a little dizzy if you aren't used to it. It's really good stuff." His eyes took on a shine. He gently held my elbow and helped me to the couch.

Setting the glass on the coffee table, I tried to get a grip on myself. My head was a little bit fuzzy. My vision blurry around the edges, and I wasn't in full control of my body.

"It must have reacted with my medication I take for my back. I'll be alright in a minute." I said, shaking my head to try and clear it.

You didn't take your medicine before you left the house. He drugged you.

I know mom. I want him to think I'm in worse shape than I am. I feel like I'm going to need every edge I can get.

Hang on, honey, shake it off. You didn't drink very much, and it won't last long. Keep your wits about you.

I'm trying.

"Let me get you a glass of water." He stood and went back toward the kitchen. As soon as he was around the corner, I stood up and faltered, tried to get my bearings and made my way toward the door. I was two steps away and started reaching my hand out when the hair on the back of my neck stood straight up. There wasn't any time between that and the shove I took from behind, slamming me into the closed door. I had been hoping I was wrong, half-convinced that my writer's mind had gone full-tilt into horror mode, and it was all in my head. Until now. As my face connected with the wood, I heard a crunching sound that could only be my nose breaking as pain shot across the middle of my face and stars exploded behind my eyes. I gasped as I bounced off the door and hit the floor, my heart pounding in my chest, unable to breathe. I could feel the blood pouring down my face and then down my throat, gagging me. The voice in my head was eerily quiet; either mom didn't know what to make of the situation or she'd been knocked unconscious. I didn't have much to say to me at the moment, either.

Whatever he'd given me was still holding on. I tried to reach up to touch my nose. My arms felt like lead. I could barely move at all. Through the tears pooling in my eyes I could barely make out the shimmering sight of a handkerchief coming toward my face.

"Let's clean this up a little. Blood is hard to get out of the carpet." He gently wiped the trail of blood that had made its way down my face and neck and into my hair, and was probably starting to pool around my head, judging from the amount I felt I was losing.

I tried to speak, but it came out in a gurgle. He situated himself behind my head and lifted me at the shoulders. "Here, let's get you somewhere that you can sit up, we can't have you drowning in my entryway." With that, he dragged me backwards, toward the door to the garage.

The hinges squeaked when he opened the door. A light came on overhead, and his hands grasped me under my arms, pulling me slowly down a wooden set of stairs. Thump, thump, thump, gently as if he didn't want to hurt me. After the fifth or sixth stair a bare light bulb came into my line of view, swinging gently above the top steps.

My body was tingling as I fought to remain motionless. If it was waking up, and I would be regaining control of it soon, I didn't want to give that away to him. Let him think I was still fully immobile.

We reached the bottom of the stairs. He turned left, continuing to drag me across the room. There were shelves along the wall across from me, but the light wasn't bright enough down here for me to see what was in the jars and cans stacked on them. The cement floor was cool to the touch. *At least I could feel that*, I thought.

Mom? Are you there?

Nothing. For the first time since right after she had passed I didn't get a response when I called her. *Now's not the time to leave me, mom. I need you. I can't do this myself.*

Bill—if that was his real name, which it probably wasn't, because right now I didn't think him lying was any stretch of the imagination—propped me up against the far wall and steadied me so I was sitting upright. I allowed my head to fall forward and tried to stay as still as possible without using my muscles. I knew my life depended on it. I write about stuff like this; it's not supposed to actually happen.

My face was still transforming from the hit; I could feel both eyes swelling shut. The tears were streaming down my face, mixing with the blood from my nose and soaking into my shirt, ruining it. Madness bubbled up, and I almost laughed out loud at the thought. *NO, don't lose control, you can't afford that right now. Get a hold of yourself.* I mentally slapped myself and clung tight to the edges of sanity with my fingernails, digging in hard.

I realized the concrete floor was cool to the touch. I felt it through my jeans. That was a good sign. Feeling was coming back.

Mr. X's shoes and pant legs came back into my line of sight. He squatted down and used an elastic cord tie down to strap me upright to the wall and hold me in place. Apparently there were some sort of hooks or something embedded in the wall behind me that he used; I wondered idly if I was his first victim or if someone else had been in this very spot before me. He hadn't been in this house for very long, and I'd not seen anyone coming or going. That doesn't make any difference. I hadn't seen him coming or going until I heard the damn chain saw... *Oh my God, the chain saw...*

A gasp escaped and I covered it with a cough, hacking up blood into my mouth. At least the blood wasn't running down my throat anymore. My shirt was ruined anyway. I let the blood run out of my mouth, pushing it out with my tongue. *Oh, yuck. I don't know how vampires do it. That was disgusting.*

Stop it! You can't do this right now, hang on Sweetie.

Mom!! Where have you been? I'm so scared!

I went home to set off the burglar alarm; the police should be on their way.

I didn't turn it on before we came over here, how did you set it off?

That's what took so long. Do you have any idea how hard it is to affect real world things when you're in the in-between? I had to use my energy to throw things at the panel and hit the correct numbers in the correct order to set it. Then I had to wait for the motion detector to engage. After that, I had to throw something through the beam's view. I waited to make sure the phone would ring, that the alarm company was calling to check on it before I came back.

Mom, the chain saw... and the leg...

Mr. X stood up and took a few steps back, standing there looking down at me. "That should hold you for now. I wasn't prepared yet, and my area wasn't complete. We're going to have to improvise. But, you're a writer; you know how to improvise, right?" He gave a soft laugh that sent chills skittering their sharp nails up my spine.

I didn't answer. I just sat there.

"Not able to talk to me yet? That's good. It means I have time."

He tilted his head to the side. "Do you hear that? Why would there be a siren out on this end of our little piece of paradise? Stay right where you are, I'll be back." He turned around and left, bounding up the stairs two at a time.

Now's our chance, Sweetie. Can you move?

Lifting my arms took all of my energy. I let them fall, choking out a cry. *Not enough yet, I need more time.*

Okay, it's going to be okay, keep trying to move them, move everything you can, get that drug through your system and get ready. We'll get out of here. I'll be back, just keep working at it. Mom? MOM!

I heard a distant door open and then slam shut. The sound was too muffled to have been the door at the top of the stairs, so I could only imagine it was the front door. I kept moving my arms, little by little, and began shaking my legs. I could feel the coolness seeping through my jeans even more, and pins and needles began piercing my body from my feet up my legs. Whatever it was he'd dosed me with shouldn't last much longer, which also meant that my face was about to start hurting even more than it already did. I didn't want that, but I did want control over my body, and I wanted that right now.

I moved around as much as possible with the cord holding me in place. I didn't know where he'd gone or when he'd be back, though I could only assume he'd gone outside to see what was happening to bring the sirens. I also knew this was probably my only chance to get away.

Reaching back, I felt around, and lucky for me it was just a hook, not a lock of any kind. I unhooked the cord and pushed myself up off the floor. Standing took real effort. I felt as if I was moving through water. The thought of him coming back down here and chopping me to pieces was more than I could bear. I pushed on through the druggy water and made my way up the stairs. Luckily he hadn't turned the light off when he left. At least I could see the steps.

It seemed like hours, but was probably a minute or less, before I reached the top and opened the door slowly. The hinges squeaked in protest. I held my breath for a few seconds, listening for sounds of him returning. I heard nothing. Stepping out of the doorway, I closed that door quickly to minimize the noise and maximize the time before he discovered my disappearance and made my way as quickly as I could through the house and out the back sliding glass door. As I lowered myself off the porch, I heard the front door open, and slam closed.

Hurrying around the side of the house, I saw the taillights of a squad car pulling away down our road. *No! Come back!!* My choices were either to chase the cop and probably not be seen by the officer and be caught by Mr. X, or to run home and barricade myself in, calling for the cop to come back. I chose option B.

As I opened my own front door I heard him howl over at his own house. I knew he'd found out I was gone. Hurrying in, I closed and locked the door, grabbed the cordless phone and set the alarm again. As quick as I could, I ran to my bedroom. It was on the far side of the house and couldn't be seen from Mr. X's direction. Opening the gun safe I pulled out my revolver and closed the safe again, spinning the dial to lock it. I let myself out the sliding glass door, closing it behind me, too, and slipped down off the side of my own patio, shimmying underneath. There wasn't much room; I was glad to see there weren't any snakes or spiders in evidence, either.

Dialing 911, the dispatcher answered, "9-1-1, what is the nature of your emergency?"

I kept my voice low in case the sound could travel around the house. "There's someone trying to kill me. There was just a policeman here; the alarm went off, and he came over. I saw him leaving but I was busy escaping from the basement of the house next door."

"Excuse me, ma'am? Did you say you were escaping from the neighbor's house?"

"Yes, he kidnapped me and was holding me prisoner. I got away and ran home, locking myself in, and now he's banging on my front door and yelling that he knows I'm here."

"Your neighbor is banging on your door? The one who tried to kidnap you?"

"The one who DID kidnap me and YES goddamn it, get that officer back up here NOW! If he finds me, he's going to try to kill me again! He has a chain saw, and I'll be in pieces!"

Disbelief came through loud and clear in her voice. "Verify your address for me, please."

"I'm calling from a landline, the address is on your screen." I rattled off my address.

"I'm sending the officer back now. Hang on, he'll be there soon. Stay on the line, please." She didn't sound like she believed me. I knew I sounded crazy, but I didn't have time to give her a play-by-play of everything that had happened.

I heard banging on my front door, and Mr. X was yelling that he knew I was in there. I heard my door slam open and crash into the wall behind it.

"He's at the door, screaming at me, and he's just now kicked in my front door."

The alarm went off again. "Do you hear that? That's my alarm! He's in my house!"

"Yes, ma'am, I hear it. Where are you in the house?"

"I'm hiding, and I'm not telling you in case he's within earshot. The cops better get here quick and catch him, because if he finds me before they do, I'm going to shoot him."

"Ma'am, try to stay calm, he's on his way."

Stay calm? "Did you seriously just tell me to *stay calm?* I've been kidnapped, beaten, am currently hiding in my own house from the madman who lives next door and is intent on killing me, and you're telling me to stay calm?!"

"Ma'am, the alarm company has called and requested we return to your residence, too. The officer should be there shortly; he's about two minutes away." She was beginning to sound like she had figured out there was a real problem. Either this sort of thing didn't happen in Aspen Grove or she was a real genius.

I couldn't hear much over the alarm going off. The sound intensified when Mr. X threw open my patio door. The light patterns through the boards of the porch changed as he stepped out and looked around. I held my breath even though I knew he wouldn't be able to hear me with the alarm still blaring.

As if they had read my mind, the alarm company turned off my alarm. I held the phone tight against my ear in case the dispatcher talked again. I didn't want him to hear any sound at all.

My heart beat double time against my chest. Time stretched thin and slowed to a crawl. I thought the breath in my lungs was going to burst out and give my position away.

He turned and walked back into the house, opening the closet door and closing it again. I exhaled as quietly as I could and took in another breath through my mouth. I heard him moving through what could only be the guest room and then back toward the kitchen. There was another back door in the kitchen. I expected him to open it and step out again, and I waited.

"Ma'am, are you still there?"

"Shhhh, I don't know where he is, and the alarm is shut off now. Where's the officer?"

"He's pulling up now."

"Tell him to get his gun out and not to believe anything the neighbor says. He doesn't have permission to be in my house. I want him arrested."

I could hear two voices now; one was obviously Mr. X's, and the other could only be the officer. I couldn't hear what they were saying, but it didn't sound intense at all to me.

"Tell him to get his gun out! This guy is dangerous!"

"Can you come out of your hiding place and talk with the officer now that you're safe?"

"How do you know I'm safe? Is the neighbor in custody? Is he in handcuffs in the back of the police car?" I began to shake uncontrollably. Either adrenaline or the after-effects of the drug, I didn't know which.

"He'll protect you. It's what we do."

Son of a bitch, she has no idea of the seriousness of the situation, and it appears that she doesn't care. She was going to be of no further help to me.

"Really? You consider disbelief and taking my call lightly as 'helping'? Thanks all the same, but I've got it from here." She didn't know it, but she'd made it to the top tier of people I would model characters after in future novels who would be there solely for me to kill. I slid out from under the porch and slipped back in through the sliding glass door.

I ignored the tiny, "Ma'am? Ma'am, are you still there?" coming from the phone and tossed it down on my bed, making my way quietly down the hall until I was close enough for the voices to turn into words.

"No, I understand. There was a cat on the window sill when I got here. It must have gotten in through the doggie door in the back. Sometimes she forgets to lock that when she goes on vacation."

"Where's her dog, then, if you're taking care of her house?"

"Biscuit is at the pet retreat. They have one at the spa where she spends her vacations. Have you ever heard of such a thing?" Mr. X laughed, his 'girls, what can you do' laugh. The officer didn't join in.

"All the same, I'll take a look around back to make sure that's what the problem was. Two alarms in a five-minute time period are unusual. Why don't you walk with me through the house, check inside as well, since I'm here anyway?" His voice was cool, professional. At least the cop wasn't as big an idiot as the girl answering the phone.

"I've already checked inside, there's nothing else to see in there." His voice sounded like he dealt with this sort of thing all the time.

"It's part of the service when we get called out like this. Step aside, please."

"Alright, but you're wasting your time."

I knew what would happen when the officer's back was to Mr. X. As I opened my mouth to yell, I heard a loud thud and another, then my end table went crashing over as X and the officer fought. I was frozen to the spot, unable to move and unsure which way to go even if I could. My eyes were still swollen almost shut, and the drug hadn't quite made its way out of my system yet, keeping me a little bit woozy.

The scuffle continued, furniture crashing and breakables shattering until a gunshot rang out. Everything went quiet. I heard nothing but heavy breathing.

I controlled my own breathing and tried to think. If it were the cop killing X, he would have called it in. If it were X killing the cop....

"Shit." In that one word I knew which one was down. X was alive, and now he was armed. My heart rate ratcheted up another notch. Any more notches and it would be out in the open.

"Sara….. I know you're here. Now look what you've done. Another person had to die because of you, and now we're in a pickle. What's a person to do when they kill a cop? Pin the murder on another person, that's what."

I took a step back, then another, feeling my way along the wall, getting closer to the bedroom and the sliding glass door. I had to get out.

"Come out, come out, wherever you are...." As if we were kids playing a game of hide and seek. "I'm coming to find you," he singsonged.

My foot caught the edge of the molding on the doorway as I stepped back. It made a soft "thunk" sound. My breath caught in my throat. I hoped he hadn't heard it.

"I hear you, my sweet."

Shit.

I backed into the bedroom and flipped across the bed, rolled off the far side and squared myself in the furthest corner of the room. Revolver still in hand, I waited, knowing he would come.

He did.

"Ah, there you are. Here I thought we were having such a nice time, and you go and run off. What kind of thank you is that for the nice dinner I cooked?" He continued walking toward me, slowly, one step at a time.

"Get away from me," I said, my voice low and steady.

"You know I can't do that. You know too much, and if everyone is going to believe you killed the cop out there you're going to have to kill yourself, too."

"I called 911. They know what's going on here."

"That's interesting; tell me what you told them," he said, making himself comfortable in the chair in the corner. He brought his right ankle up to rest on his left knee, laying the cop's gun across his calf and resting his arms on the arms of the chair, taunting me.

"I told them my neighbor kidnapped me and was trying to kill me. I told them to send the cop back, that you were breaking into my house."

He tapped his fingers. "Now, see, you don't really have a neighbor. The house is, by all accounts, empty and for sale. I'm the one who took the sign down after I'd watched the house for several weeks, seeing no one had been looking at it and no one had visited it at all in that time. I also know you live alone, hardly ever leave and never have company. So, the location and, in particular, you, were perfect for my plan. I have to polish my procedures, and I can do that. I will do that, with practice."

Sweat popped out across my brow. "What procedures?"

"Mmm. The procedure necessary to build the perfect woman, of course. The body parts have to be removed with precision, and they have to be of perfect proportion in length and overall size to match what's already been harvested. No one woman will ever be as perfect as Eden, but with time I believe I can come close to making one, with the best parts of many women."

My mind reeled. Perfect body parts harvested to make the perfect woman? "You can't possibly think you are going to be able to build a perfect, living, breathing woman." My voice quavered. "It's not possible to create life in that way."

"You misunderstand. I don't want a living woman. I want the perfect woman. The perfect woman isn't alive. She's quiet and subservient and sits there unless I want her to move, in which case I'll move her myself. My dear, I'm talking about stuffing her. I'm a taxidermist."

If I hadn't been sitting, I would have fallen down.

He smiled and waited.

"How… what…. You're crazy, you know that don't you?" I croaked out.

"Many leaders in their fields were thought to be crazy for years before technology caught up with their ideas. I prefer to think of it as 'advanced,' not crazy." His eyes glittered. He was certifiable in my book.

"We've talked long enough. It's a shame I won't be able to use part of you in my perfect woman. I've never seen eyes quite your shade before. But, there will be others. Now you'll have to commit suicide to make the scenario work. Come out here where we can position you correctly."

I raised my revolver and held it with both hands. "I don't think so."

He sat up and grabbed for the cop's gun still resting on his leg.

He'd done enough damage to me over the past several hours; I didn't wait for him to do more. Six shots rang out. Five hollow points entered his chest through five small holes, jerked his body in a macabre dance, and exited through a much larger area through his back and my chair. The permanently surprised look on his face was the last look he'd ever give. The sixth bullet marked his forehead with a slightly off-center hole, one thin trail of blood tracing its way down past his eye and across his cheek. Certainly more blood would have run out and down his face had it not been for the sixth hollow point bullet tearing out the back of his head, splattering brains all across my wall and leaving an indentation that allowed his head to tilt back further than normal.

I sat where I was for a minute, watching for any movement from him. When I was relatively sure he wasn't super human and going to yell, "Surprise!" and shoot me, I stood up and moved carefully around the bed, never taking my perfectly colored eyes off him.

The analytical side of my brain knew he was dead. The mystery writer side needed proof. I pressed a finger to his neck, searching for a pulse and finding nothing. Reaching across I checked the other side, again finding nothing. Having read and written too many murder stories, I took a shirt from the dresser and wrapped it around the barrel of the cop's gun and carried it with me to the living room. I needed to check on the officer.

As I rounded the corner from the hallway into the living room, my ears had been trained for any noises behind me. It was a shock to see the officer's chest rise and fall, shallow, but there. I stumbled over and dropped down to the floor next to him, checking his pulse. There it was! He was alive!

Leaning down I keyed the microphone that was strapped to the shoulder of his uniform. "Help! Please help, an officer's been shot, he's breathing but unconscious. Please send an ambulance!"

The dispatcher's voice came back. "Ma'am, please stay where you are, an ambulance is on the way. Can you tell me where he's been shot?"

I looked closer at him. "In the shoulder, just to the outside of his bullet proof vest."

"Is that the only wound?"

"I think so. I only heard the gun go off once."

"Can you tell if the bullet went all the way through?"

"There's not much blood on the carpet, just on his uniform, so I don't think so."

"Is he still bleeding?"

"I think so."

"Okay, I need you to get a compress and put pressure on the wound, try to stop the bleeding."

"Okay." The coat closet was closest. I grabbed a ski cap and scarf and used those. "I'm pressing on the wound."

"Good. Keep up the pressure."

The officer made a guttural noise. "I think he's waking up."

"Don't let him get up, talk to him, have him stay still. The paramedics should be there any time."

I heard the siren getting closer. The officer's eyelids fluttered, and he tried to roll. I laid the phone down next to me and gently held the officer still. "Shhh, shhh, you've been shot, stay down. Lay still, the paramedics are on the way. Can you hear the siren? They're just about to the driveway. Be still, you're going to be just fine." I kept gentle pressure on his good shoulder to help him stay down and to let him know he wasn't alone.

"Are you still there, ma'am? Ma'am?"

I picked the phone back up and rested it between my shoulder and my ear. "I hear them pulling up. I also need to tell you there's a dead man in my bedroom."

"I know, ma'am. I was still listening on the phone and heard everything that went on in there."

I didn't hang up the phone? Maybe she wasn't as big of an idiot as I thought, continuing to listen. "You heard him say he was going to kill me?"

"Yes ma'am. It's all on tape. We continue recording until the call is disconnected. That hasn't happened yet."

"Oh, thank God."

The paramedics looked in the window on their way up onto the porch. As they rushed in they took one look at the officer, another look at me and immediately called for a second ambulance. As they stabilized the officer, another police car pulled up. The second officer came in, looked at his friend and backed away to let the paramedics finish their job. They loaded him onto the stretcher and wheeled him out to the ambulance, then left quickly for the hospital with full lights and sirens.

I picked up the gun by the barrel that was still wrapped in a t-shirt and held it out, butt first. "Do you have an evidence bag? This has fingerprints on it that you might need."

The second policeman looked closely at my face for a moment before saying anything. His name tag read 'Brighton.'

"I do, in the car, but I'll take it with the shirt for now. Would you mind telling me what happened here?"

"I will, but first I want to show you something. Please."

I walked down the hall and into the bedroom, looking back once to make sure he was following. I really didn't want to go back in there at this point by myself. I'd spent entirely too much time alone with Mr. X and wasn't interested in any more.

As we rounded the corner, Officer Brighton got his first look at my handiwork. He looked at me and said, "You did this?"

I nodded.

"With your eyes swollen almost shut, you still managed to do this?"

I nodded again.

"Good grouping."

I couldn't help it. I laughed. The relief flooded my system at the outcome of this situation and I found his comment to be the most comical thing I'd heard in a very long time.

He pulled out a pen and a small spiral notebook. "Why don't you start at the beginning?"

Walking over to the bed I held up one finger to him, picked up the phone and put it to my ear. "Are you still there?"

"Yes, ma'am."

"Would you mind telling Officer Brighton here your part of the story while I go wash some of the blood off of my face? He's asked what's happened here today."

As I handed the phone to Officer Brighton, I couldn't help but notice that he was cute. Tall, thin, and obviously smart to be able to pick up on what was going on as quickly as he did.

He took the phone, and I took another t-shirt and a pair of yoga pants out of my drawer. Closing myself in the bathroom, I took my time washing my face gently. My eyes were closed to slits. The black and blue was going to be pretty in a day or two.

After I was as clean as I thought I could get myself, I changed clothes.

When I came back out, Officer Brighton was standing by the sliding glass door looking out at the view. He turned to face me. "I'm sure there's more to the story. From what I've already heard it sounds like you've had quite the day. I'd be interested in hearing it if you're up to it."

"Let's talk in the kitchen. He's a little disconcerting, sitting there like he's listening to us." I jerked a thumb toward Mr. X.

"The coroner is on his way. I'll stay with you until the body's been taken away."

The second ambulance arrived without lights or siren. Officer Brighton asked if I wanted to go to the hospital first; I said, "no," if he would take me after my statement that would be fine. He stepped away and talked with the paramedics for a minute before they left.

We went into the kitchen and sat down at the table. He took out a voice recorder and raised his eyebrows in question. I nodded. He turned it on, and I told him the whole story, starting at the chain saw and ending where he came in the door. He nodded a few times but didn't interrupt, taking written notes occasionally. We were interrupted twice, once when the Crime Scene Unit came in with their cameras and gear, and then again when the coroner arrived.

Once I finished my story he closed his notebook, put it in his pocket, and turned off the recorder. He looked intently at me. "That's definitely an eventful day. Do you happen to remember what realtor had the sign in the yard next door? I'd like to get permission to look inside that house, as well, before I leave."

"I don't remember. It was white with red writing and had a little blue house or a bird or something, that's all I know. I didn't pay too much attention, except to hope no one bought it so this area would stay quiet."

He took his cell phone out of his pocket and walked out to the porch. After a few minutes he came back in, pocketing his phone. "I found the realtor's name, and she's given me permission to enter the property. Will you take me through it and show me what happened where?"

I took a deep breath, blew it back out and nodded. "Yes."

We crossed the yards and tried the front door. It was locked. "I went out the back door when I got away. Let's try that."

Around back we went, up on the porch and to the door. It opened. As we walked through, I retold the story from when I arrived to when I left. We went down the stairs into the basement and for the first time I saw the area where I'd been tied. He'd dragged me backwards toward the wall, so I hadn't seen anything when I'd been brought down, and I hadn't wasted time looking around when I escaped. This was the first I was seeing of this…

There, along the wall, were seven large glass containers, backlit and filled with a hazy fluid. Inside of each floated a different body part. There was a sign nailed above. Around the edges were crudely drawn and painted flowers. The words in the center read, "Garden of EDEN."

THE WATCHER

The new water heater was heavenly. I stood under the spray for longer than I'd been able to with the old heater. Who knew a shower could feel this good? I'd certainly forgotten!

As the water began to cool, and my fingers turned into prunes, I reluctantly shut off the water. I grabbed a towel and dried off before slipping into my comfy, ratty old green bathrobe and twisting my wet hair up into a matching terry cloth wrap.

I wiped a circle of steam off the mirror and checked my reflection. Since changing jobs and moving here, I'd noticed the dark circles slowly disappear from under my eyes, and I was starting to see the sparkle return to them. This had been the best thing I could have done for myself. Not to mention finally finding a doctor who correctly diagnosed the reason I was tired all the time. With that thought, I opened the medicine cabinet, grabbed the small brown bottle and shook out a thyroid pill, downing it quickly with a glass of water.

I made my way into the kitchen and poured my first cup of coffee. As I blew gently across the steaming liquid, I anticipated the strong acidic bite of the morning's first sip. It smelled delicious. I raised my favorite mug to my lips and was about to reach nirvana when the doorbell rang. I certainly wasn't dressed to receive company even if I wanted it.

Who could it be at this time of the morning? I wondered idly. Mentally reviewing my calendar for the day, I couldn't remember anything that would require anyone to show up in person. The contractor wasn't supposed to come by until tomorrow to measure for new windows, and though I don't speak Spanish, I understood the gardener's motions and hand gestures yesterday, accompanied by the almost illegible invoice, to mean he was through with his part of the back yard design. Thinking about the secret walled-in garden that awaited my arrival through the sliding glass back door almost had me ignoring whoever dared interrupt my Saturday morning ritual. *If only I'd gone out there a minute sooner I wouldn't have heard the doorbell at all.* As if in answer to my thought, the doorbell rang again.

With a sigh, I set my oversized mug down on the recently replaced grey granite counter top and made my way down the short hall and through the living room, my slippers flap-flapping on the hardwood floors with each step. "Coming!" I called out.

My peek through the long skinny window next to the door showed me a slice of the front yard, sidewalk and street out front. There was a mostly-white panel delivery van parked at the curb advertising Woodland's Wonderland Flowers and More. I'd never heard of that business, but Perryridge Manufacturing had transferred me to Oklahoma just six months ago, so I couldn't expect to know every business in town.

Tucking the edges of my robe closer together, I tightened the belt and opened the door. Where there should have been a person's face was a huge arrangement of vividly-colored flowers. Roses, carnations, tiger lilies, calla lilies, sunflowers and baby's breath. Lilacs, daisies and even a bird of paradise was sticking straight up out of the middle, and it was all surrounded by leaves and greenery. I breathed deeply; the intoxicating smell wrapped its invisible tendrils around me, bringing a flash of memory from long ago.

"Ohhhh," I exhaled, "what gorgeous flowers. I do believe you have the wrong house, though, as much as I hate to say that."

The vase jostled a bit, and a small white square appeared to levitate out from somewhere deep in the middle of the arrangement. Plump fingers came into view, pinching the edge of the tiny square envelope.

"Are you Sass Otterbery, 3T Pensach Way?" The voice from the other side of the flowers sounded like it should be accompanied by a ground-shaking rumble.

I frowned. "Sasha," I corrected absently, "but the rest is correct…"

The hand tucked the card envelope back into the arrangement and thrust the vase forward. "Then these are for you."

"Oh, okay then…" I stammered, reaching out to catch the vase before he let go. Burying my face in the flowers for a long second,

I inhaled the sweet scent again, filling my senses. "They're beautiful. But who would send me flowers?" I murmured.

Coming back to reality, I remembered my manners. "Hold on, let me get my purse, just one sec." I took a step back into the house and turned, setting the vase on the hall table to free my hands. As I carefully set it down, I ran my hands up to the stem of the vase to make sure it was settled. "Ouch!" I jerked my hand back. A dot of blood on the tip of my index finger was growing; I lifted my hand to my mouth and sucked to make the bleeding stop. The room seemed to shimmer for a moment as if the sun were reflecting off of a shiny secret.

I stepped back to the door, pulling my wallet from my purse where it hung on a hook behind the door; I took out a five-dollar bill and handed it to the man, who I now saw was shorter than my five foot four frame, looked to be in his mid-50's, and had the most intense hazel eyes I'd ever seen. They almost seemed to be lit from within and staring straight into my soul. I blinked several times, rapidly. He smiled, apparently used to the reaction I'd just given him. Without another word he touched the bill of his ball cap in thanks, turned on his heel and made his way back toward the van. I was still watching the odd little man as he climbed into the driver's seat and slammed the door. As the engine roared to life, I swear I saw him wink at me.

I leaned my head out the door and glanced up and down the street at the neighbors' houses to see if anyone else had witnessed the little man. Though it was normally busy with people leaving for to work at this time of the morning, there wasn't anyone around today. *Of course not, it's Saturday.* As I closed the door and flipped the lock, a wave of nausea swept over me and I leaned back against the door. The room shimmered again, a golden light flickering from nowhere and everywhere at once.

Stars swam before my eyes as my living room pulsed and shimmied. What had moments ago been a room with yellow walls and a welcoming feel was now cold, drab, and grey, overrun with stacks of newspapers, magazines, moldy take-out containers and random shoes lying around. The ashtray on the coffee table was overflowing with butts and ashes. A lit cigarette languished on the edge as if its smoker would be back any second. A burst of flickering lights and a rush of heat closed in on me from all sides. I closed my eyes and bent over, certain I was about to pass out. Taking slow, deep breaths seemed to push the nausea back. I stood still for a moment, making sure I wasn't going to throw up.

After what seemed like an hour, but was probably more like a minute or two, the episode passed and I felt I could open my eyes without a repeat performance. Putting a hand to my head, I checked for a temperature; none that I could feel, though my skin was clammy. *Guess I was closer to passing out than I thought. What WAS all of that? How depressing, and why would I see an ashtray? I don't smoke...*

I shook it off. The scent from the flowers permeated the room. I picked them up and took them with me to the kitchen to freshen up their water before I moved them to their new home on the dining room table. When I set the vase in the sink, I felt another prick. "Ouch!" Yanking my hand back, I saw the spider as he launched off of my thumb and touched down in the sink. He scurried away in an attempt to escape the inevitable. I reached for the water sprayer and just as I pressed the button to let loose a stream of water, the spider looked up at me and I saw his face—it was the face of the flower man, his same little crooked smile and piercing eyes, this time filled with what I could only imagine was remorse. With a swish of the water, I washed him down the drain.

The nausea returned with a vengeance. I dropped the water sprayer and grabbed the edge of the counter to keep myself from falling as a wave of heat and pain splashed across me. I sunk to the floor, both arms wrapped around my stomach, and instinctively curled into a ball. *What the hell?*

As the pain began to subside, I push-pulled myself across the linoleum floor and crept toward the living room. My cell phone was in my purse behind the front door; I needed to get there, call for help. Something was horribly wrong. For the first time in my adult life, I found myself wishing I didn't live alone.

The cramping intensified; I pulled my legs up underneath my body and rocked-scooted an inch at a time toward the front door; rough Berber carpeting scrubbed the skin from my knees with every movement.

Without warning the floor creaked, groaned and buckled up. It rolled like the wave at a baseball game, and I rolled with it, onto my side and then my back. It was all I could do to keep from vomiting as the view of my ceiling flashed and rippled, then wasn't my ceiling anymore, and the walls slammed in, stopping within two feet of where I lay.

I must have passed out. The next thing I felt was an air mask being placed over my face and cold hands on my arm. My eyelids felt heavy; I labored to open them.

The light was bright and all around me. Was I dead? No, I was in an ambulance, strapped to a gurney and had it not been for the blanket covering me, I would have been embarrassed by the yellow and white bunnies on my pink flannel pajamas. Only I didn't remember owning any flannel pajamas, at least not since I was in kindergarten.

The air mask was keeping me from being heard. I tried to raise my arm to lift the mask from my face, only to find that my arms were pinned next to my body underneath the straps. The sirens warbled through my semi-consciousness, shooting holes in my brain. I wanted it to stop. I'd never been a fan of lying on any type of gurney. It made me think about surgery and the horror stories told about being awake, but paralyzed, during the procedure, and no one in the operating room realized it but the patient.

A bump in the road jarred the ambulance, and my head lolled to the side. Adrenaline slammed through my body; the paramedic was the flower man. His mouth tilted into the crooked smile and his intense, just-this-side-of-freaky hazel eyes stared deep into mine. Then, he winked.

"She's awake," his voice rumbled, his gaze shifted to something or someone behind me. I had no energy and no control over my body; I couldn't move to see what it could be. I'm not sure I would have looked even if I'd have been able. I didn't know if it were my fear of gurneys, of surgery, or a newfound fear of the flower man, but something had me paralyzed.

A disconnected voice came from over my shoulder. "Here, Bob."

Flower man reached a hand over the top of me and out of sight, bringing back with it a hypodermic needle filled with a milky white substance. He tapped the needle several times and I watched the middle of the tube bend where his finger came in contact with it. *This isn't happening, no way,* I told myself. *Hypos aren't made of rubber. I don't think.* At this point, though, I couldn't be sure of anything.

While I was talking to myself, flower man Bob lowered the needle toward my arm. Right before it dipped out of my sight, it turned into a wasp, wings flapping wildly, head twisting about. I felt it sting me in the fleshy part of my upper arm. I sucked in a deep breath and my eyes tracked back up to flower man Bob's. I half expected him to wink at me; instead, his eyes twisted, stretched and shimmered from hazel to electric green, the pupils elongating, reminding me of a snake. The transformation continued as his forked tongue flicked out of his mouth, tasting the last drops of whatever it was that remained in the needle. Above his head, the wasp circled slowly, making its own transformation into what looked suspiciously like, well, flower man Bob. Correction, flower man, spider head, paramedic, snake man, now wasp guy Bob.

My vision faded out, thankfully, and everything went black.

I was floating. This feeling reminded me of my mom and the swimming lessons when I was young. She could float on her back and close her eyes, and I remember wanting to learn how to do that, too. She looked at peace when she did that; I wanted to share that feeling, the feeling I imagined she was immersed in by the smile that played at the edges of her lips. I always told myself she was a mermaid and could flip over in an instant, slice through the water, and I would see her legs turn into a tail and fins as she dashed playfully away, leaving reality behind and me with it. She would have never left me, not if she'd had a choice…

The memory swirled and slipped away as I floated closer and closer to consciousness. I stayed as still as possible in hopes that whatever was happening above the surface would continue on by and not make me open my eyes. I didn't know where I was; I only knew that it was cold and I didn't think I wanted to be there.

It was too late. The last vestiges of my dream-like memory slid down the mental drain and the hard surface beneath me made itself known. Still unwilling to risk opening my eyes, I hesitantly tried to lift first my right hand and then my left. As I suspected, neither moved higher than an inch or two; my legs followed the same pattern.

The fuzziness around the edges of my brain retreated. I tried to pull it back up like a warm blanket to cover my psyche but couldn't quite reach it in time. With nothing else left to do, I opened my eyes.

There was nothing to see. It was pitch black. I blinked several times until I was sure I was actually opening my eyes, and that the darkness was real. It took a few seconds for my eyes to adjust; the first ray of light was coming from my left; I turned my head and saw a small vertical rectangle and the outline of a door, the light stealing around the edges like a thief in the night.

While I waited for my eyes to finish adjusting, I listened hard. From the other side of the door I could hear a faint beeping and a telephone ringing. The ringing stopped; the beeping didn't.

There didn't seem to be any immediate danger; I was alone at the moment, so I paid closer attention to my restraints. They felt rough against my forearms through the thin cotton sleeves of my gown. A shiver slithered up my spine as a cold breeze whispered across my body; every part of me felt like ice except for my feet. The wool socks were scratchy but at least they kept my toes warm.

Turning my head toward the direction the breeze had originated, I could just make out a fan oscillating on the table about fifteen feet from me. It had red streamers that held on for dear life to the bent and dinged mesh cage across the front while they danced to the tuneless whirring of the blades spinning around and around inside. The fan at grandma's house when I was a kid looked just like this one. Only it made a squeaking noise right before it reached the end of its path.

The fan reached the end of its cycle and reversed direction. I almost expected to hear that squeaking noise. I watched the streamers flail about, twisting ineffectively against the breeze, following wherever the fan turned to go. The breeze blew across me again, bringing with it another uncontrollable shiver.

I'd been so caught up in the plight of the dancing streamers that the sudden loud bang behind me came as a complete surprise, followed by the fluorescent lights across the ceiling blazing to life, temporarily re-blinding me. I cried out and squeezed my eyes shut, my arms jerking ineffectively against the restraints as I tried to cover my face.

Squeak, squeak, squeak... splash, plop. Swish, swish, swish, swish...

I pried one eye open just enough to see out through a sliver between my eyelids. A stainless steel door was propped wide open and held in place by a dirty yellow mop bucket. That explained the first noise. Looking around, I saw the source of the rest.

A woman of Native American descent wielded a mop as if it were a weapon against the germs on the floor. She wore a grey housekeeping uniform with a red belt that looked suspiciously like the ribbons on the fan. Her hair was so black it was almost blue, and shiny, so shiny it almost hurt my eyes. Or maybe that was left over from the lights. She wore ear buds attached to something in her pocket and slapped the mop around the floor to the beat of whatever song was being piped into her ears. Her hair swung back and forth to the same beat.

Apparently she hadn't heard my cry, and still hadn't seen me. "Hello!" I cried out, my voice hoarse. I could barely hear me, how did I expect to get her attention, especially through her music? Summoning as much strength as I could muster, I jangled the restraints against the table and called out again. Still, she didn't hear me.

As I tried to decide if there was something I could do, or if waiting was my only option, the fan's breeze slithered over my ice cold skin again. Shivering, I watched to see if she would feel it too. Her hair swirled up, waving in the air. The motion was reminiscent of cobras being coaxed out of their baskets by a snake charmer playing a flute.

The room tilted and the snake charmer popped in as if summoned, sitting cross-legged on the floor with his back to me, the music floating out of his instrument as audible as the door crashing open moments earlier. Her hair continued to dance long after the fan's breeze left it alone, forming itself into the likeness of snake heads, becoming clearer with each passing second.

As she mopped, she backed up so as not to step on the freshly washed floor. The snakes in her hair continued growing larger, coming closer to me with each step she took. The snake charmer lifted himself to his feet in one fluid motion with only the power of his legs; his fingers continued seducing the flute and, by extension, the snakes. He backed around the table where I lay, and as he turned to keep the snakes in his sight I saw a now-familiar face. Bob the flower man-paramedic-everything else was now the snake charmer.

My breath caught in my throat; I tried to scream, but had no voice. Every step he took back, she took back, the snakes swaying nearer to me. Fear coursed through my veins, slamming home with a burst of adrenaline. I jerked my hands up, up, up, and managed to pull my right hand free of the restraint. Fumbling with the restraint on my left arm, I took my eyes off Bob the flower man paramedic snake charmer for just a second to see what I was trying to do. When I looked back, he was no longer there.

Whipping my head back around, I saw the snakes weren't charmed anymore… they were hissing at me. The largest one in the middle struck lightning fast, leaving me no time to move out of its way. As its fangs pierced my shoulder, pain shot in and radiated in every direction. The other snakes hiss-laughed; their fangs were sticking straight out of their mouths and venom was beading on the tips.

As the cleaning lady moved around and away, the snake let go and then it was just her hair again. She hadn't heard one sound that wasn't through the ear buds. She backed out of the open door, snagged the bucket of water with her mop and squeak, squeak, squeak, she was gone down the hall.

My shoulder burned. I'd lost feeling in my hand. *Why did it have to be the hand that was free from the restraints?* I screamed inside my head. The poison from the bite made its searing presence known as it worked its way through my system and toward my heart.

Then, fierce cramping erupted in my stomach. *Oh God, I'm going to die!* The fan blew across me again, and the air was hot.

Hot enough to make the walls cry; there were tears running down them in streams. The table beneath me heated up. The restraints became pliant, and I pulled against them; they stretched to let my other hand out and then, in turn, I pulled each ankle free. Perfect timing, as another wave of cramps clawed in an attempt to break free from my intestines.

As I curled up, I ran out of table and fell unceremoniously to the floor, crashing down on my unbitten shoulder. Sweat popped out on my forehead and stained the underarms of my parka. I whimpered and curled up as tightly as possible.

White shoes came into my line of sight—nurse's shoes! I freed one hand from its hold on my belly and reached out to touch, unsure if they were really there or if this were another horrible nightmare. My hand shook from the strain of holding it out. The tips of my fingers brushed down, coming into contact with… air. The shoes stepped back, and the legs crouched down until I could see a face swimming into view…..

Swimming…. Swimming…. Something grabbed my ankle and yanked me under the water; very cold, very salty water. I couldn't breathe. I hadn't gotten a deep enough breath because there was no notice before it happened! *Oh my God I'm going to drown!*

The hand that was clamped around my ankle had talons for fingers. They were stabbing into my flesh and muscle. The pain was excruciating; it took everything I had to keep what little breath I had in me, to hold onto the oxygen that was left, not let it go… if I let it go, I'd be dead in no time. Drowning was said to be one of the worst ways to die, and I did *not* want to go out that way.

I could see the sun above, through the few feet of water over my head. I was so close to air if I could only reach it. I kicked my feet, striking the hand that gripped my ankle over and over again. I must have hit a nerve or something because all of a sudden it loosened its grip and my ankle was free! I frog-kicked as hard as I could to get as far away as possible, scooping through the water with my arms in the butterfly motion we'd been taught while I was on the junior high school swim team. My lungs were on fire, the burning sensation of zero oxygen and a need to let out a worthless breath no longer worth holding drove me to the surface.

I burst out of the water, and gasped for breath, my lungs screaming for air. The stars shooting across my vision left no doubt that I'd almost passed out. I choked on the water that I hadn't realized I'd breathed in with the oxygen and flipped over to swim on my back while I regained some strength in my arms. My legs had always been my strongest feature; working my way through college as a waitress had gained that for me.

I felt something slide past my foot as I kicked out. It almost felt like… tentacles? *No, God no!* My kicking picked up intensity, the thought of being dragged back under the water was more than I could bear. I rolled myself back over onto my stomach and swam for all I was worth.

When my hand stroked down and touched what could only be sand, I dropped my legs down and stood. The water was less than waist deep, and I was so close to shore I picked my knees up high with each step and ran as quickly as possible to the beach. I kept going until I hit dry land; then I kept going until I couldn't go anymore.

My legs gave out, dropping me without warning. I was sure my limbs had been transformed into overcooked spaghetti. As I lay on the edge of the sand next to the boardwalk, I felt like I'd just competed in a triathlon. The sand beneath me and the sun above were warm on my skin. My vision began to grey around the edges. Exhaustion covered me like a soft blanket, and I willingly let it take me to into the dark.

~~*~*~*

I woke to the repetitive beeping of the alarm clock. Reaching my arm out from under the covers I found the snooze button and slapped it, silencing the obnoxious noise. I laid there completely cocooned under the covers while I tried to wake up and focus. *That was one hell of a dream*, I thought, laughing softly. *Wow. I really need to eat dinner earlier and go to bed a little later.*

As reality crept in on my semi-wakefulness, I heard footsteps and muffled voices nearby. My breath caught in my throat as my heart beat a staccato double time; there shouldn't *be* voices or footsteps. Not if I were at home where I thought I should be.

Cautiously I slid the covers down past my forehead, my eyebrows, and then my eyes. Dim light was filtering through a window, peeking around the edges and through the small slit of an opening where the blackout drapes hadn't quite been pulled tightly together. I could make out the interior of the small room: twin size bed along the opposite wall from the one I was currently in, milk crates holding up a sheet of plywood to form a makeshift desk, and what I could only assume was either a closet or a tiny bathroom hidden behind a sheet on a clothesline. It was painfully obvious that this wasn't my room. I'd never seen it before.

A male voice whispered softly; a female voice responded with a giggle and shushed him. I couldn't understand what they were saying, but the gist of the conversation was clear enough. He was apparently telling her everything she wanted to hear, and it was working if the sounds that were beginning on the other side of the tiny room were any indication. I had to get out of here, and quick, or I would find myself the unwilling witness to their intimacy. *How had they not heard my alarm clock?* I thought.

Slipping quietly from the bed, I scooted my feet around on the floor and found a pair of flip flops. I only hoped they were mine. *How could they be, though, if this weren't my room?* I didn't want to think about that. Feeling near the foot of the bed, my fingers grazed a bathrobe. I stood up slowly so as not to disturb the other couple, and slipped the sleeves over my t-shirt and boxer shorts and tied the belt on my way toward the wall with the outline of a door.

As I grasped the knob and turned, I opened the door onto a scene from a cheesy 1980's college movie... a crush of people, loud music emanating from a 'boom box' at one end of the hall and an exit sign over where I was sure the stairs would be at the other. I pulled the door shut behind me and made my way as quickly as possible toward that end.

"Hey! It's the new girl!" a male voice shouted over the din. "Where are you going so fast?" the same voice called as he closed the distance. "I've been hoping you'd come out and join us!"

I tried not to look, afraid it would be Bob the flower man paramedic snake charmer turned coed. If I could keep moving, maybe I could get to the stairs and get out of here before... a hand grabbed my upper arm as a voice whispered in my ear. "Hi, didn't you hear me? I was calling you."

Jerking my arm away, I whirled around. "Don't EVER grab me like that!" I screamed into the face of... some random guy. "You do NOT have permission to TOUCH me!"

Swinging back around, I ran for the stairs, pushing people out of my way as they laughed and sang and drank from their red plastic cups.

I was so freaked out it took at least ten seconds after I reached the end of the hall before I realized there wasn't an exit at all. It was a dead end. I looked up to find there wasn't even an exit sign anymore. The only thing here was a keg, several college guys filling their cups, and a girl in a bathrobe and flip flops sinking down into the corner, tears streaming down her face. The guys by the keg didn't pay any attention to the girl. They didn't even seem to see her at all. There was only one person who did.

"Are you okay?" he said softly. "I didn't mean to scare you." Two things struck me at once. His eyes were very blue; they were showing genuine concern, and he wasn't Bob anybody.

"No, I'm not okay. I'm freaked out," I answered, not sure why I was talking to this guy at all except for the fact that I was in a place I'd never been, surrounded by people I didn't know, and he seemed to be the only person who could see or hear me.

He squatted down in front of me, still keeping his distance. He tilted his head in thought. "Is there anything I can do to un-freak you out? I feel like it's my fault you ran away."

I looked at him and felt almost normal, or as normal as I could feel with what had happened to me lately. His dishwater blonde hair was cut short, and the dimple in his right cheek reminded me of a boy named Teddy I'd gone to school with in the fifth grade. I wondered what had ever happened to him.

"Can we start over?" he asked, still speaking softly, although with the volume at which the music was playing it was amazing that I could hear him at all. "My name is Tony." He held out his hand.

"I'm Sasha." The smile I gave him was weak, but it was all I had. I hadn't felt a stick when he'd grabbed my arm before, but I also didn't trust people after everything that had been going on. I scrutinized his hand, not seeing anything but skin. Hesitantly I reached over and took it. "Hi."

"Hi." He smiled, flashing that dimple again. "Would you like something to drink?"

I shook my head. "I've been having a pretty rough day. Alcohol probably isn't the best thing to add on top of that. Thanks all the same."

"I've got Dr. Pepper in my room. Would you like one of those?" His teeth were straight, white, and something out of a fashion magazine.

"Okay. Thanks."

"Do you want to follow me, or wait here?"

"I'll wait here, thanks."

"Okay. Be right back." He raised himself up slowly, almost as if he thought I would bolt. I nodded.

I stayed huddled in my corner, knees drawn up. I was feeling better with a wall on two sides of me. Fewer angles of approach from directions I wasn't watching.

The party was in full swing. I found it odd that no one paid any attention to me at all. Well, besides Tony, that is. It was as if they couldn't see me or something. Maybe it wasn't that, maybe they were busy enjoying their lives and being self-centered college students. That was more likely.

He must live in the same building, I thought, as he was gone for less than two minutes. He sat down a respectable distance away from me and held out the can. "Here you go."

"Thanks." The can was cold and felt good as I rolled it across my forehead. I popped the top and took a long pull.

"So. You come here often?" His laugh was lighthearted and easy; his comment intended to break the ice. It didn't work. Instead, it ratcheted up my anxiety to the next level.

"What do you mean by that and what do you know?" My voice sounded high and tinny to my own ears; I wondered if I sounded like a mad woman to him.

His brow creased. "I... I'm really not sure what's going on with you, I was trying to start a conversation. If you'd rather I left you alone, that's okay, just say so." He rose in one slow, fluid motion, holding his hands up, palms facing me, and took a slow step back.

I closed my eyes and rolled my neck. Taking in a deep breath I tried to calm myself. This was the first person who had been nice to me in the midst of whatever it was that was happening, and I needed help.

"I'm sorry. Please, come back." I looked at him and gave another weak smile. "I'm having a *really* bad day so far. I apologize for reacting like a psycho."

"Hey, we all have bad days. I had one yesterday. The prof threw a surprise Chem test. Epic fail." Tony sat back down where he'd been sitting a moment ago. I was surprised we could hear each other over the distance between us and the noise of the surrounding party. "So tell me about your day. You have a surprise test, too?" His gaze was level with mine. He looked like he wanted to know, not like he was asking to be polite. What could I tell him, though, without sounding like I was completely around the bend? Nothing that had happened was even remotely sane.

"It's been one thing after another," I heard myself say. "From before coffee this morning until... well, until I met you, nothing has made any sense."

His eyes softened. "That sucks for sure. Listen, you want to get out of here, go somewhere we can hear each other talk?"

My breath locked up in my chest, and I could hear my heartbeat pounding in my ears. I felt a little freaked out again, and my face must have shown it.

He held his hands up again. "Just talk. Really."

The cacophony *was* getting louder and more irritating as the seconds ticked by. Forcing my breath out, I nodded.

As he stood, he reached his hand out to help me up. I took it and felt the stick. *Noooooo!* He pulled my hand to help me stand and at that moment my fingers decided to turn to rubber. I remained sitting and my fingers, then my hand, and up my arm began stretching, pulling, stringing out, followed by my shoulder and then my torso. The air around me pulsed and shifted. Walls, people, even the keg, appeared as if someone had installed fun house mirrors all around me. I looked up at Tony and watched as his face began to shift, his cheekbones bulging out and his jaw shrinking, stretching, and finally dripping down to the floor.

My arms looked like wet noodles, sliding around. I had no control over them or any portion of my body anymore. I slid into a puddle of me, becoming one with what was left of the undulating floor. Tony's face contorted, his chin sliding back up and continuing past his nose and around his eyes, turning him into one big forehead with eyeballs. His gaze stayed locked on mine, never losing their concerned look. That was the last sight I saw before I slipped down through the floor and into total darkness.

Sasha lay on the bed wearing a hospital gown and covered by a thin sheet, currently deep in REM sleep. Her arm and chest were hooked up to electrodes that constantly monitored her heart rate and breathing. The tiny wire disappearing into the center of the shaved patch on her head transmitted her every thought in perfect video and was being recorded by the computer attached to the other end. There was a currently-empty bed next to hers. The room was small compared to the gallery above her. A large plate glass window allowed full view of everything going on in the room to anyone who wanted to watch. Not that many people were in attendance; this was a private test, one that was only known to three individuals, none of which were Sasha.

A woman dressed in pale blue scrubs, her hair pulled back into a bun, checked the printout currently being recorded and tapped a few keys, entering a new command into the computer. The large screen showed a view looking out through Sasha's eyes and it appeared she'd now gone into a scene where she was running.

"I told you this would be fun." Bob cackled and looked over at Tony.

"You were right, as usual." Tony smiled a dark smile that didn't reach his eyes. "She gave us so much information. You chose well. How did you find her?"

"It took me a while to identify a viable candidate. I had to wait until someone came in with a prescription for pills that resembled ours." He ticked off the requirements on his fingers. "It

needed to be a woman with a refillable prescription so I could follow her and watch her routine, make sure she lived alone, and she needed to be somewhat of a recluse so no one would notice she'd gone missing for a couple of days. Once I'd identified someone who matched our needs, she needed to come in for a refill when the timing was right. I had to be alone when I filled the prescription in order to switch out the pills."

"Why did it have to be a woman?" Tony asked, his eyes flat and empty.

"They're more fun to stalk." Bob stated matter-of-factly. "If they happen to catch you at it, they don't turn around and approach you, they run away. I'm not interested in getting beaten to a pulp, thank you very much."

"Good thinking."

"The next thing we need to do is figure out how to get audio. The video is great, but I want to hear what they're hearing, too, even when I'm not in the scene with them." Bob was lost in thought.

"We've had her for over a day now, we need to take her home and get the next candidate in here. Do you know where they are, or who?"

"Yeah, she's about done. I've got her correct medicine to replace our pills and will switch that out when I take her back. I'll check on the next one on my way back. I think we can have her in place by Tuesday if she stays on her normal routine."

"Good. I want to do the next one. You can be the cameo appearance."

"I don't know if you're ready for that. I want to do one more, make sure you've got the rules down. You almost lost her in there."

Tony was quiet for a minute. "I'm getting some coffee, you want some?"

"Yeah, thanks." Bob stayed by the window, watching Sasha's nightmare on the screen.

Tony walked into the break room and pulled two mugs from the cabinet, then two pills from his pocket. "I said it's my turn, asshole," he said as he smashed the pills into powder and poured

*the dust into one of the mugs. Filling them both with coffee, he
stirred in cream and sugar then carried them back to the window.*

Blowing on his own mug, he handed Bob's to him.

"Thanks." Bob blew on his own mug and took a drink.

*Within minutes Bob was lying on the floor, clutching his
stomach. "What did you do to me?" he gasped between cramps.*

*Tony squatted down in front of Bob, reached over and stuck
him with the fingertip syringe. He watched as sweat popped out on
his brow and his eyes began to swim. "I said it's my turn to be The
Watcher."*

*When Bob's eyes glazed over, Tony called out without turning.
"He's ready."*

*The woman in the pale blue scrubs rolled the stretcher in and
helped load Bob onto it. "I'll get him hooked up." She pulled a
small brown bottle out of the pocket on her shirt and held it out.
"Here are the pills to swap for the girl's."*

*"Thanks. I'll get her home while you get things ready here. I
want to use the audio lead on him. That should make it even more
interesting, don't you think?"*

She nodded. "I do. Is it ready?"

*"We'll find out, won't we?" The smile he gave could chill ice
water.*

~~*~*~*

The alarm clock's incessant beeping was cut short by my hand
shooting out from under the covers and knocking it off the
nightstand. As it crash landed on the floor, I heard the plastic break
and scatter. Didn't matter, I hated that one anyway. When I
shopped for a replacement, I would insist on testing them out so I
would know what sound to expect when it went off every morning.

I opened my eyes and looked around. My room, I was in my
own room with my own drapes, television, closet door… and I was
clammy and uncomfortable. Flipping the covers back, I noticed the
large sweat stain on the sheet where I'd slept. Apparently my fever
had broken overnight. Wait, I don't remember a fever.

I also don't remember Sunday. The last thing I remembered
for sure was getting up and taking a hot shower on Saturday.

The alarm clock had been set for only Monday through Friday; if it were beeping, it was a weekday. *What day is it, really, or is this another nightmare?*

The series of nightmares came flooding back. She shuddered involuntarily. *What an odd series of dreams, surely it was just because of the fever. I hope that's the end of them!*

Reaching over and picking up my phone, I checked the date and time. It was Monday. I'd lost a whole day. I must have really been sick to have slept through an entire day! I took a mental check and decided there was no way I was in any shape to go in to the office. My head was pounding and my stomach was upset. My forehead was still clammy, too. I dialed my boss's number and called in sick.

A hot shower would help. I stumbled into the bathroom and turned on the water, then reached into the medicine cabinet for something for my head. My thyroid medicine bottle was laid on its side. *When did I leave it like that?* I thought. *That's so unlike me.* Popping the lid, I took one of those as well and set the bottle upright in the cabinet.

ONE TOO MANY

The table was set, the candles ready to be lit, and the beer stein frozen the way he liked it. Everything was perfect; she thought. As she waited for him to come home, she checked the meatloaf one more time. The oven had been turned to warm for almost forty-five minutes; she worried that it would dry out before he arrived.

He was late. It was never a good thing when he was late. Not for her, anyway. Had he worked late? Stopped for a beer? Gambled on a game and gone by to see the bookie? She could only hope he'd won and would be in a good mood when he got home.

As the seconds ticked by, she grew more and more nervous. She fidgeted, wringing her hands. She wanted tonight to be perfect; it was their anniversary, after all. Pacing back and forth, she smoothed her apron, straightened the place mats, checked the cans in the pantry and adjusted their alignment; all the while keeping an ear open for tires crunching on the gravel drive out front.

Darkness fell, leaving her alone in the quiet. She switched on the lamp in the corner of the living room to keep the shadows at bay. She didn't like the shadows when he was late. Her nerves were inexplicably raw, as well. She didn't like that feeling, either, especially when she didn't know what was causing it.

She didn't dare turn on the radio; what if she didn't hear him approach?

~~*~*~*

The headlights shone through the front window as his car turned into the drive. She looked away. The high beams were on, and it hurt her eyes to see them coming straight at her. The glare off the front window showed a streak where she'd cleaned and missed a spot earlier. There wasn't time to fix it; she hoped he wouldn't notice. She'd done so well lately.

Walking quickly now, a woman on a mission, she hurried to the kitchen and popped a top, pouring the beer perfectly into his mug. He didn't like the foam to be too thick. They'd spent days working on her technique so she could pour it perfectly for him. When he was happy, she was happy.

He stumbled up onto the porch, catching the toe of his work boot on the edge of the top step, pitching himself forward, and catching the door frame with outstretched hands. She heard him take the Lord's name in vain, and cringed, not from his choice of words, but from the slur and tone with which he uttered them. Also, she knew God wouldn't hold his transgressions against *her*. They weren't her words. He'd been drinking, and from the sound of it, it hadn't been beer.

She set his beer mug down by his place at the head of the table and rushed back into the living room to open the door. He watched her approach, through the pane of glass in the door, and just as she was about to grasp the doorknob, he slammed it open into her unready arm and hand. The door smacked into her face with a resounding thud. The dull crack echoed in her head, rattling her thoughts as well as her bones. She involuntarily stumbled back and cried out, covering her eye with her good hand, feeling the lump swell beneath her fingers.

He approached, a gleam she hadn't seen in months shining in his eyes. Whether it was whiskey-borne or the real Richard showing through, she didn't know; what she did know was it wouldn't end here. It never did. He'd promised it would never happen again. They'd both cried. She'd believed him and promised to stay.

"Are you alright?" His words didn't match the inflection. He asked because he knew he should. He didn't really care. Why would someone who cared watch his wife walk across the room to open the door for him and slam it into her face when she got close?

And then he laughed.

His tone made her glance up with her good eye. The raw meanness on his face caused her to step back. She bumped into the wall, afraid to move. She stood there, pressing her back flat against it, absolutely sure that he would beat her to death tonight.

If she let him.

Something in her brain shifted. She could swear she heard it, the quiet snick of everything sliding into place. She definitely felt the difference, like liquid courage flowing through her veins. It was animal kingdom, fight or flight; the certain realization that it was now or never.

"I'm fine. Thank you for asking. If you'd like a shower before dinner, I can make everything perfect and have it ready and waiting for you when you're done." She lowered her hand from the injured eye, allowing him to see what he'd done to her while she stared intently at the floor. Her concentration was less on him and more on what was happening within her own brain, her own body.

"You do that." The tone of his voice told her he knew what he'd done, and he knew she was cowed. He got off on feeling superior, and stood where he was until he was sure she wasn't going to look up at him again. Then he ambled off toward the hall and bathroom.

Without lifting her head, she slid her gaze up and watched him from under hooded lids until he was out of sight. Raising her face once more, she spoke softly. "Oh, you can bet I will." *Runners, on your mark, it's game on.*

Peeling herself off the wall, she tilted her head to the side and cracked her neck; the sound of bone on bone, in her mind, transformed into the sharp report of a starter pistol being fired. Go!

Hurrying back into the kitchen, she checked the meatloaf. It was ruined, but that didn't matter. Slipping the frozen dinner box out of the freezer, she set the microwave for ten minutes and let it recreate what he'd assume was her own homemade version.

Turning the burner on under the potatoes, she let them reheat for a few minutes as well until the steam was rising from the water. The potatoes needed to be just warm enough to melt the butter. While those two dishes readied themselves, she opened a can of corn into a separate pan and fired the burner to life under it.

As soon as the potatoes were warmed through she dumped them into the strainer in the sink, gave the water time to drain out, and then returned them to the pot. Moving quickly to the kitchen doorway, she listened; the shower was still running. Good. Hurrying back, she reached into the pantry and grabbed the box from the top shelf. She poured a generous amount into the potato pot and returned the box to its place. Adding half a stick of butter, she plugged in the hand mixer and whipped the potatoes to the consistency he preferred... no lumps but not entirely smooth either.

The microwave beeped, signaling the end of its time. Quickly she transferred the lump of pseudo-meatloaf into her own pan and spooned gravy over the top. Stirring the corn, she tasted a bite. Warm enough, not too hot. She turned off the burners and moved everything to the table, lit the candles, fixed his plate and stood next to his chair, holding his meal in her hands.

Not a minute had passed before he lumbered down the hall. Rounding the corner, hair still wet, he was dressed in his good jeans and a new shirt, one she'd never seen before. She knew better than to comment. He didn't allow her to buy new things, and said it was because she didn't go anywhere so it didn't matter what she wore. Lately she'd noticed he had more than one new shirt, and she was sure he had new underwear, too. Not that he needed them. His closet was bigger than hers and overflowed with clothes he'd never worn. She didn't know where they came from since he didn't shop, but found she didn't really care anymore either.

Pasting a smile on her face, she watched him approach.

He stopped in front of her, sniffing the plate. "Smells good. Set it down."

Playing the part of the perfect wife, she gently set the plate down next to his beer, taking care to turn it so that the meat was at the 6 o'clock position, potatoes at 2 o'clock and corn at ten. Just the way he liked it.

He smiled that cat-like smile at her , and motioned for her to fix herself a plate and take her own seat. She took as much time as she dared; she didn't want to piss him off or give him any reason to move from his chair before he'd eaten. She chose her food carefully, taking the most rubberized piece of microwaved meatloaf and a small spoonful of corn. He was drunk and didn't notice.

Slowly she adjusted the napkin in her lap and picked up her fork. Taking small bites, she chewed each one for an extra long time and waited.

He ate the way he always did when he'd been drinking, shoveling it in as if it didn't have a taste. Tonight she didn't mind; in fact, she preferred it that way. Get as much into him as possible before it took effect.

She listened to the second hand tick on the clock. To her, it was the loudest sound in the room. It took him twelve minutes to eat everything on his plate. Being the doting wife that she was, she stood up and served him seconds. He belched loudly, pounding his fist against his chest several times. "Good stuff. Thanks babe."

He picked up his fork and scooped up more potatoes, stopping halfway to his mouth. Staring at the blob, he squinted, then clenched his teeth. "Is … this … a … lump?" He enunciated, letting a beat fall between each word. His eyes raised slowly until they met hers.

She didn't say anything. Come ON, work if you're going to, now's the time. Please, please, please, please, please … she repeated it quietly, over and over, a mantra now.

Slowly he pushed back from the table and stood, his right hand still gripping the fork. "I asked you a ques-…" His eyes glazed over, and his left hand moved up to rub his belly. "I asked…" Sweat appeared on his brow as he took another half step toward her. He swayed like a pendulum before casting forward and hitting the floor, hard.

His breathing became labored. Sweat trickled down his face and appeared in semi-circles under his arms.

She stayed where she was, safe for the time being in her chair at the table, where he couldn't reach her from his position on the floor. She watched him try to focus on her, on anything really, unable to regain control of the situation, at this point not even having connected the dots on what was happening.

"Help me…" his voice was garbled, almost unintelligible as it made its way around the white foam that had begun to bubble out near the corners of his mouth. He turned his head and spat. Turning back, he looked at her with clear eyes for just a moment, long enough for him to see the neutral expression on her face while she watched the light bulb above his head come on. His brain finally registered what was happening.

He flung out his right arm, slinging the fork at her as mashed potatoes flew off and split into clumps before landing at her feet. She glanced down and then back at him, locking eyes. A small smile worked its way across her face. She let him see it.

"Why, yes, that does look like a lump."

She said nothing else, nor did she look away. The wheels were in motion. There was only one acceptable outcome. Anything else meant certain death for her. The ticking of the clock soothed her in a way little else had during their twelve years of marriage. He'd hit her one too many times. Now he would pay.

His breathing slowed. The white, bubbly foam around his mouth moved in and out rhythmically with each breath. The pure hatred in his eyes would have scared her had it shown up while he was in control. He wasn't, and it didn't. In fact, it had the complete opposite effect. She found herself elated at his inability to do anything about it. It was about time he felt a fraction of what he'd caused her to feel over the years. His eyes glazed over again before his eyelids fluttered closed. They stayed that way, even as the bubbles continued to slide in and out of his mouth.

Time stretched on; she had no idea how much had passed while he lay there and moaned. She sat and watched. There was nothing she'd rather do than wait for him to die. The clock continued to mark the passage of time, though she no longer felt the need to watch it. She had all night.

Reaching out with her foot she pushed his leg, just enough to make him open his eyes. In the same tone he'd used on her earlier, she asked, "Are you okay?" Then she let a predatory smile fully engulf the lower half of her face, a look so foreign to him that he didn't even know what it meant. The smile never quite reached her glittering eyes. Something else she'd learned from him.

She tilted her head to the side and cracked her neck. The fear she'd so often felt was evident in his eyes for a split second before the light behind them extinguished. It was the last expression they ever showed, and the one she most looked forward to every time she'd dreamt about his death.

She dragged him by the collar from the dining room through the kitchen and toward the back door. Every time she'd thought about this, dreamed about killing him, she'd anticipated the task being more difficult, thought he would be heavier She never really thought she'd go through with it; didn't think she had the nerve.

Maybe she wouldn't have if he hadn't laughed. Funny what makes a person snap.

Is it premeditated if you dreamt about it, even if you weren't planning to act on it? She wondered. Not that it mattered. What's done is done, the bell can't be un-rung. There was nothing to do now but move forward.

Stepping over his lifeless form, she made her way to the front door and locked the doorknob and the deadbolt. Reaching into the coat closet, she pulled her black windbreaker off its hanger and slipped it on. She picked her keys up out of the bowl on the hall table and pocketed them.

Back in the kitchen, she stood looking down at him. Was this a dream? Would she wake up and he'd be there, as always, looking at her with thinly veiled derision? Reaching out with her foot, she toed his ankle. His foot flopped over, then back. Nope. Not a dream.

She reached down and started to grab his collar again. *Since he's gone*, she thought, *he wouldn't need whatever money he had in his wallet, would he?* She shoved his hip and shoulder over enough to get access to his back pocket. Holding his body at that angle with her leg, she wrangled his wallet out of his pocket. Flipping it open she took out all of the cash except for two dollars. That's all he'd let her carry in her wallet; probably so she couldn't leave him, she thought now, looking back. Considering the wad of bills he had, it couldn't have been any other reason.

She flipped through the rest of his wallet. Driver's license, two credit cards, two bank cards, a receipt for $47.26 from the Zippy Mart with a phone number scrawled across the back, and a myriad of business cards, mostly from people she didn't know. The last slot held a confirmation for a hotel room reservation and a photo of a blonde woman with short sassy hair and a dimpled smile. The reservation was for next weekend in Baltimore. Glancing up at the calendar on the wall, she squinted to bring it into focus. Next weekend he was penciled in for a convention in Tallahassee. She'd have to check the calendar against their credit card receipts and see how long this had been going on.

Her eye throbbed; a dull headache settled in. She would tend to that as soon as she'd finished this.

Replacing everything where she'd found it except for the majority of the cash, she shoved the wallet back into his pocket. Feeling across the outside of his other pockets she found his keys, some change, and a wadded up piece of paper. The same stuff she found when she did laundry every Saturday. She reached in and wiggled the keys out, leaving the rest of his crap where it was; she didn't really care what else he was carrying around anymore.

Grabbing his collar again, she finished dragging him out the back door, dropping him on the porch and turning to lock the door behind her.

Down the steps, thump, thump, thump, she followed the winding paved pathway through the copse of trees, past the park bench he'd bought her for Christmas the year they bought the house, and around the fire pit. It was such a beautiful night; the stars were plentiful and the moon was almost half, just enough to see her way without needing a flashlight.

The path ended where the dock began. His body hadn't made much noise as she dragged him along the path. Now that they'd reached the dock, though, she heard his heels hit and bounce off each individual board, the opening between them catching enough of his heels to give his feet a little bounce. Thuck, thuck, thuck. The noise was a bit macabre considering the source. She reached the end and let go of his collar. The hollow thud that followed as his head hit the wood was satisfying. He deserved no better; in fact, he deserved much, much worse.

She tilted her head and looked down at him, considering. There were two boats to choose from, one on each side; a rowboat for fishing, and a ski boat for the rest of the water activities. Firing up an engine at this time of night was bound to attract attention. Pushing him with her foot, she shoved first his head, then shoulders, and part of his torso off the dock and down into the rowboat. Gravity took over, and he slid the rest of the way in. He landed in an ugly heap. Good.

Turning back, she returned to the boat shed and, using his keys, opened the padlock that held the door. The hinges squeaked as the door swung open. There was enough moonlight for her to make out the majority of the items stacked and leaning inside. Extra boat paddles, life jackets, an old first aid kit, fishing poles and nets, a coil of rope, a pile of tarps and a gas can. The clothesline she'd hung across the corner still had her swimsuit draped across it where she'd left it to dry the last time she'd been out on the boat. Underneath the bench, along the back wall, she found what she'd been looking for – a metal bucket with one end of a chain cemented inside. This was the original anchor that had come with the boat. It hadn't been good enough for Richard; he'd gone out and spent an exorbitant amount of money on a gold-plated replacement. She doubted it had ever seen the water. At the time, she'd thought it was a waste of money. Now, she was glad he'd replaced this bucket with something else. It was exactly what she needed.

Picking through the small box of miscellaneous items, she pulled out several carabiners, or D clips as he referred to them, and pocketed them before she leaned down and grabbed the loose end of the chain. She gave it a good yank. The bucket tipped over and rolled out from under the bench. She hefted it up; it was heavy but somehow felt right in her arms. Like a toddler, only not. She giggled. Picking her way around the extra life vests and scuba gear, she kicked flippers and goggles out of her way and made it back to the door.

The adrenaline must have been starting to wear off. Her arms were getting tired of lifting and dragging things.

When she reached the rowboat, she lowered the bucket down, inch by inch, carefully setting it next to her now-dead husband. It wouldn't do to knock a hole in the floor, not before she finished the task at hand. A tiny little giggle bubbled up and escaped before she pressed her fist to her mouth. Hold it together, she told herself. Now is not the time to crack up.

Another giggle escaped her lips. If she weren't careful, she'd be belly laughing before long. Tamping down her feelings she shook her head, trying to get a grip on herself. Looking down at him, she couldn't be sure, but in this light it looked as if his skin were already turning pasty, losing its fake, tanning bed tan. She nodded approvingly.

Her head throbbed; she reached up and gingerly touched her eyebrow. The knot was a good size. Carefully moving her fingers down and around, she felt for any further damage. Her cheekbone, below the eye socket, was also sore and sported a lump. No wonder her eye was swollen almost closed. She had a slit through which to see, but that was enough. She had one good eye; that's all it took to get the boat out and finish what she'd started.

Hurrying back to the shed she stepped inside, grabbed the extra length of chain hanging from the hook by the door, closed the door and re-locked the padlock. Taking his keys from the lock she flipped through them and found the key to the ski boat. Twisting it off of the ring, she leaned down into the larger boat, pulled up the back seat and dropped the key down in with the life jackets. He'd had to have this boat, though it hadn't been away from the dock more than a dozen times in the two years they'd owned it. The last time he'd taken it out was last weekend and he'd insisted she stay home. He'd given her a list of chores to do instead of taking her out for a sunny day on the water. Looking back on it now she was sure he hadn't spent the day alone.

Stepping down into the rowboat she set down the chain untied the rope from the dock and pushed off. As they began to drift away, she settled herself on the bench and locked the oars in place. The lake was five miles across. Their house was at the edge of the north cove, and their closest neighbors were far enough away to give the illusion of seclusion. She looked around for evidence of any other life form and found none.

Slowly she rowed the boat out of the cove, across the 'bottleneck,' and into the larger expanse. The water was quiet and smooth. No other boats were out at the moment. Thankful for that, she realized she would have a hard time explaining this if anyone else pulled up near her, especially if a taller craft saw what she was hauling. It would be equally troublesome explaining the lack of a lantern to alert them to her presence.

Putting her back into it, the boat picked up speed. She felt the power in her arms, the muscles working in a familiar rhythm. As she rowed, her mind drifted back to the summer she turned twelve and the rowing lessons her father had given her. That was the happiest summer of her life; she'd been old enough to spend time fishing with her dad and young enough not to realize her parents were hiding his condition from her. Looking back now, the memory was bittersweet. Oh, how she wished they'd told her...

maybe she could have... deep down she knew there was nothing she could have done. Pancreatic cancer, stage four, was a death sentence no matter what the doctors did back then. At least she had the memories of that summer; she knew that was what he had aimed for, and it was a bullseye.

Coming out of her reverie, she realized she'd rowed far enough. The shoreline could only be seen in the dots of light from house windows and porch lights reflecting off the water's edge, and she was over the deepest portion of the lake. Pulling the oars up and in, she began wrapping the chain for the anchor around her husband's legs, securing it with a carabiner. Wrapping the extra section of chain around his neck she secured that one to the first chain with another carabiner.

Looking around once more to be sure she was still alone, she lifted the anchor bucket over the edge of the boat and lowered it into the water. As she let go of the bucket's handle it took off, dragging the length of chain behind it. She grabbed the chain to slow its progression and keep it from rubbing against the edge of the boat. With one hand she held the chain; the other lifted his bound feet and edged them over the side. As soon as his feet were over the side she let go of the chain again. This time it didn't drag against the boat; instead, it slipped almost soundlessly into the water. His ankles and legs jerked as the bucket extended the length of the chain.

Scooting across the boat to the other seat, Sara lifted his head and pushed it over the side of the boat, as well. His own weight took it from there, pulling his body over and out, splashing into the water and disappearing below the surface. The last thing she saw were his back pockets with his wallet sticking out of one. Rather fitting actually... she'd wanted to see the end of him for a long time now. The giggle bubbled just below the surface again, threatening to come up and explode out of her. She couldn't afford that yet. Sound traveled at night, especially over water.

As the weight dragged him down it also dragged the weight from her shoulders and took it, as well, down into the deep. Pulling his keys out of her pocket she flipped through them one last time, mentally running through what each of them unlocked. There was a car key; the spare was in the drawer in the hall table. A house key; she had one, didn't need his. Another house key… whose was this? She thought about it for a second and realized it didn't matter. None of these keys mattered. Holding the key ring over the edge of the boat, she lowered her hand down close to the surface and let go. Ploop. They sank out of sight almost as fast as he had.

She waited a minute, then two, then a few more to make sure the wrap of the chains would hold him down. The gentle lapping of the water against the side of the boat was hypnotic. A cloud drifted across the moon, casting darkness over the small amount of light she'd had.

Thinking she'd waited long enough, she readjusted her position and set the oars back in motion. When she reached the dock she tied the boat back just the way it was, the way he'd made her learn. It wasn't the right way to tie a boat, but it was his way, it was the way he'd done it, and the way it should be if the boat hadn't been used this evening at all.

Stepping up and out, she made her way back toward the house. The bench overlooking the lake beckoned; she stopped and sat, just for a moment. Her arms and shoulders were tired; she would be sore tomorrow, but nothing like she would have been had he... had she not stopped him from beating her. A smile played at the corners of her lips. She rose and continued along the path and up the steps onto the porch. Reaching into her pocket she pulled out her keys and let herself into the house, locking the door behind her.

A knock on the door woke her from her sleep. She looked at the clock and rubbed her eyes, disbelieving what she was seeing. Nine-thirty in the morning? She never slept past six o'clock, even when her alarm wasn't set to go off. This was the first good night's sleep she'd had in longer than she could remember.

The knock repeated, more insistent this time. Sliding out of bed, she pulled on her robe and tied it as she made her way down the hall. Looking through the peephole she saw a man and a woman, both in uniforms.

She called out loud enough to be heard. "Who's there?"

"Mrs. Jameson?"

"Yes, who are you?"

"Aspen Grove Police, Ma'am. Could you open the door please?"

"How do I know you're really the police?"

"I'll hold my badge up to the peephole and you can look at it. Will that work?"

She put her eye to the hole once more and saw the badge well enough to read the number on it. "I'll just be a moment while I call the police station and verify you are who you say you are."

"That's smart, Ma'am. We'll be right here."

After doing just that, she returned to the door and opened it. "Thank you. What can I do for you?" Her face wore a confused expression, brows drawn together slightly, concern lines evident around her mouth. Her hair was tousled from sleep, and a slight mark crossed her face where her pillow case had been creased underneath her cheek.

"Officers Donovan and Malasky. Ma'am, what happened to your eye?"

She'd forgotten about the shiner. Her hand went to her eye and, as it touched the lump, she winced. "The door hit me. I ran into it. It was an accident. I should have been watching."

Donovan's eyes narrowed, giving his rough, worn face a definite edge. She stepped back involuntarily.

He realized before she did what her response meant. His face softened; his eyes went sad and understanding. "Ma'am, may we come in? We'd like to ask you a few questions if you don't mind."

She grasped the collar of her robe tight near her throat, shaking her head, her eyes wide. "I need to change into appropriate clothes."

He nodded. "We'll wait right here."

She closed the door and returned to her bedroom. Dressing quickly, she made a detour through the bathroom and got her first look at the black eye. Damn. He'd gotten her good this time. She quickly returned to the door and let the officers in.

They stepped in and looked around. "Is your husband home, ma'am?"

"He's not, no."

"Do you know where he is?"

She shook her head, tears welling in her eyes.

Officer Donovan sat down on the edge of the recliner. Officer Malasky took that as her cue to lead. She kept her voice soft, non-confrontational.

"Would you mind telling us about how the door hit you?" Malasky lowered herself to the couch, leaving Sara as the only one standing.

"Richard came home last night after it was already dark, and I tried to open the door for him, and he opened it at the same time. I was in the way."

Donovan looked at the window next to the door and then glanced at his partner. She was already looking at him. Sara knew by their exchanged glance that they had both come to the conclusion that Richard would have seen her there by the door. There was no way he wouldn't have known. They knew it wasn't an accident.

The tension was thick enough you could cut it with a knife.

"Would you like some coffee?" Sara asked. "I can make a pot." Standing, she turned toward the kitchen.

"No, thank you, we're fine."

She remained standing and clasped her hands in front of her. "Alright, then. Well. You haven't said why you're here."

Donovan cleared his throat. He took out his notepad and pen. He looked down as if reviewing something on the page. "We'd actually like to talk to your husband. You said he's not here. Do you know where we can find him?"

"I don't understand. Why do you need to talk to him? I told you it was an accident."

"It doesn't have to do with that, ma'am. He may have some information in an ongoing investigation. We'd just like to ask him a few questions."

"He... he didn't say when he'd be back." Her voice caught in her throat.

They both looked at Sara and waited. Silence was uncomfortable for most people; given enough time, they tried to fill it with words whether they wanted to or not. It worked.

"We... he... last night, after the door hit me, we sat down to dinner and ate. After that, he said he was going out. He deserved to have some fun after the week he'd had."

The officers looked at each other. Today was Wednesday.

Sara caught the exchange. "I thought the same thing, but before I could ask him how bad a week could be with only two days gone by, there were headlights pouring in the front window and a car honked. He told me not to wait up, and he left. The car fishtailed on the gravel when it left, so whatever it is must have been important." She blinked a couple of times, holding back the tears. "Look at me, you only asked ... you didn't want to hear my life history. Sometimes I rattle on. Richard doesn't like it when..."

This time she didn't fill the silence. She dropped her gaze and lowered herself to the edge of the couch, waiting.

Officer Malasky got up from her seat and moved closer, perching carefully on the edge of the coffee table directly across from her. Reaching out, she touched Sara's hands gently. "He didn't come home, did he?"

One tear tracked down her cheek. Without looking up, she shook her head.

Donovan cleared his throat again. "The ongoing investigation we're interested in speaking with your husband about is a missing persons report. A call came in last night saying that he'd been missing for 48 hours. We're required to check out reports, so we'd really like to know when the last time you saw your husband was."

Sara looked up, confusion creasing her brow. "He was here last night. He did this to me," she said, motioning toward her face, "and then he went out. He left without explaining himself, so the answer to your question is I saw him last night." She gasped, realizing what she'd just said. "I mean, he was here when this happened, but it was an accident. Wait... who could possibly think he's missing? Who filed a missing person's report?"

Donovan started to answer. "Missy Rodri-"

Malasky cut a quick look toward Donovan, effectively silencing him. Instead of answering Sara's question, she said, "Is that his car in the driveway?"

Sara looked at Donovan, then at Malasky, before she nodded.

"Do you mind if we take a look at it?"

"I don't know what good that will do, and he's a very private person."

"There may be a receipt or something in there verifying that he wasn't missing during the period that was reported. If we can establish the report as false, we can close the case and be gone before he gets home." The unspoken message being that they didn't want their presence to cause her any trouble.

Sara looked at Officer Malasky and thought about it for a few seconds, then nodded. "Okay. It shouldn't be locked. He never locks it."

The three made their way outside to Richard's car. The officers pulled rubber gloves from their shirt pockets and pulled them on. Donovan opened the driver's door and stuck his head in, Malasky went around to the passenger's side, and Sara stayed a few steps back.

She could hear them talking quietly to each other inside the car but couldn't make out what they were saying. Donovan backed out with a small piece of paper pressed between thumb and forefinger. Turning toward Sara, he held it out. "Whose credit card ends in the numbers 4293?"

"He doesn't let me -- I don't have a credit card. It must be one of his."

"The date on this receipt is yesterday."

"I told you he was here last night."

"Yes, you did."

Malasky straightened up from the passenger's side of the vehicle, stepped back and walked around. "Mrs. Jameson, are these yours?"

Sara looked down at what Officer Malasky was holding in her gloved hands. There was a pair of lace thong panties, embroidered with the letter "A."

As many things as she was prepared for them to find, this was totally unexpected. She took a step back, the tears welling up and overflowing. She'd thought he was seeing someone on the side, and then the upcoming trip he had planned, but proof in her face like this was not something she was prepared to handle. She leaned over and threw up.

Officer Malasky held her hair and gently rubbed her hand up and down her back. When Sara's stomach was empty, she slid to the ground. Malasky helped her down and knelt next to her. The tears were flowing freely.

"They aren't yours, then." It was more a statement than a question. "I'm so sorry."

She didn't have anything to say. Sara leaned against Malasky and whispered, "Why?"

From one woman to another that one word asked a multitude of questions: Why was he having an affair, why was a report filed by one woman while another woman's panties were in the glove box, why didn't he love her enough to be faithful. There was no answer for any one of them, let alone all of them. Malasky held her and rocked her. Meeting Donovan's uncomfortable gaze over the top of Sara's head, she shook her head once. Donovan understood. Moving off, he called it in. The case was closed.

When Sara's tears were cried out, she shuddered and took a shaky breath. "I'm sorry, I … I'm sorry."

Malasky helped her stand. "Is there anyone we can call to come sit with you?"

She only shook her head.

"When your husband comes back, please give us a call. We'd still like to talk to him. Would you do that for us?" Malasky took a business card from her pocket and passed it to Sara.

She took it, nodding once. "Yes," she whispered.

"If you need anything," she continued, referring to Sara's domestic abuse, "anything at all, you call me. My cell phone number is on the back of that card as well."

Sara looked at her, took her hand and squeezed. "Thank you."

Malasky watched Sara walk into the house and close the front door softly behind her. The latch clicked.

The officers got into their patrol car, turned it around and rolled down the drive. Sara curled up on the end of the couch and picked lint off of her pants while she waited. Finally, after what seemed like an eternity, she heard the gravel crunch and looked up without moving her head, following their progress with her eyes. The look she'd seen from her husband for years, the look she'd grown to fear, the look that had become hers as she watched him walk down the hallway last night after he'd laughed.

Her eyes glittered.

THE ORGANIST

"We can put him on the transplant list. For now, that's all we can do." Dr. Hargrove laid his pen down on top of Brian's file.

"He's never going to *live* long enough to wait out the list! The tests show that he's only got fifteen percent of his lung capacity left. It's getting worse, and there's nothing you can do except put him on the damn list?" I knew I was shrieking, but I didn't care. I couldn't believe what I was hearing.

"I'm sorry, Ms. Millinger. Brian can still breathe on his own; that puts him at the lower end of the list. Since he is under twelve years of age, he will be placed on a different list than the adults. If he were on the twelve and above list there would be very little hope. As it stands, he's in fifth position, if we get him on that list now. Potentially, he'll be in a good position to receive a donation within two years' time." He leaned back in his chair.

Jumping up, I paced the length of his office. "You don't understand. His breathing is getting worse by the day. He doesn't do more than wheeze. The pain on his face means I'm a failure as his mother. I'm supposed to protect him, keep him safe. Being put on the donor list doesn't make that happen. Getting a new lung, that's what would take away that look, would take away his pain." My palms were sweating; my own breath was short. My blood pressure was rising steadily, and I could feel it pounding in my chest, booming in my head. My entire body was getting hot. A flush rose up my neck and across my face.

He nodded slowly. "I understand your concern, Ms. Millinger. Brian is in pain, of this there is no doubt. He is not, however, the worst case. Now, if his oxygen intake drops below eighty-nine percent and he becomes lethargic..."

My hand flew up and, palm out, I stopped his bottled speech. "YOU don't get to tell me how Brian has to get WORSE before he can get BETTER. YOU only get to tell me you can help him." Tears welled up in my eyes, overflowing in streams down my cheeks.

The dam broke, and my voice cracked. "I can't do this. I need him to be able to breathe. He needs to be like other boys, running and playing, falling off his bicycle. Climbing trees to swing out on the limbs and scare his mother half to death. He needs to experience life, and I can't fix him. I need help. Help me save my son."

It seemed my outburst had little effect on him. He nodded again and leaned forward, pushing a stack of papers across the desk. He set a pen down on top of them before looking up at me.

"That's what I'm trying to do. My hands are tied, here. There are rules and directives in place to make sure the neediest patient receives the first available organ. To get Brian on the list, you'll need to sign these papers so we can get the process moving. Please, Ms. Millinger, for Brian." He spread his hands wide, indicating that the ball was back in my court. The look in his eyes had softened, taking the edge off my hate and leveling my blood pressure.

There had to be something else I could do. Right now I couldn't think. Coming back around to the front of the chair, I dropped down into the chair, drained of all energy. I looked at Dr. Hargrove, then down at the pen. My hand shook as I picked it up.

The clock on the wall ticked loudly, reminding me that each second that went by was another one gone from Brian's life. I didn't bother to read the documents in front of me. Half of them were in legalese, which I wouldn't have understood anyway. Right now I didn't care. I had to do something to help my son. Tick tock. Flipping through the pages, I signed everywhere that was marked. It seemed as if there were fifty pages. Why so many just to help another human being live?

When I'd finished signing, I set the pen down and laid my head down on my arm on the edge of his desk. He reached over and placed his hand over the top of mine. It was warm and soft, callous-free. To me that identified a man who had not seen one single day of hard labor in his life. At that moment, I felt very old and worn out.

"If you'll wait here, I'll have my secretary make the call to UNOS and get the process moving. I'll be back in a few minutes." His chair squeaked as he rose. I heard the papers I'd just signed rustle as he picked them up and then the door close softly behind him.

A minute or so later the door behind me opened. I didn't bother to raise my head; I was still gathering my strength. It was too much work to lift it. I felt paper slide underneath my hand. A second or two later the door closed again. Turning my head to the side, I looked around; I was alone. I closed my eyes again. I was utterly drained.

The next thing I knew, Dr. Hargrove was tapping my arm.

"Ms. Millinger?" I grudgingly opened my eyes. My eyeballs felt like sandpaper had been scrubbed across them. I raised my head and blinked several times, trying to clear them.

"I'm sorry, I must have dozed off. It's so hard, I never sleep anymore. I can't..." I took a shuddering breath.

As I leaned back in the chair, a business card fluttered to the floor. Looking down at it, I noticed it only had a name on it in plain block letters, with a number printed below. I picked it up and held it out to the doctor. "This fell off your desk."

He shook his head. "That must be yours, I don't recognize it."

Remembering the page I'd felt being slipped under my hand while I rested earlier, I picked up the card and slipped it into my purse. "Perhaps it fell out of my purse. Is the paperwork filed? Is Brian on the list?"

Dr. Hargrove nodded. "All set. Good news for Brian, only four children are on the list now, including him. A donor presented this morning, and the child at the top of the list is currently being prepped to have the lung implanted. Here's a pager that I'd like you to keep on at all times. If you need to leave Brian with a sitter for any reason, please leave the pager with the sitter, as well. The moment it goes off he'll need to be brought to the hospital. Organ transplantation is time sensitive. Tissues, including organs, die quickly without oxygen and blood. To keep them viable, they must be transplanted as soon as possible."

I nodded. Reaching out, I took the pager and made sure it was turned on before slipping it into my purse. With another shuddering breath, I rose from the chair. "I apologize for my outburst earlier. Brian is... I am..."

He patted my arm. "No apology necessary. You're under quite

a bit of strain, and that's understandable. If you have any questions, please don't hesitate to call."

After I'd sent Brian's babysitter, Mrs. Kowalski from next door, home, and Brian was settled in for the night, I went over in my mind what Dr. Hargrove had said about the child at the top of the list. He'd survived long enough to make it to surgery. I had to think positive about Brian making it to the finish line, too.

My thoughts turned to the business card. If Dr. Hargrove hadn't given it to me, then who had and more importantly, why? I wished I'd looked up sooner when I heard the door open.

Retrieving my purse from the back of the chair, I dug through until I found the card. I read it again. All it said was "Henderson" and a seven-digit phone number. No area code. I assumed it was a local number. I wasn't sure why, but I found myself curious about how it had come into my possession.

I dialed and waited. The phone rang once before the call was picked up.

"Yes." The voice on the other end answered curtly. The woman had a slight accent; I wasn't familiar enough with different countries' dialects to identify the accent from one word.

"Today at Dr. Hargrove's office, I was given a business card with this number and the name 'Henderson' printed on it."

"Wait." Again, one word. A breathy huff and the phone thunked down at the other end.

I waited. Several minutes went by, and I'd begun to think I'd been forgotten when I heard rustling and a male voice.

"This is Henderson."

His voice didn't have the touch of accent that had been evident in hers. This voice had a deep timbre, melodic and hypnotizing in its richness.

"Hello?" he said. I realized I hadn't spoken. He probably thought I had hung up.

"Hello. Yes. Mr. Henderson, I was given your name and this number during my visit to Dr. Hargrove's office today. I'm not entirely sure why. Perhaps you can shine some light on that reason.

May I ask who you are, and what you do?"

"Henderson. No Mister, just Henderson. I am in the business of procurement. Your turn. Who are you, and who gave you my card?"

Procurement? I was no closer to an answer, any answer, than I was before I dialed the phone.

"My name is Stacy Millinger and I have no idea who gave me your card. I was resting my eyes while I waited for Dr. Hargrove to come back, and the card was slipped under my hand. I wish I had looked up and seen who it was. I might have been better prepared for this phone conversation."

"Dr. Hargrove's office. Yes. Well, tell me about your reason for visiting the good doctor."

He was now much further along in the information department than I was. This was definitely an odd conversation, but I'd made the decision to dial the phone, I might as well follow through and see where it went. Taking a deep breath, I dove in.

"My son, Brian, is sick. He needs a lung transplant, double would be best but one will save his life. The doctors don't know for sure what causes the 'condition' he has and haven't been successful in reversing the effect. They only know that if his lungs continue to atrophy the way they're doing, he'll die before his eighth birthday. We were at Dr. Hargrove's office to fill out the paperwork and get on the donor list."

"Your son, how old is he?" His voice softened. My throat closed. It was hard to talk about the disease itself. I found it even harder to talk about what it was doing to Brian. Thinking about his tiny little form struggling to breathe, the possibility of his dying from this vicious, undeserved attack on his body...

"Six." My voice cracked. It was all I could do to get that one word out.

In the background on his end, I heard a drawer closing and paper rustling. He didn't speak for at least a minute. That was fine with me; I had trouble getting myself under control. It had been a long day. I'd spent most of it flying down the emotional roller coaster then chugging back to the top for another terrifying drop.

"I would like to meet Brian. Would that be alright with you?"

"Why do you want to meet my son?"

"Perhaps I can help him."

My heart skipped a beat. I had no idea who this man was or how he could help, but I couldn't deny the spark of hope that one sentence lit.

"How?" I whispered.

"I'd like to talk with you about that, though not on the telephone. In person would be better."

"Alright. Tomorrow morning we have an appointment, but Brian and I will be home after lunch. Can you come by around two o'clock?" Chugga, chugga, chugga, chugga... the roller coaster stuttered back toward the top of the hill, fueled by adrenaline and faith.

"Two o'clock it is, then. What is your address?"

I gave it to him, and we hung up. There was so much adrenaline flowing through my veins; I was jittery and my skin itched. I was suddenly wide awake. Wider awake than I'd been in the full four years since Brian's condition had made itself known.

Doing what any woman with excess energy would do, I cleaned the house from top to bottom, except for Brian's room. I didn't want to wake him. By the time I finished, the adrenaline had worn off, and exhaustion was setting in. I stripped down and crawled into bed, anticipating tomorrow's meeting.

~~*~*~*

The doorbell rang at exactly two o'clock. Brian was playing with his cars in the living room.

"Can I get it, Mama?" He rasped, his eyes shining bright. People rarely came to our door, so he didn't have many chances to answer it. I didn't have the heart to tell him no.

"Let's both get it. I'll go with you, and you can open it, how's that?"

His entire little face lit up. "Okay!"

Taking his hand we walked each other to the door, swinging our clasped hands in rhythm to our footfalls. He reached up and pulled the handle, tugging slightly to get the door started. I grabbed the door itself and helped. Too much exertion and he wouldn't be able to breathe at all.

As the door swung open, Brian peeked around the edge, and though I couldn't see it from this angle, I knew he had a smile on his face. He loved surprises. What he saw caused him to step backward.

"Mama, it's a stranger," he stage-whispered. "I thought it was Mrs. Kowalski." Backing around behind me, he kept hold of my hand.

The gentleman at our door was probably in his mid-sixties with a round, portly belly. The greenest eyes I'd ever seen twinkled at us from beneath bushy white eyebrows. As he removed his bowler hat, white tufts of hair sprung out all over his head as if someone had cranked the handle on a jack-in-the-box.

"Henderson?" I questioned.

He bowed slightly, his eyes never leaving mine. "Indeed. It's a pleasure to meet you, Ms. Millinger."

I reached over and unlatched the screen door. "Please, come in."

As he pulled the screen open and made his way in, Brian peeked out at him from behind my leg.

"You must be the man of the house," Henderson said, holding out his hand for a shake. "Mr. Millinger, I presume?"

Brian giggled softly. He looked up at me for confirmation and when I nodded, stepped out from behind me. He stood up very straight and shook hands. With more seriousness in his voice than his age should have allowed, he answered. "I am Brian. Want to play cars?"

Henderson appeared to consider his invitation seriously. "I would like that very much. Can we play with them on the table? Getting down to the floor is easy enough, but getting back up gives me trouble."

"Can we, Mom?"

"Well, I think that's a fine idea. Let's use the breakfast nook."

Brian scooped up his cars while Henderson followed me through the archway.

"Would you care for some coffee?" I asked over my shoulder.

"Lovely, thank you."

As I bustled about in the kitchen getting the coffee pot started, I heard soft murmurs from around the corner. When I rounded the wall, the sight before me stopped me in my tracks. There was my son, propped on his knees on a kitchen chair, leaning on the table and setting up a race track with Henderson's help. Their heads were tipped together, conspiratorially, and though I could hear their voices I couldn't make out the words.

"What do we have here?" I asked, stepping closer, inspecting a piece of track.

Brian looked at me with wonder-filled eyes. "Henderson brought a race track, Mama. He didn't even know I had cars!"

He leaned closer to me, motioning me in. I leaned down, and he cupped his tiny hands around my ear.

"I think he's Santa," Brian stated quietly.

Turning my head, I looked at him. "You never know," I said and winked.

Brian winked back at me, grinning from ear to ear.

~~*~*~*

After the three of us had played cars for half an hour or so, Brian was struggling to breathe. It was time for him to rest awhile.

"Brian, I think you should take it easy. What do you say I tuck you in for a nap?"

He shook his head slowly. "No, Mama, we have company. I get to stay when we have company."

"Normally you do, except when it gets hard for you to breathe. Are you having trouble?"

He started to deny it, but changed his mind and nodded instead.

"Carry me?" he asked, wheezing.

"Okay." I picked him up and motioned to Henderson that I would be right back.

When I returned, I said, "Thank you for playing with Brian. He doesn't get to do much of that with other people."

Henderson's satchel was on his lap, and he was extracting a single sheet of paper. He laid it on the table next to the track and reached back inside, withdrawing a gold pen.

"Brian is a bright young man. I'm glad I had the opportunity to meet him. It's been a long time since I've played cars with a new friend, too." He smiled brightly.

"Would you like more coffee?"

"No, thank you, I've plenty."

I lowered myself into the chair that Brian had just vacated. "Alright, then." Clasping my hands together on the table in front of me, the paper and pen between us, I said, "Please tell me how it is you think you can help my son."

He set his satchel on the floor next to his chair and mirrored my position, clasping his own hands before him. "As I've said, I'm in the procurement business. I have the unique gift of being able to find what others need."

I didn't understand, so I remained quiet and waited.

"This morning I found a race track for Brian, which is his to keep whether we are able to help one another any further or not." He tipped his head in my direction.

"Go on." A tingle started near the bottom of my spine.

"Yes. Brian is in definite need of a lung. In order to determine his severity, I needed to meet him and see for myself. I agree that his condition makes this a dire necessity and that he, and by extension, you, qualify for my services."

"And what services, exactly, would those be?" The tingle moved steadily upward.

"Procurement. Specifically, of a lung for Brian."

My breath caught in my throat. Did I just hear him right? Was he offering to sell me a body part for my son?

"I… I'm not quite sure… at all… what you're saying Henderson." I stammered.

"Yes you are, Ms. Millinger. I'm saying exactly what you think I am." Again, he waited.

I'm sure my thoughts were transparent and displayed in living color across my face: Disbelief, shock, hope, delight, fear, and finally, resignation.

"I can't afford to pay for services such as yours, Henderson. I can barely make the rent and co-pays for Brian's doctor visits. I don't have two dimes to rub together at the end of the month, let alone the hundreds of thousands of dollars I presume your service costs."

He reached out and gently inched the one page document

closer to me.

"My services do not require cash for payment. This contract sets out specifics of our deal. If you'll read it before you make a firm decision, I believe you'll be surprised at your ability to make the sacrifice."

I stared at him for another moment, not sure at all if I wanted to read the contract. I knew I was at a turning point in my life; a fork in the road. One branch was most certainly right, the other horribly wrong, but how was I to know the difference when I couldn't see farther ahead than where Brian and I now stood? The last thing I wanted to do was lead Brian the wrong direction. His life depended on my choices, and I was so far out of my league in the decision-making department.

"You are wise to consider all possibilities, Ms. Millinger. I'm only asking that you read the one-page document. If you disagree that this would be the answer to Brian's predicament, I will collect my things and be on my way. It will be as if this conversation never took place. If you find that you are agreeable to the terms as set forth, we will sign the sheet and consider our agreement bonded by our signatures and each other's honor."

The tingle raced up and down my spine faster than Brian's cars along the track. I reached my hand out and pulled the paper closer to me. There were three paragraphs, a space for today's date, and two lines for signature.

I read through the document quickly. He watched me read and calculated my response; I could feel his eyes on me the whole time. Stunned by what I saw on that sheet of paper, I looked back up at Henderson, eyes wide.

He waited. Once again that ever bouncing ball was in my court and what happened next depended on what I said or did.

"I need some time to consider. Can you come back tomorrow? I can..." I croaked, my throat suddenly dry.

He shook his head slowly. "I'm afraid that's not how this works. It is a one-time offer that expires if I walk out the door without your signature. The decision is already made; you know it, and I know it. We only need to know which direction you've decided to take in helping your son live. My waiting list for Brian's new lung is much shorter than the national database list."

My breathing was ragged. My heart hurt. "How long is your list?" I managed.

"There is currently no waiting list, Ms. Millinger. Brian would be at the very top and have my full attention."

I closed my eyes. Searching deep, I knew he was right. I'd already made the decision. Brian was my whole life. My hand reached out in search of the pen before I'd even opened my eyes.

"Brian, wash your hands while you're in there, please. Dinner is almost ready." I stood at the end of the hall and listened. First I heard a flush, and then the faucet turned on. Satisfied that he'd heard me and was doing as I'd asked, I returned to the kitchen and finished putting the food on our plates.

As I carried them into the dining room, my son was standing near my chair, watching my purse.

"What are you doing, honey?" I asked, setting the plates near our places.

"I'm listening to the bees."

"What bees, sweetie?" I walked around to where he was standing, thinking this might be a new game he'd come up with on his own.

"The ones in your purse, Mama. They're buzzing."

"The ones in… Oh, the bees are buzzing!" I hugged Brian tight, picked him up and swung him around in a circle. I laughed loud enough to startle him. "Honey, that sound is the pager. Let me check and make sure, but I think we just heard your lung come in!"

I set him down gently and grappled with my purse, digging through for the pager. My fingers found it, and I yanked it out, checking the display. The hospital's main number was shining brightly.

Brian stood there, unsure of what to do. "My lung?" he rasped. I could tell by the tone of his voice and level of wheezing that he was getting excited.

"Stay calm, baby, and get your shoes. We're going to the hospital! I'll get our coats and meet you by the front door." It was my fault he was getting excited; I should have been better prepared for this eventuality. Shouldering my purse, I rushed toward the front door.

I reached into the closet by the door and pulled out the overnight suitcase I'd packed weeks ago, shortly after Henderson's visit to our home. In it was everything Brian would need during the first couple of days at the hospital. Slipping on my own shoes, I pulled his jacket and mine off the hangers. As I closed the door, I saw Brian, shoes on, holding his favorite teddy bear.

"Can Puppy go? He's scared to stay home alone." Brian plunked a thumb into his mouth. He hadn't done that since he was two.

"Absolutely, Puppy can go. He can even sit on your lap under the seat belt." I helped Brian into his jacket and grabbed the suitcase in one hand, Brian's hand with the other, and tried to contain my excitement as we crossed the threshold and stepped onto the porch. It felt as if a new day were about to begin.

I pulled the car into a parking space in the hospital parking lot. Brian had fallen asleep on the short drive; any amount of adrenaline had that effect on him these days.

"Wake up, baby, we're here." I rubbed his arm as I unbuckled the seat belt from across his car seat. He stirred.

"I'm tired, Mama," he wheezed, words barely audible.

"That's okay, baby. I'll carry you." I would come back later and pick up the suitcase once he was out of surgery and moved to a regular room. Sliding my purse strap up higher on my left shoulder, I lifted Brian up and held him tight against my chest, adjusting his sleeping form so he could rest his head on my right shoulder. Bumping the door closed with my hip, I punched the lock button on my key fob and the car answered with a twin beep.

Across the parking lot, two figures were walking toward me. As they stepped into a pool of light cast by one of the overhead lights, I saw it was Henderson and an intern.

"Ms. Millinger, we'll go in this way," Henderson said, redirecting their path along the side of the building and down a sidewalk. The intern reached for Brian, and I let him take over.

Brian was slight in build, but heavy when carried asleep.

"He's sleeping," I whispered. I hoped he understood my unspoken wish to be careful.

"Yes, ma'am. I'll be gentle." He responded quietly as he cradled Brian in his large arms, dwarfing him in size.

Once I was sure Brian was safely in good hands, I returned my attention to Henderson. "Why are we going in back here?" I questioned, a bit wary.

"This is a shorter route to the surgery suite. Please, follow me. We don't have time to spare."

I wasn't sure what was causing my discomfort, but the feeling along the base of my spine was back. All of a sudden I really wanted to carry my son again, myself, though it was too late. The intern had much longer legs and a wider step; he'd made his way down the sidewalk and through the door at the end before we'd reached the halfway point.

By the time we cleared the door, and I had gotten my first glimpse of the white tiled hallway, we saw the last glimpse of the intern as he carried Brian into a room near the far end of the hall.

Henderson motioned toward a room to our right where several chairs, end tables with magazines, and a television mounted to the wall could be seen. "Please wait here. I'll check on progress and come back to update you as soon as I know something."

"Wait," I called, catching his sleeve as he continued away. "I'd like to be with Brian until they take him back."

He stopped and turned to face me. "They've already taken him back. He's on a time schedule, and there's precious little left. Excuse me, I'll be back."

I let go, and he nodded before moving down toward the end of the hall and the door through which Brian had gone. I watched until he disappeared. I was suddenly and completely aware of the quiet that covered this wing like a blanket.

~~*~*~*

"Ms. Millinger?" The doctor in scrubs closed the distance as he removed his rubber gloves with a snap. His face mask hung loosely around his neck, and shadows clung tightly to his lower eyelids.

"Yes. How is he? Can I see him?" I stood, rubbing my lower back. The waiting room chairs weren't comfortable after a few hours. I'd spent time sitting, then pacing, and then sitting again.

"He's in recovery. It was touch-and-go there for a while; we weren't sure his body was going to accept the new lung, but as of right now he's stable and we're cautiously optimistic."

Tears sprang forth, threatening to fall. Relief flooded my entire body. Bryan was through surgery and on his way to being able to breathe. "Oh, thank you. How long will he be in recovery?"

"They'll watch him until he wakes up, and once the recovery nurses are certain he's going to remain stable, they'll move him to ICU. I suspect that will take another four to six hours or so, depending." He stifled a yawn. "I can either have someone come and get you, if you'd like to stay, or give them your number so they can call you when it's okay for you to see him."

Four to six hours. I hadn't eaten or slept, and the clock on the wall showed it was closing in on six o'clock in the morning. Coffee would help, I decided, now that the unknown was known, so I opened my purse and shuffled through the random contents until I found an old receipt and a pen.

"Please ask them to call me if I'm not back when they come looking. I'd like to freshen up and grab a cup of coffee, but I shouldn't be gone long." Passing the scrap of paper with my scrawled writing on it to the doctor, I breathed a sigh of relief.

He turned and strolled back down the hallway, rubbing the back of his neck. The long night had apparently caught up with him, as well.

~~*~*~*

I walked out to my car, punched the button to unlock it and slid behind the wheel. Though a trip home for a shower and a change of clothes would feel good, I decided to stop at the coffee shop around the corner for breakfast and a go-cup instead. Better to stay close to the hospital in case he was moved to a room sooner than the doctor anticipated.

The minute I opened the menu my stomach growled. It

reminded me how long it had been since I'd eaten.

Though I tried not to eat like this on a regular basis, having the stress lifted from my shoulders after so long left me famished. I ordered the truck driver's special. It came with everything I wanted, and then some.

I made quick work of my breakfast, clearing the oversized plate. To offset the day's worth of calories I'd just consumed, I promised myself I would eat a salad for dinner. After dropping enough money on the table to cover the tab and a generous tip, I headed back out to my car.

The sun had come up, and the temperature began to follow. In the tree nearest my car, an unseen bird mimicked the sound of a car alarm.

When I arrived back at the hospital, the parking lot was a beehive of activity. I circled the lot twice before finding a space on the far side of the building. Climbing out of my car, I crossed the lot and headed toward the door we'd entered through last night. The intern who had carried Brian rounded the corner, spotted me, and headed in my direction. I smiled.

"Good morning," I managed to get out before the look on his face registered. My face fell, a certain dread dragging me down. A sharp stabbing pain pierced my heart.

"Ms. Millinger, it's Brian…"

Who else could it be? The wail trapped in my mind flooded my body, my brain, and finally found my mouth.

"*No!*" was all I managed before the air was squeezed out of my lungs, and I was unable to breathe. My legs weren't strong enough to hold up the weight of my grief. They gave out and unceremoniously collapsed. He caught me before I hit the ground, pulled me against him and held me until I regained a modicum of composure.

"Where is he? Where's my son?" I whispered, using what precious little air I could draw in.

"I'll take you to him." He loosened his hold, inch by inch, until he was certain I was able to stand and walk. Moving his arm to my waist, he supported me that way. I was grateful; without his support at this very moment I would have slumped like a rag doll, unable to take a step, let alone cross the rest of what seemed like miles to the building.

Neither of us spoke as he led me around to another, separate entrance. This door swung open before we reached it—apparently someone had been waiting for us.

The smell was overwhelming; it hit me as soon as we entered. No amount of cleaning or air freshener spray could cover up the unmistakable smell of death.

The intern took me to a row of chairs along one wall. Everything here was institutional—free from any comfort, as there wasn't a way to ease the pain of those in the beginning stage of grief. The people who passed through here were either unconcerned with such trivial matters or not in a position to care about such things. He lowered me down into one of the hard plastic seats, patted my shoulder and went through the swinging door across the hall. Through the slim opening, I saw the edge of a grey desk and a sliver of a person in a white coat.

"Brian," I whispered. Pain rolled over me in waves. "Oh, Brian, what have I done?"

A woman in olive green scrubs sat down next to me. Neither of us talked until the tears that poured down my face began to slow. She pulled some tissues from the box she carried and handed them to me. I took them and blew my nose.

"Thank you."

"I'm very sorry for your loss, Ms. Millinger." Her voice... I'd heard it before.

"What happened? He was... the doctor said he was stable and that I could see him when he got out of recovery." I looked at her, searched her face, her eyes, for the truth.

"He was stable. An aneurism burst and we could not control the bleeding."

"An aneurism? Other than his lungs, he was perfectly healthy. I don't understand." Her voice unsettled me as much as her words. I searched my memory but couldn't put my finger on where I'd heard it before.

"For some things, there is no explanation." The accent! She was the voice on the phone, the woman who had answered Henderson's number!

"Where is he?"

She stood and led me down the hall and through another door. The room contained a blue plastic chair, a large window inset into the long wall, and a speaker box on the wall. She pushed the white button on the speaker box and the curtain covering the other side of the glass was drawn back. I saw my baby boy laid out on a steel table, covered to his neck with a sheet. He looked so tiny and pale.

I pressed my palm to the glass. "Did he suffer?"

"No."

Her one-word answer did nothing to comfort me. As hard as I tried to control the flood, all I could do was feel it rising, roiling, gurgling up and over me. A sob escaped. With both hands pressed flat against the glass, the pain pressed in on my heart from all sides.

"How could this have happened? He was recovering, the doctor said…" The tears poured out again.

"They did everything they could to save him." She wasn't helping, shoveling out the company line. How dare she tell me they did all they could? My baby was still alive twenty-four hours ago, and now he was as cold as the air in this room. I turned and stared at her, incredulous.

"How can you stand there and *say* that to me? 'Everything they could' didn't include saving his life! He's dead! My baby is gone, and they're going about their day like nothing happened, as if everything were alright. Well, let me tell you something," I glared at her, stabbing my index finger within inches of her face, "*NOTHING* is alright, it will never be fine again!"

The tears flowing down my face now were not those borne of sadness; I was angry. The level of unfair perpetrated on me, on my son, my innocent, sweet son, was beyond anything I'd ever imagined could exist. They had taken *everything* from me, and they weren't going to get away with it.

Turning on my heel, I stalked out of the room, the building, and across the lot to my car. I slid in behind the wheel and yanked the door shut. The phone call I was about to make was best made in private.

I dug through my purse and pulled out my cell phone and the white business card. The phone on the other end rang once, twice, three times before it was picked up.

"Yes." Henderson himself answered the phone, sounding irritated.

"Brian is dead. I want to know what went wrong, and I want to know why."

After a short pause, I heard a long sigh. "I don't know what went wrong, I'm going to talk to the doctor and find out after they've had a chance to do an autopsy."

"You promised me..." my voice cracked. I tried again. "You promised he would be better, and now he's lying on a cold slab in the morgue and I'll never hold my baby again."

Another pause, then his voice turned cold and business-like. "I promised a lung. I didn't promise he would live. Ms. Millinger, our business is concluded at this time. I will be in contact when it is time to settle up your end of the contract. My condolences on the loss of your son."

I turned the key in the lock and opened the door. The house felt as if it, too, were in mourning. Without conscious thought about what I was doing, I found myself standing on the step stool in the doorway, reaching up, stretching on my tiptoes. My fingers felt it, and I stretched a little bit further before being able to grasp it.

Pulling the box down, I stepped off the stool and carried the box to the bed. There was a fingerprint scanner instead of a lock. I'd taken every precaution to keep this safe, secure, and out of Brian's hands. I was a good mom. I set it down gently and placed my finger on the scanner, holding it still, waiting several seconds until the telltale click announced that it was unlocked. Flipping the lid up, I removed the revolver from inside. With the precautions I'd taken, I saw no reason to store the bullets in a separate location. I opened the cylinder and loaded it.

The gun had belonged to my father. It was one of the few possessions he still owned when he passed away. Most of his belongings had been sold to pay the assisted living facility expenses for mom's stay after the Alzheimer disease advanced.

With gun in hand, I walked slowly toward Brian's room. At

the door, I paused, crushing sadness washing over me again. I almost felt as if I could deny the truth by not stepping inside. My analytical mind knew this wasn't true, but I wasn't thinking analytically; I was waffling between denial and acceptance. Nothing would bring him back; I knew this. The only relief in sight was on the far side of revenge.

I made myself step in. His room was clean: stuffed animals lined up on his bed, backs against the wall so they would sit up straight; race track assembled at the foot of his bed, and his superhero bed sheets, mismatched because he couldn't decide on just one, were pulled up and as straight as he could make them. The tears welled up in my eyes again—he was the tidiest six-year-old, and now he was all alone. Even his pajamas were folded and waiting for him on his pillow.

Crossing to the bed, I lifted his pajama top close to my face, inhaling. The collar smelled like him. Overwhelmed, I sank down onto the bed, curled into a ball and buried my face in his smell before the anguish took over. I finally allowed myself to grieve, sobs wracking my body, and tears I thought were already cried out renewed, draining my body completely.

I must have fallen asleep; it was dark when I opened my eyes. The pajama top was still clutched in my hand, and the revolver laid next to me on the pillow.

The thought came unbidden. Brian should be buried in his favorite pajamas. I folded this pair and returned them to his pillow, picked up the gun, and made my way downstairs. As I passed the chair where my purse hung, I tucked the gun down inside and continued on to the laundry room. Turning the light on, I opened the dryer and dug around until I came up with his blue flannel footie pajamas. Shaking out the wrinkles, I folded them and tucked them under my arm. Another thought came, and I returned to Brian's room.

Under the teddy bear at the end of stuffed animal row, I found his baby blanket. He didn't know—hadn't known—I was aware he still slept with it. On his fifth birthday, he'd made a big deal about being a big boy and gave me a speech about how he was too old to sleep with it anymore. We'd washed and dried it, and he'd taken me to his room to watch him "be big." He carefully moved his socks and underwear to the side and gently placed his blanket in the back, moved his clothes in front of it, and closed the drawer. Then he'd turned to face me and brushed his hands off like he'd just accomplished a difficult task. A week later he'd taken it back out. I saw it when I checked on him in the middle of the night. By the time I'd gone in to wake him the next morning, the blanket was nowhere in sight. I'd let him keep his secret. Now it would go to his grave with him. Pulling the blanket out of its hiding place, I folded it and tucked it under my arm with his pajamas.

I needed to get these things to the hospital before anything else so Brian would be taken care of properly. I took them downstairs and found a tote bag, setting them inside. Business first, then revenge.

The drive to the hospital was quick. There was limited traffic after ten p.m., and the lights were all green. I parked my car at the far end of the lot, away from the emergency entrance and close to the familiar walkway. Light spilled from windows on all three levels, bright enough to light my way.

Rounding the corner, the sidewalk fell into shadow. There were no windows on this side of the building to relieve the darkness.

As I neared the end of the sidewalk, luck was on my side. An orderly stepped through, holding the door for me. I nodded my thanks. The moment I entered, the events of the last twenty-four hours flooded my memory: the "bees" in my purse, our excited trip to the hospital, the large intern carrying Brian ahead and away... my heart squeezed in on itself at the thought, and tears threatened to overflow again. The memory of the doctor coming out to reassure me and, ultimately, the intern bringing news that destroyed my world, causing full-blown rage to flood my system. The senseless loss that could not, would not, be explained to me. How dare they brush me off as if I did not matter, like my feelings were unimportant?

Standing in that hallway, I felt the heat of my rage burst into flame, consuming every fiber of my being. Red encroached the edges of my vision; I now knew what was meant when someone "saw red."

Before I realized I'd moved, I was pushing my way through the swinging door through which Brian had been carried last night. I found myself in a surgery preparatory room. The large window between this room and the next allowed an unobstructed view into the surgery suite. There was a team in place, in the middle of a procedure. They didn't know I was here.

Henderson, with his white tufts of hair and electric eyes, stood facing me on the far side of the operating table. I strode over to the door between the two rooms and pushed. It didn't budge. The lock holding it closed thunked against the door jamb, drawing the attention of those inside. They looked at the window, and at me.

"Henderson!" I bellowed, the red closing my vision down further by the second.

He walked toward the window and pushed a button on the voice box inside.

"Ms. Hillinger, I cannot speak with you right now. We're in the middle of a procedure."

"You *will* speak to me now. You *owe* me that."

"Ms. Hillinger. Call me tomorrow. I will take time then to answer all of your questions." He turned away.

Being dismissed in person was the last straw. The red completely covered my vision; everything was covered in a coating of blood red.

Dropping the tote bag with Brian's clothes inside, I reached into my purse and withdrew the revolver. I tapped the barrel on the glass.

Henderson turned back, apparently unaffected by the sight.

"You will come out here and talk to me now, or I will shoot you. I am prepared to take your life because you took my son's."

He stepped back to the speaker. His eyes should have shown fear; instead, there was boredom, as if he'd been there and done that before.

"Call me tomorrow, Ms. Hillinger. I did not take your son's life. His surgery did not go well. There is always a risk of death. Furthermore, you cannot shoot me. This glass," he tapped a finger on the glass, "is bullet proof."

Bullet proof glass. In the operating theater. My mind churned through every possible reason they might have used to justify this expense. Every path led me back to one answer. This one. They knew what they were doing was wrong, and they anticipated this very outcome. The boredom on his face, his response to my announcement, it made perfect sense now. He *had* been here and done this, before. I wondered how many times before; how many parents, siblings, children, friends, lovers... how many others?

My rage extinguished, leaving complete calm in its place. The full weight of the situation crushed my last hope. I had nothing left to live for. My son had been my entire life, my everything, and he was gone. I wanted to be with Brian again.

Putting the barrel of the gun under my chin, I enunciated my last words.

"Then collect your contract payment now. Take what you want."

The click of the trigger was buried under the roar of the blast. Bright light filled my sight, blocking out all of the red and everything beyond as the bullet exploded, taking skin, tissue, and bone with it on its way out.

~~*~*~*

Weightless, I couldn't remember where I was or what had brought the utter peace. I was floating.

A tiny voice called out to me. I turned my head to see.

"Brian!" Swimming toward him, I moved as quickly as my un-body would let me. A tether, attaching me to wherever I was, stopped my progress. Reaching my hand out I tried to touch him, but couldn't quite get there. I began to slide backwards, unable to control my movements. I heard his voice.

"I'll be waiting."

The light hurt my eyes. I tried to raise my hand to shade them and found myself unable to move my body at all. I closed my eyes, the only defense I had left.

A shadow moved across my lids. Opening my eyes again carefully, I saw Henderson.

"Good, you made it," he said. His eyes twinkled as he smiled down at me.

As what I'd done came back to me in a rush, I gasped. "I killed myself. Why did you save me?"

The skin around his eyes crinkled at an unspoken joke. "Don't you remember? You told me to take what I wanted. Some organs are no good from the moment of death. The contract gave me one organ; your spoken words gave me so much more. Your gift is generous; I thank you, and several others whose lives will be spared because of your donation thank you. Though as you wish, I won't make you stay to hear it from them. I'll let you go after we've finished the harvest."

He backed out of my line of sight, revealing a view of the mirror above. It took a moment before I could make sense of what I was seeing. My body was sliced open from collarbone to pelvic bone, and two different doctors were busy removing my kidneys. My cavity was already missing one lung and my liver, and the surgeon standing next to my head cradled my heart in his hands, waiting his turn to cut.

FOOLS ROULETTE

I call it Fools Roulette. It doesn't have anything to do with gambling, not really; it does, however, have to do with people who piss me off.

There's something about knowing you can stop stupidity in its tracks that makes you feel all warm and fuzzy, and godlike. Yeah, that's it, godlike. That's a good word for it. I like that feeling. Let me backtrack a little bit, you're looking at me as if you think I'm crazy. I can assure you; I'm not.

It was a Saturday morning last summer during that unseasonably mild week when the temperatures were perfect for being outside up until around three o'clock. I couldn't stand the thought of being trapped inside the house with nothing to do, so I slipped into my favorite sun dress and put my sandals on. Locking the door behind me, I took a stroll with no destination in mind, only enjoying a carefree, gorgeous day.

I wandered aimlessly down Main Street along with a handful of other people doing the same. The warmth of the sun, a slight breeze ruffling my hair, and the chirping of the birds in the trees lining the street made for a perfect day.

As I walked, I looked at the wares in the windows. The western store was stocking their fall clothes already; the jewelry store clerk was taking a necklace out of the window for a customer, and the thrift store seemed to be doing a brisk business from the looks of it. As I started to pass the antique shop, I saw it and stopped. There in the window was the most beautiful fountain pen I'd ever seen. I didn't know anything about fountain pens; I'd never been interested in them before, but for some reason this one stopped me in my tracks.

I stood there, for I don't know how long, just staring through the window like a kid in a candy store. I remember thinking I really shouldn't be spending the money, but how often in my life am I going to come across something this … perfect? I probably couldn't afford it anyway, but it didn't hurt to look.

When I opened the door, a bell tinkled overhead. The shop was quiet in a library sort of way; it was as though it was holding its breath, waiting for something. That's the only way I could describe it. The air was filled with anticipation. I shook that feeling off; an inanimate object couldn't feel anticipation.

The lighting was bright and cheery and not from overhead but from lamps of all shapes and sizes dotted around the cozy room. There were some with pretty stained glass shades, giving a different glow to the light. I knew my entrance had been announced, and as I waited for the salesperson to find me, I took my time looking around. There was a roll top desk with a patina on the wood that left no doubt the piece was old, though it was in great condition. There was a player piano, a case with rings and necklaces, another display case with brooches, several small silver boxes with their lids open to show off their velvet interiors, and a wooden Indian stood watch in the corner. I hadn't seen one of those in years. Stepping over, I ran my hand down his arm. The wood was smooth as silk.

I hadn't heard him approach. "He's been with me a long time," he said, his rich baritone rippled over me. Normally I don't care for people standing behind me, but something in the tone of his voice conveyed comfort and security.

Without turning, I responded. "There was one that looked just like him in the soda fountain where mom used to take us when we were little."

"He actually came from a soda fountain that was being remodeled."

I turned to face him. He appeared to be in his late forties, maybe early fifties. His smile reached all the way up to his eyes, making me think he had just shared a secret. I smiled in return.

"What a coincidence that would be, if he were the same one... good memories." I looked back at the Indian again before turning toward the window display. "What caught my eye and brought me in was the pen in the window. What can you tell me about it?"

"Mmm, yes, the pen. Quite beautiful." He moved soundlessly to the window and picked up the pen with its case. I moved closer to see it better, and he held it out for me to take. As the case settled into my hand, I was surprised by its warmth. The sun was out but not shining directly in the window; the store was comfortable, as well. I remember thinking how odd that was, but dismissed it in the next thought.

"This pen was originally part of a set, as you can see by the case. There's a space for a mate, which sadly did not come with it when I acquired the pen. There is a description behind the liner with detailed information." He grasped the corner of the insert and gently slid it out. "It is a Waterman 452 1/2V, red ripple fountain pen. What is even more interesting is that this very pen is said to have been used by Mamie Addlemeier to write her *Out of the Dark* series. Have you read her work?"

"I haven't, though I know she lived here in Aspen Grove, and she was thought to be crazy. That's all I've heard." I reached out with one finger and stroked the pen from cap to end. It was smooth and felt... right, somehow. It felt as if it were singing to me through vibrations. As strange as that sounds, it felt good.

He motioned for me to sit in the wing chair to my left. I did. He sat in the matching chair. I rested the pen and box on my lap, cradling it gently.

"She did live here, up on the hill at the end of Archer Lane. The Addlemeiers have lived in that house for generations. Her great-great-grandfather was our town founder and built the house so he could see threats before they reached the town. Mamie had always been a loner; not because she wanted to be, more because other children didn't want to play with her. She had three sisters, all of whom were older than she was by a good margin. They all married and moved away. She stayed with her parents until they died, and then lived on in the house until she passed away, as well. During her adult years, she was seen in town less and less, choosing to sequester herself away. She had a maid named Aurora who kept the household running. Now, Aurora had been with the family since before Mamie was born. Her mother, Sarah, had been the Addlemeiers' maid before her, and when she passed, Aurora was sixteen and was offered the position. She took the job and stayed on, living with the Addlemeiers. As Mamie became more and more of a recluse, Aurora did the grocery shopping and took care of anything Mamie needed from town. Legend says there were weeks at a time where Mamie didn't come out of her room and that maniacal laughter could be heard randomly through the door. That part had not been verified and was most probably added by a storyteller; Aurora was close-lipped and didn't talk out of turn. Whatever strange things, if any, happened in that house were taken to the grave by one or both of the ladies."

He rested his elbows on the arms of the chair and steepled his fingers.

"About the time Mamie would have been twenty-three or twenty-four, her first novel was published. This started the *Out of the Dark* series that would eventually become twenty-seven volumes over the next thirty years or so. The money made from the sales of her books kept the bills paid and both Mamie and Aurora comfortable. Mamie passed away from cancer when she was fifty-five. When Mamie died she left everything to Aurora. The royalties from book sales alone were enough to let her stay in the Addlemeier home without having to take another job. The legend goes on to say that Aurora took on the characteristics of Mamie and began writing her own stories."

The tone and cadence of his voice had lulled me into a trance. The quiet that descended when he stopped talking broke the spell, and I found myself openly staring at him. I blinked several times and cleared my throat. At some point during his story, my finger had resumed its stroking motion along the pen.

"I don't remember hearing the part about Aurora being the beneficiary of Mamie's will, or anything after that. I've intended to pick up the first book in the *Out of the Dark* series for a while now but haven't found one since they're out of print. The library doesn't carry a copy, either, which I found strange, since she's local."

His smile returned. I hadn't realized it had disappeared. He leaned closer, as if telling me a secret. "Then today is your lucky day. I happen to have a copy of her books here, as well. If you're interested, that is."

"Um, I am, though I'd like to talk about this pen first." The longer I touched it, the warmer it got and the more comforting it became. My fingers itched to hold it and write something, anything.

As if staring into my soul, he looked deep into my eyes for a long moment, then down at the pen in my hands. "It would appear the pen has chosen you," he said, his voice so low I had to strain to hear.

"I'm sorry?" Surely I'd misheard him.

It was his turn to blink. "I believe there's a price tag in the box. Let's have a look." He reached over and pulled a white tag from under the edge of the lining. "Here we are. Looks like this pen is… well, this can't be right. But it must be, as it's right here on the tag. The going price for this pen and its box today is $17.88."

The pen almost hummed under my finger. "Really? That sounds unusually low, much lower than I'd expe… I'll take it." At that very moment in time I would have hocked everything I owned and paid one hundred times that much.

"Wonderful. Let's get this wrapped up for you then. Join me at the counter?" He stood and moved gracefully toward the register situated on the marble-topped credenza along the side wall of the store. From just beneath the counter, he pulled a small square box. "This came to me when the pen did, and goes with it to you now. There's a small bottle of ink and two different nibs. I believe there is a small amount of ink already in the bladder though you'll want to fill it if you intend to write for long. If you aren't familiar with filling this type of pen, there are instructions in here as well."

As he rang up my purchase, I found my fingers itching to hold the pen again. I pulled my wallet out of my purse and counted out the exact change. This purchase would leave me with $13.73 to make it until next Friday; if I ate chicken salad sandwiches I would make it just fine. Good thing Jerry paid us minimum wage, as the tips made at the diner weren't much at all.

"Have you thought any more about Mamie's *Out of the Dark* series? I have them right here under the counter if you'd like to see them." His smile gave his eyes that secret-sharing look again before he ducked his head down and straightened back up with the first leather-bound volume in his hands.

Before I could stop myself I reached out and touched the aged leather. It was a smooth dark brown and had a thin leather string-tie to keep the front and back covers closed when not in use. The title was indented on the front by what appeared to be a leather tool stamp. I traced my finger over the lettering; it, too, was smooth with age.

The bell over the door tinkled as another customer entered. I turned at the sound and saw an older man wearing a thin sweater over his button down shirt, plaid pants and a bowler hat. His white hair poked out in tufts around his ears. He shuffled more than walked and tipped his hat to me before he continued on his way to the player piano.

Realizing I was still stroking the lettering on the cover I pulled my hand back and coughed nervously. "I apologize; I seem to be very touchy-feely today. It is a very beautiful book, and though I would love to have it, my budget doesn't have room this week. Maybe they'll still be here when I'm able to justify the cost. I shouldn't have bought this pen right now, either, but..." Lifting my wrapped package off of the counter, I lowered it carefully into my purse.

He disappeared below the counter again and came back up without the book. "Perhaps they will still be here. Kismet works that way."

The bell tinkled overhead as I left the shop. I felt rejuvenated, and with a renewed sense of purpose I was anxious to return home.

~~*~*~*

When I arrived home I slipped into an old t-shirt and a pair of comfortable yoga pants, then gathered a couple pads of paper and set them on the end table next to my favorite chair. It was oversized and overstuffed, and I'd gotten it for a steal from a yard sale down the block a few months earlier.

After pouring myself a glass of iced tea, I settled in and grabbed my purse, pulling out the package that held my new pen. I was a kid on Christmas morning; the excitement built with every second of unwrapping.

The second I laid eyes on it again my fingers began tingling; I couldn't get it out of the box and into my hands quick enough. The warmth wasn't my imagination; neither was the need. As I fit the pen to my hand and settled my fingers comfortably around it, I felt a warm vibration travel up my arm.

Have you ever had tunnel vision? I experienced it that afternoon for the first time in my life. When the warm vibration made it to my brain, I felt as if a dam had burst. The pen wrote smoothly and kept up with my thoughts, though I don't know how. That was a first, as well, the information streaming onto paper as quickly as my thoughts were created.

I'm not sure what time it was when my pen ran dry. I came out of "the zone" and looked around. The part of the street in front of my house that I could see through the window next to my chair was very dark and very quiet. I don't remember turning on the lamp, though I must have. It cast a soft glow in a circle around the chair and end table, and was the only light that was on in my house.

Suddenly I realized how badly I needed to use the restroom. I jumped up and promptly fell flat on my face. I'd been sitting with my legs crossed underneath me in the chair, and they'd fallen asleep. I couldn't feel either one of them. Luckily I missed crashing into the coffee table by a few inches. I lay there and shook my feet and legs, trying to bring blood flow back into them. The pins and needles said it was working. I still had to pee very badly and couldn't wait for my legs to wake up. I crawled on my hands and knees to the bathroom and made it just in time. Who knew a bladder could hold that much?

The bladder! That's why the pen quit working… I hadn't filled the bladder with ink like he'd told me to do. I face palmed myself and finished my business.

I wandered through the house, making sure the doors and windows were locked. My habit was to do this each day before the sun was completely down; I hadn't done it before sitting down to try out my new pen, and the amount of time that had passed between then and now was a little bit disconcerting. The fact that I'd spent such a large chunk of time writing and my hand didn't hurt at all was amazing; normally I had hand cramps before my shift ever finished at the diner, and that was just from taking orders for seven or eight hours. Well, there was the carrying of plates and that huge tray, too, but writing wasn't easy by the end of my shift either.

The instructions for refilling the pen with ink were easy to follow. I managed to do it right the first time and didn't spill the ink at all. Score one for the klutzy girl!

I set the pen down and returned the instruction sheet to its pocket in the box. My glass was empty; I took it back to the kitchen and refilled it. It wasn't surprising, but I didn't remember drinking it at all; in fact I didn't remember the last few hours at all, either.

Returning to my chair, I got comfortable and picked up the pad of paper and pen. When I touched the pen, it felt... charged, somehow. The warm feeling radiating from the pen up into my hand and arm was stronger and more intense; I wondered if I imagined things or if I was a little bit crazy. Touching the nib to the paper, the pen began to write again—long, flowing strokes, ink beautifully swirling across the page, my eyes following it as if I weren't the one writing, simply an innocent bystander watching it happen.

From somewhere far away, I heard a doorbell. *The neighbors must have company*; I thought, and kept watching the ink attach itself and soak into the pages, one beautiful line after the other.

I don't know how much later it was, though the sun was up and shining through the front window, when the phone rang and broke my concentration. I didn't want to stop watching the ink; it was captivating. The phone rang again. I pushed it out of my mind. The third time I reached over and answered it to stop it from bothering me.

"Hello?" I croaked.

"Beth? Where the hell are you?" Oh, crap, it was Jerry, my boss. I looked at the clock. Seven o'clock. Already?

I made a snap decision, one I hadn't made before and wasn't entirely comfortable with, but did it all the same. "Jerry, I'm sorry, I'm sick as a dog, throwing up everywhere. I should have called, but I haven't been able to leave the bath... oh, no, not again, gotta go." I hung up on him. I'd never called in sick for work before when I wasn't deathly ill; I don't know what came over me, except that the pen was still in my hand, and it wanted to write.

The pen wanted to write? What an odd thought. I meant *I* wanted to write. I think. Setting the phone aside, I flipped to a new page and touched pen to paper.

The ringing of the telephone interrupted my concentration again. *Days can go by, and nobody calls; why is it when I'm busy doing something I want to be doing, the damn thing rings off the wall?*

I answered it with an irritated, chopped "hello."

"Beth?"

I cringed inwardly. "Hi, Roxie." My current shift partner at the diner; I'd probably left her in a lurch today when I decided not to go to work. She was a nice girl, but not quick enough to cover the whole diner through a breakfast and lunch shift on a Sunday, let alone the church crowd that would have filled the place to capacity after services were over.

"Jerry said you were sick. How are you feeling?"

"I'm not eating yet, but I think I'll live. How was work? I'm sorry about leaving you alone today." That wasn't exactly a lie; I hadn't eaten a bite all day and my stomach was currently letting me know.

"It's okay. A girl came in to apply for a job just after Jerry called you, so he gave her a test run. She caught on quick, especially for her first day. I don't know what we would have done otherwise."

"Jerry hired someone to take my place?"

"No, Carrie's leaving, remember? She'll take her place. He just had her start because we were short staffed. How could he replace you? You've been with him for a long time, and you hardly ever get sick or ask for time off." She paused. "Do you want me to bring you some soup?"

What I wanted was to hang up the phone and get back to writing. "No, my stomach has settled down, it must have been a virus or something. I'm going to make some toast and see if that stays down. I appreciate it, though."

"Okay, well, I just wanted to check on you. See you tomorrow?"

"Yeah, see you tomorrow. And thanks for checking, I appreciate it."

After we hung up I stood in the kitchen and ate a sandwich and some chips. My body was achy, though that was probably from sitting in one spot for so long. The clock said it was after three o'clock in the afternoon; apparently I'd lost seven hours this time. I flexed my fingers; they weren't sore, and neither was my hand.

When I finished eating, I thought I would check the mailbox. I slipped on my sandals and opened the door. There was a package on my doormat, about the size of a cereal box. It was wrapped in brown paper and tied with twine. There was a tag flapping idly in the breeze; all it had on it was my name, no address, nothing else. I looked around but didn't see anyone. I wondered how long it had been here. Stepping around it, I went to the end of the drive and picked up the stack of flyers and junk mail from the mailbox. Flipping through them, I saw nothing important and dumped them all in the trash can on my way back to the house. Picking up the package, I took it inside with me, closing and locking the door as I went.

I held the package up near my ear and shook it gently; nothing rattled or ticked. Setting it down on the footstool by my chair, I went back into the kitchen and grabbed my iced tea glass.

The twine was tied in a bow. It untied rather easily, and the twine fell away, the brown paper packaging the only thing between me and whatever was inside. I lifted it carefully and turned it over; there wasn't any tape at all, just the paper flaps folded over each other. Lifting each edge carefully, I unwrapped the gift. I pressed the edges of the paper fully away; it was the back of a leather-bound book. A small gasp escaped my lips. Could it be *Out of the Dark?*

Gently I lifted the book and turned it over. As I'd hoped, it was the first volume in the series. Tracing my fingers over the lettering, I wondered who would give me such a rare and special gift. I laid the book carefully on my lap and flipped over the paper wrapping. There was no writing on it anywhere. The tag that had been attached to the twine was lying on the floor under the edge of the footstool. I picked it up and turned it over; all it said was "To Beth." There wasn't an address or any other information.

Setting the wrapping off to the side, I untied the leather closure and carefully opened the book. The smell of the old pages greeted me; I'd always loved that smell. Turning to the first chapter, I began to read. It was written in Old English handwriting; this could only have been the original book. The very first ever created. The shallow indents left by the pen could be felt on the page.

I closed the book cover carefully and moved the volume back onto its wrapping. The smell of the pages, the ink, and the leather combined to intoxicate. Inhaling deeply, a feeling of innate calmness infused me. Picking up my pen, I touched it to paper and began to write.

The next time I came up for air, the clock read almost four o'clock. I couldn't believe I'd lost that much time again. This was the craziest thing I'd ever experienced.

Laying the pen down on the stack of pages, I stood up and moved around. My back and legs were stiff. Not a huge surprise there. I would have been flabbergasted had they not been. It would probably be better if I spent a few minutes on my feet, I thought, so I wandered into the kitchen and washed the dirty dishes. The laundry had been piling up for days, so I sorted that and threw a load in the washing machine. While that was going, I straightened up the bathroom and took a few minutes to pull up the covers and make the bed.

Now would be a good time to grab a shower and shampoo my hair so it would be dry before I went to bed. I didn't like to sleep on it while it was still wet, as that gave me some serious bed head.

After my shower, I pulled on a pair of boxers and a comfy t-shirt. Sitting back down in the living room, I moved the pen to the side and picked up the pages I'd written. The writing didn't look like mine; my script was generally much messier. This writing was tight, compact, and quite legible. *Interesting.* There appeared to be close to a hundred pages, and flipping through them showed me the same script throughout. The first page was written in a sweeping style; after that, it settled into a precise, controlled flow and the writing on the rest of the pages didn't appear to waver or lose control, as if someone had taken extra care to make sure it was legible. *Not 'someone,'* I thought. *Me.*

The story's time frame was current day and took place right here in Aspen Grove. It drew me in from the first sentence, creating a dark-haired girl, a fair-haired boy, and a night they would never forget.

By the time I'd finished reading, it was a quarter after eight. The story was almost finished; it lacked the final scene, and as I could see it in my head, I picked up the pen and wrote. As the ink dried on the final words, the minute hand on the clock ticked to straight up ten o'clock. Stacking the pages together, I set them in the top drawer of the desk, put the pen in its box, set it on top of the manuscript, and closed the drawer.

I knew I should have thrown the load of wash into the dryer, but I was so tired I could hardly keep my eyes open. I could do that in the morning. The moment my head hit the pillow, I was out cold.

The alarm went off at five o'clock a.m. I awoke refreshed and full of energy. Since I'd showered last night, I had an extra fifteen minutes to myself this morning without having to rush around. The wet laundry got moved to the dryer, and a new load started, dishes from the drainer were put in their proper cabinets, and I even had time to sweep the kitchen.

By the time I left for work, I was humming with energy and happiness. It was going to be a gorgeous day.

When I arrived, Jerry was pulling into the parking lot. Hopping out of my car, I made it to the door before him and unlocked it with my key.

"Good morning!"

"You look like you're feeling better today." Jerry eyed me suspiciously. "Was it a twenty-four hour bug?"

"Must have been, because I feel great today. I haven't slept that well in a long time." I replied, holding the door open for him. He went through, and I flipped the CLOSED sign to OPEN.

"Good. We missed you around here. A new girl came in to apply for Carrie's job, and I put her to work. She did okay."

"Roxie called to check on me and told me. That was perfect timing on the new girl's part. So, tell me about her. What's her name? Who is she related to?" Living in a small town has a different flow, a different way of looking at newcomers; everyone knows everyone else, lived near, or went to school with someone from the family. Instead of asking, 'where are you from,' we ask, 'who are your parents.'

We went about our opening routine: Tied on the aprons, turned on the grill to heat, made the coffee, chopped the potatoes and vegetables, turned on the oven and mixed up the dough for the dinner rolls. Even though the sign said we were open, everyone knew we didn't start serving until six o'clock.

"She's not from around here. Her name is Donna. The only history she gave was on her application, and it says she's from Arizona. Says she's been a waitress before, and from the job she did yesterday, she has been. You know she actually used that big ol' tray to carry the plates? She didn't stack them on her arm like the rest of you."

"Hmm," I answered, noncommittally. New in town doesn't happen very often. We're out of the way, off the beaten path.

Accidentally stopping off in Aspen Grove wasn't something we were used to. You had to work at it to get here.

"Carrie's last shift is tonight, so she'll officially start tomorrow night. You'll meet her at shift change then."

The sirens could be heard before we saw the red and blue lights on top of the police cars fly by. They were headed west, out of town.

We looked at each other. It wasn't often both cops on duty lit them up at all, let alone at the same time.

"Look at that. I wonder what's going on." Jerry perked up. Nothing like emergency vehicles to get the speculation started.

"Petey will be by later, I'll ask him." Petey McClure was the chief of police, had been for as long as I could remember.

We finished our prep work as our first customer walked in.

I saw him pull into the lot and step out of his squad car, adjusting his hat on his head before hitching up his gun belt and britches and strolling toward the door. He wore the same black uniform his officers wore, with a bullet proof vest underneath. The effect gave his chest a squared off, muscled look. His cowboy boots were well worn and permanently dusty; the heels showed a wear pattern that evidenced his bowlegged gait.

Pulling his favored mug from the shelf, I filled it with coffee. As the bell over the door tinkled, announcing his arrival, I turned and gave a wave, weaving between tables, following him toward an empty one.

"Hey, Chief, what's happening?"

He removed his hat and set it on the table. Running a hand over his near-bald head, he smiled up at me. His wrinkled face, tanned like leather from enjoying the outdoors, put his age at somewhere between fifty and seventy. No way to narrow it down more without asking.

"Hi, Beth. Missed you yesterday. Roxie said you were sick?"

"Yeah, I wasn't feeling well. I'm great today, though." I smiled back at him, setting his coffee cup down on the table in front of him.

"Good to hear, young lady. Yesterday's chicken fried steak wasn't near as good since you weren't here to make it." He didn't bother to reach for the menu; he always ordered the same thing.

"You're so sweet to say." I laughed.

"Wouldn't say, if it wasn't the truth, you know. Since you're here, I trust you made the stew this morning?"

I nodded, confirming his question.

"Bring me a bowl of that, and some cornbread if you've got it."

"Had a piece or two put back for you, knowing you'd be by for it."

"You're too good to me, Beth."

"So, Jerry and I saw you and Tito headed out of town this morning in a hurry. Anything happen that you can share?"

Petey lifted his mug and took a sip. "We don't have all the details yet. Leroy Jones called and said one of his cows was down, her back end had fallen into a hole. After he had winched her out, he went over and shined his light down in. There was a body in it. He called me. Tito and I went out and took a look. The hole didn't look like it had been dug all that long ago. I called it in to the sheriff's office since Leroy's field is technically outside city limits. Sheriff came out and cordoned it off. The crime scene unit was on their way when I left."

"Wow. Who was it, could you tell?" My head was spinning.

"Never seen him before, not that I could tell anyway. Old Maizy, Leroy's cow, stepped pretty good on his face. We'll have to wait and see what the coroner comes up with."

I shuddered. "That's scary."

"Yep, it is. Until we get a handle on it, be careful, you hear?"

"I will. Thanks, Petey. I'll go get your stew. Do you want me to save you the last slice of coconut cream pie?"

"You talked me into it."

~~*~*~*

After shift, I stayed at the restaurant for a little while, talking with Carrie. The only time we usually saw each other was at shift change; though since she was leaving I wanted to wish her well. Mid-afternoons were the normal slow time, so we had a few minutes to ourselves. She was going to live with her mom, up north, since her dad was in poor health, and her mom needed help. She didn't know if she would be back, and there wasn't anything keeping her here since her divorce last year, so she'd sold her house and had a moving truck in the parking lot. She would be taking off right after the diner closed.

When I finally made it home, I showered and finished up the laundry before sitting down. I knew I'd put it off as long as I could. Slowly, I reached out and opened the desk drawer. Withdrawing the manuscript, I took it with me to the armchair and got comfortable. I wasn't sure I wanted to re-read what I'd written, but I knew it needed to be done.

Taking a deep breath, I blew it out and turned to page one.

The story read exactly the way I remembered: The girl, the guy, a drive in the country, a flat tire, by the time the tire had been changed it was getting dark, they resume driving, he suddenly blurted out that he couldn't live with the secret any longer; he loved her too much to lie to her, told her he slept with her someone else. They looked at each other, neither saw the deer running across the road, the sickening crunch of bone and glass when he'd hit it, the pulling onto the shoulder, him getting out to check for damage, the way she slid across to the driver's seat, put the car in gear, and the satisfying crunch of his bones as the grill cracked his skull and the tires reduced his legs to jelly. Back and forth until she was sure he wouldn't cheat on her, ever again. The way she'd folded his broken body into the trunk and driven until she'd found an unlocked shed, a shovel, and work gloves. A dark night, a cattle field, and a body dragged underneath the barbed wire fence. A hole dug deep and an unceremonious burying. The way she had the presence of mind to drive back to where she'd borrowed the shovel and return it to its rightful owner and the one tear that slid down her cheek at the loss of what might have been.

This story is freakishly realistic. What about it is bothering me?

The more I thought about it, the stranger I felt, and the more convinced I became that it was not what it seemed. *My mind is working overtime. This is what I get for writing a murder mystery. I can fix this.*

I got out of the armchair, moved back to the desk, placed the story in the drawer and picked up my pen.

The next morning I woke up still tired, as if I'd run a marathon through the night. The story I began creating last night was a love story. The portion I managed to get on paper was beautiful; flowery, poignant, touching in a first-love sort of way. That alone should have helped me to sleep like a baby. Every time I closed my eyes, all I saw was a dark figure digging a hole in a cattle field.

A shower helped a little. When I pulled up at the diner, Jerry's car was already there, and I could see him inside. Hopefully he'd started the coffee.

The bell on the door tinkled, announcing my arrival. "It's just me," I called out, flipping the sign to OPEN before heading for the back. The welcoming smell of freshly brewed coffee met me halfway across the room. A quick detour and a few seconds later, I was in heaven.

Jerry stepped out from the kitchen. "I thought I heard the door. What are you doing?"

"Infusing my body with a little bit of liquid life, Jerry." I blew across the top of the mug, anticipating sweet relief. I was not disappointed. "Ahhhhhhhh."

Crossing his arms across his chest, he squinted his eyes. "You look tired. You're not sick again, are you?"

"I don't think so. Just didn't sleep very well, that's all." For some unknown reason, I didn't want to share with anyone the strange turn of events.

"Well, whenever you're ready, I was about to start the dinner rolls…"

"Don't do that, I'm coming." It was our little secret that he couldn't make a decent dinner roll to save his life.

We fell into our usual routine, and by the time shift change came around I was on fumes.

The bell tinkled. A petite brunette came in and made a beeline for me. With a wave of my hand, I encompassed the entire, currently empty, dining room.

"Sit wherever you like, I'll be right with you."

She smiled. "I'm not here to eat. Hi, I'm Donna. Jerry hired me for the dinner shift."

I looked back, this time focusing on her. What I saw had me blinking several times. She was the spitting image of the young girl in my story: slightly shorter than me, with long hair that reached her hips, accentuating her slender waist. Her round, cupid-like face gave her an air of innocence. I couldn't have written a more accurate description of her had she been standing in front of me when I'd done it.

"Ah, sorry, switching gears... hi, Donna, nice to meet you. I'm Beth."

Her smile widened, a dimple showing in her cheek. "That's okay, I do the same thing."

"Oh, good! We'll get along just fine then." I returned her smile. "I understand you covered for me the other day—perfect timing, coming in to apply. Jerry and Roxie were impressed with the way you dug in and picked up the slack. Is there anything you aren't sure of, something I can help you with? I'm happy to stay for a bit, in case you need help before Jan gets here. She'll be your shift partner tonight." I was rambling, but I couldn't help it. The resemblance was uncanny.

"Can you show me where we keep the extra condiments? Do we refill at night?"

"Yes. Each shift rolls silverware; night shift refills sugar, ketchup, salt and pepper shakers. Jan will help you with it, but we keep it over here." I led her toward the back room.

"So what brings you to Aspen Grove?" My voice sounded tinny to my own ears; I hoped she didn't hear the excitement behind the words.

"I was driving through and thought it looked like a quiet town. So far everyone has been super nice."

"Where are you from?"

"Arizona."

It was like pulling teeth to get any real information out of her. "Do you have family nearby? I mean, are you passing through, or do you plan to stick around awhile?"

"I don't know." She grew quiet; I got the feeling she didn't want to talk about herself. I can take a hint.

"The people here are nice, though we don't get too many strangers. We're far enough off the highways that most people haven't even heard of us. You probably got to play twenty questions with the morning crowd, so the dinner crowd will already know there's someone new in town. News like that travels fast around here. They'll ask all sorts of questions until they're satisfied, so a word to the wise: if you don't want to share personal information, make something up." I winked conspiratorially.

She smiled a forced smile, looked around at everything else before her gaze returned to me. "Thanks."

"If they press, mention my name. That'll slow them down."

A look of confusion crossed Donna's face.

"I make them toe the line around here. It's something they've come to expect, and once they've been called out on their behavior in the middle of a crowded diner, they don't want to have it happen again."

The tension broke; her spontaneous laugh was infectious. "Thanks, I appreciate that."

When I arrived home, I couldn't sit still. The new girl, the dead body, the mirror image with Donna on one side and my character on the other, combined to keep me on edge and ping-ponging around my house.

Finally, I settled at the desk. My mind quieted as soon as I picked up the pen.

When I surfaced again, several hours had passed, and I had finished the most romantic love story. *There,* I told myself. *If it's a coincidence, no one will fall in love. If it's not, tomorrow should prove it.* Maybe I shouldn't have modeled my character after someone I knew, but this was a good thing, right? Besides, I needed to know. What could it hurt?

Climbing into bed, I tossed and turned for half an hour before falling into another restless sleep.

Jerry pulled me off to the side around eleven thirty. Not one to waste time, he got straight to the point. "Jan called. She's got whatever bug you had. She's not coming in tonight. Can you stay?"

"You want me to pull a double?"

"That's what I just said, isn't it?"

"Jeez, no need to get cranky."

"I get nothing but grief from you girls…"

"I'm just kidding, Jerry. I'll stay, okay?"

He turned and stalked off, mumbling something about selling the diner and moving to a cabin in the woods.

~~*~*~*

The rest of the morning shift went by quickly. When Donna arrived, I made a point to catch her alone. There had to be a way to find out more, to get her to open up. For now, I would play it by ear.

"How's it going?" I began, affecting a nonchalance I didn't feel.

"Good, thanks. How about you?" She stowed her purse in her locker, closed the door and turned to sit on the bench to tie a shoe.

"Pretty good. We haven't had much of a chance to get to know each other yet. I was wondering if you wanted to grab a drink after shift."

She looked up at me as she tied. A shadow crossed her eyes and was gone almost before I registered it. As if sizing me up, or deciding internally, she didn't say anything for several seconds.

"Alright, we can do that. Do you want me to meet you somewhere?"

Ah, of course. She didn't know. I smiled. "Jan caught a virus or something, and called in sick. I'm pulling a double today. We can leave after close."

"Oh, okay. I'm going to go set up. See you out there." She grabbed her apron off the hook and moved toward the dining room.

This was fortuitous, Jan calling in sick. With any luck, I could get Donna to disclose some little detail that would either confirm or dismiss my theory. She looked like my character, but I could be seeing things that aren't there. I needed real proof.

~~*~*~*

The chairs were up on the tables, and the floor was vacuumed. I turned the sign to CLOSED while Donna put our aprons away. She came back out.

"Ready?"

"Yes." I looked around once more to be sure everything was done. If I were going to have a beer or two this evening, I didn't want to leave a mess that would have to be cleaned up in the morning. Since tomorrow was my day off, I'd feel twice as bad about it. Assured that everything was done and in its proper place, I nodded.

"Jerry, we're out of here," I called.

"Good night." The disembodied voice floated out from the office.

Grabbing my keys, I locked the door behind us before turning toward the parking lot.

"Where's your car?" I asked, seeing only Jerry's pickup truck and my car.

"I walked," she said, "my car is in the shop."

"We can take mine," I replied, looking at her. "Mechanical trouble? Bob Miller is the best in town, if that's the problem."

"No, I don't think so. I hit a deer a few nights back, and there's been a rattle ever since. I took it to Darrell. He came in the other day and said he could take a look at it for me. He's supposed to call me tomorrow."

She hit a deer... Another piece that matches.

We climbed into my Taurus and buckled up.

"Where do you go around here when you want a beer?" she asked as I pulled out of the lot.

"Down to Charlie's. That's where the locals go, and since you're local now, you qualify to be let in on the secret." I smiled, but she didn't see it. Her face was turned toward the side window.

"How far is it?" Donna watched the buildings go by, disappearing and being quickly replaced by countryside.

"About five more minutes. Don't worry, I'll drive you home after."

"Speaking of home, is there a place to rent that's um..." she hesitated, "cheaper than Mary's Boarding House? I'm not making much in tips yet, and my savings will be gone soon."

I watched her from the corner of my eye. She stared straight ahead, not even blinking.

"You're staying at Crazy Mary's?" I asked in mock horror.

Donna turned in her seat to face me. "She's crazy?" Her face was serious.

"Does she still light every candle in the house and then blow them all out, three times each night before bed?"

Tucking her hair behind her ear, she tried to cover a smile. "She does."

"What about tater tots with every meal? Does she still do that, too?"

She nodded, covering her mouth now to contain her laugh.

"Then there's the basement stairs that creak at midnight... does that still happen, too?"

Her eyes went wide. "Yes! What's up with that?"

"Bubba lives in the basement, he comes up for the plate she leaves him in the microwave."

"You're kidding... someone lives in the basement?"

I shook my head. "Not kidding at all. Bubba is her son. He has internet down there, and a television, and a Nintendo, if Joey over at the thrift store is telling the truth. He was hit by a car when he was fifteen, and hasn't moved a foot out of her house since. Nobody is really sure if he's an invalid or just lazy. He hasn't been seen. There was a lady who rented a room from Mary a few years back who kept hearing the stairs squeaking, so one night she waited in the hall behind the coat rack and watched. She saw someone come out through the basement door, the light back washing him. He carried an empty plate to the sink; she heard him set it in, and then he opened the microwave door and took out the full plate. She saw him carry it back down the stairs, closing the door after him, and she says she heard a lock close on the other side."

"Oh. My. Gosh. And here I thought I didn't need to use the lock on the inside of *my* room's door."

"I don't know if any of that is true, but I do know Bubba went missing after that accident. We've got to get you out of there."

She put her fingertip in her mouth, chewing on the corner of her nail. "Where can I go?"

"Well, there's Miss Claire's over on Elm. She rents out a room or two, and last I heard she had an empty one. I can take you by tomorrow to meet her, if you like. She's lived in this town all of her life and will be more likely to rent to you if I take you there than if you go by yourself."

Donna let out her breath. "Thanks, I appreciate it."

I pulled into the parking lot at Charlie's and shut off the engine.

~~*~*~*

We'd each had two beers, when another round showed up at the table. We looked at each other and then at the waitress.

"I don't think we ordered those. Did we?" I said, feeling relaxed but certainly not drunk.

"You did not. Those gentlemen at the end of the bar sent them over." She motioned over her shoulder and turned sideways so we could see past her.

"Oh, they did, did they?" I laughed, picking up my new beer and saluting Boss and Tubby with it.

"Go ahead and do it, salute like I did, or they'll come over here with their feelings hurt," I told Donna.

She raised hers like I did. They smiled and waved. Turning back to me, she said, "Okay, who are they?"

"Boss and Tubby are brothers. They work out on the farm at the edge of town, the place where the body was found the other night. They're harmless, if you're polite. Otherwise, they don't know where the line is and want to talk to you for hours about what they did wrong that made you not say thank you." Which reminded me… I leaned halfway across the table.

Donna did, too.

It was now or never. "Did you hear about that? The body they found?"

She started to shake her head, but stopped. Instead, she whispered, "Who found a body?"

"Well. Leroy Jones, the farmer who owns the land, was missing a cow. He went looking for her, and found her alright, out on the back forty. She had her hind quarters sunk down in a hole. Leroy went on and winched her out of there. He didn't remember there being a hole there, so he looked in to see if there was an underground stream or something. What he saw was a body."

"Really. Tell me more." She took a swig of her beer. Was it my imagination, or was she fishing for information herself?

"Petey and Tito, that'd be the chief of police and one of his officers, the one who happened to be on duty when Leroy called it in, went out and took a look. Petey was in the diner later on for lunch, and I asked him about it. He said the sheriff was called and is handling it, since the land where the body was found is in the county, not in the city limits." I took a swig of my beer, watching her as I did.

There wouldn't be a better time to ask, I thought, so before I could change my mind I did. I looked her in the eye and kept my voice low.

"Who was he?"

Donna backed away. "What? I don't know. Why would you ask me that?" She had that cornered look on her face again.

I nodded. "That's what I thought."

She started to get up, looked like she was going to bolt, then thought better of it and sat back down. The internal disagreement was evident, if only to me. I waited her out.

"I have to go to the bathroom. I'll be right back." She stood and made her way down the hall, past the sign with the arrow.

I'd either really messed up, and she would climb out the window and be gone for good, or she would be back and trust me.

Ten minutes went by, then fifteen. I was starting to think she'd bolted, when she finally came back to the table. She looked like she'd been crying; her eyes were rimmed with red, and her face had been splashed with water. The tendrils of hair around the edges were damp and curling.

"Can we get out of here?" she asked without looking at me.

"Yes." Now, not only did I have a pen that wrote stories that came true, I was about to know more about the body.

I waved at Missy, the waitress, on my way by. She waved back. The beers would be on my tab, and I'd pay for them on payday.

We got in the car and headed back for town. Donna stared out the window, an air of dejection around her.

"Are you ready to go back to Crazy Mary's, or can we talk a little while?" I asked quietly, reassuringly.

"We should talk. I'm a little bit scared to go back to Crazy Mary's, to tell you the truth." She sniffled out a small laugh.

I smiled at her attempted humor. "Why don't we go to my house, I've got a spare room you can use tonight if you want. No one will hear our conversation that way, either."

"Okay. I need to know, before anything, if you can keep a secret."

Without so much as a thought, I responded. "Yes, I can. Your secret will be safe with me. I promise." I meant every word.

~~*~*~*

When we walked in, I motioned to the living room. "It's not much, but it's mine. Make yourself comfortable. Would you like a beer?"

"Yes, please. This may take another one or two."

"We've got six." I called, grabbing two bottles out of the refrigerator and the bottle opener from the drawer. When I walked back into the living room, she was facing the couch, checking out the painting hung on the wall behind it.

"That was here when I bought the place. I rather like it, so it got to stay."

"It's nice. I like it, too." She turned and took her beer before sitting.

I kicked off my shoes and pulled my feet up underneath me on the other end of the couch. She followed suit.

"So, what happened?" I asked, more than merely curious. I hoped my question hadn't come out as anxious as I was on the inside.

Donna took a deep breath and let it out slowly. "Caleb and I started 'going together'," she air-quoted the phrase, "before either of our parents would let us date. He was so cute, and nice, and smart. We had a lot in common, and when we both turned sixteen we were allowed to go to the movies or out to eat, as long as he had me home by ten o'clock. Even one minute past curfew and I got grounded for weeks."

Her eyes were looking in my direction but focused on the past. I stayed still, not even lifting my beer, so as not to break her thought process. The joy in her memory was evident.

"One evening, we were supposed to meet a couple of friends and grab a pizza. The friends cancelled out at the last minute, and we found ourselves with a free evening. We could have gone for pizza anyway; we'd done that before, but this night something felt different. There was tension in the air, one that had been building, but was now at a level... well, we were at a crossroads. We could continue to do what our parents wanted, and that was to abstain, or we could follow our hearts and explore the unknown. As you can guess, we chose option two."

Donna peeled the label from her bottle, lifting it and chugging half of it down. She continued.

"It was everything a first time should, and shouldn't, be. We'd driven up to Lookout Point, neither of us sure of anything, being that it was a first for both of us. To make a long and terribly embarrassing story short, we wound up in the back seat of his car, and managed to do the deed before we ended up in the back seat of a police car."

"Oh no, what happened?"

"We were so caught up in each other and what we were doing that our hormones took total control, and neither of us heard the crunch of tires on gravel as the car pulled up behind us. We hadn't known that a cop patrolled up there. When the flashlight beam lit us up like Christmas, neither of us had a shred of clothing on. They let us get dressed before they put us in the squad car and called our parents."

I gasped. "They didn't..."

She laughed. "They did. When I got home, let me just tell you, being grounded for a month was the least of my worries. Caleb never did tell me what punishment his parents gave him."

"That's awful. I could see the Chief doing that, too, though, if for no other reason than to keep teen pregnancy out of the picture, if he could."

"Funny you should mention that." She grew wistful again. "Several weeks went by and I realized I hadn't gotten my period. Mom made me keep a calendar, and right then I was glad. I checked it and counted the days. I was six days late. That wasn't a big deal, normally. My cycle hadn't regulated yet. But being that we'd had unprotected sex, well, I was a little bit worried."

She held her hand up, fingers estimating an inch of space for her little bit worried.

"Two days later, when I was about to go to the drugstore for a pregnancy test, I got my period. I've never been so happy to see it in my life. I hadn't even told Caleb I was late, with as little time alone as we got to share. Even after I'd outlived my grounding, my parents didn't seem to trust me. Through the rest of my junior year, they found a way to keep Caleb and me from being alone together. I guess they thought they could control what we felt for each other. Occasionally we'd sneak off during lunch hour, but only to be alone with each other. The most we did was hold hands. We decided, or rather *he* decided, we should wait to go all the way again until after graduation. He made it sound so romantic at the time. I had no idea he was sleeping with someone else."

"Your parents kept that tight a rein on you all the way through senior year? That's pretty harsh."

"No, they eased up over time, but something didn't feel the same anymore. Caleb didn't want to take the chance, he said, and we should wait. I went along with it. I was so in love with him. I felt like such a fool when I found out I was the only one waiting..."

Her eyes welled up with tears. I turned and grabbed the tissue box from the end table and offered it. She took the box.

"Through my senior year I worked as a waitress and saved money for a car. Our plan, or so I thought at the time, was to leave town and start a life somewhere else. I was so stupid; I didn't see it."

"You weren't stupid, you were in love. We all get blinded by love. What happened then?" I spoke softly. She was wracked with grief and guilt. I didn't want to make her feel worse.

"Graduation came and went. The day after, I had my car packed with my things and space for his. I went to his house at noon to pick him up, as we'd agreed. He was outside, on the porch, no suitcases, just him. He met me at the car before I could get out. He said, 'Go.' I asked where his things were, and he got forceful, saying 'Just GO.'"

Donna pulled a tissue from the box and wiped her eyes. "I'd never seen him like this. We were out of our town, and through the next before I spoke again. I asked if he was okay, and he told me his father had kicked him out of the house. I wanted to talk about it, but he refused. Next thing I knew, he was asleep."

She stopped long enough to down her beer.

"Which way is your restroom?" she asked.

"Through there, first door on the left." While she did that, I took our empties into the kitchen and replaced them with full bottles. As I popped the second top, she returned.

"So, he slept until almost sundown while I drove. I didn't know where we were headed; we'd talked about deciding that as soon as we were in the car and moving. That was the plan, anyway. By the time we reached Amarillo; we had needed gas. I stopped and stretched while the tank filled. He'd woken up and got out to stretch. He said he would drive awhile, so I let him. I was getting tired anyway. We grabbed a burger from some drive-through I'd never heard of and got back on the road. I dozed off. The car blew a tire, startling me awake. Caleb pulled over and got out to change it. By this time, it was pitch black out. When he got back in the car, I asked where we were. He said outside of Oklahoma City. We weren't on a highway; that much was obvious. I pressed him on where outside of Oklahoma City, and he muttered something about a detour. For some reason, he was really mad. I don't know if it was the flat tire or what, so I asked him. He gripped the steering wheel tight. I asked again. He said he needed to tell me something. He told me he loved me so much; it was killing him to keep the secret."

She stood up and paced, becoming increasingly agitated.

"I asked him what he was talking about. He said he'd been sleeping with a girl we'd gone to high school with. I was in shock, and speechless. He took that opportunity to tell me she is also pregnant with his child."

Her pacing ground to a halt directly in front of me. "I couldn't believe what he had just said to me. We were going to have a fairy tale. Instead, he slept with the slut of the school. He looked at me, probably because I wasn't talking or crying, or even screaming at him, and that's when it happened."

Donna rubbed her eyes and resumed pacing. "I saw it out of the corner of my eye. A deer ran right in front of us, and he was looking at me instead of the road. We hit it. Caleb slammed on the brakes. The deer tumbled into the ditch and, without missing a beat, jumped up and ran away. He pulled to the side of the road and got out to look for damage."

Her stride slowed. She resumed her seat on the couch, picked up her beer, and drank it all down in one breath.

"I was so mad. All I could think was how betrayed I felt. Next thing I knew, I was in the driver's seat and was backing over him. I don't know when he got behind the car. Last I remembered he was bent over, looking at something on the front bumper. I may have run him over once already; I don't know. My memory is blank."

Lifting the empty bottle, she looked at it like it should be full and set it back down. I went to the kitchen for another for her. When I returned, she reached for it.

"Thanks. I'll replace your beer. This is harder to talk about than I thought."

You're moving along just fine. And yes, you did already run him over once or twice. I don't know which thump you're currently remembering. "No problem."

"At this point I'm officially freaked out. I am in a situation I never even considered having to wonder about, and I've not only got a dented fender, I've got a dead boyfriend. Or ex-boyfriend, I guess, since there's no way I could stay with anyone who cheated on me."

It would appear the alcohol was finally getting to her. Donna was becoming more animated, gesturing with her hands while she talked and really getting into the story. It almost felt like she'd stepped outside of the situation and was telling me the plot of a movie she'd watched.

"Since I'd backed over him, I had to pull over him again just to get the trunk near him. In case you hadn't noticed, I'm not that big. He was a good six inches taller than me and fifty pounds or better heavier. So I got the trunk near where he was, and I got out of the car. I was scared. This was a road I didn't know, the only light was my own headlights, and I had one definitely dead body on my hands. Okay, so, I pop the trunk and struggle to get him inside. I think it helped when I heard what sounded like a wolf howl. Do you have wolves around here?" She didn't wait for an answer before continuing.

"Whatever it was, I got this adrenaline rush and hauled Caleb up like a sack of potatoes and in the trunk he went. It wasn't pretty, but it was done. Then I thought, what am I going to do with him? I couldn't drop him off at the bus station."

Her words were beginning to slur, and for some reason she found this funny. Perhaps it was from the release of pressure, telling someone else about what had happened and lifting it off her own shoulders.

I prodded her along. "So what did you decide to do?"

"What? Oh. Caleb. I drove around for a little while, until I came to a little community. It was down the road a little ways from where I'd been on the side of the road. There was a dark, dark house. They had a shed. I tiptoed," she giggled. "I know that was silly, but I didn't want to wake anybody. I tiptoed all the way to the shed, and thank goodness it wasn't locked, I just thought of that now, but I got inside and closed the door behind me. There was a light, so I turned it on, and found a shovel. There were these gloves, the kind the workers wear, yeah, work gloves, so I borrowed those too. I went back to my car and drove to an empty field. I waited a few minutes to be sure no one knew I was there. When nobody came, I got out and shimmied through the fence. I'm glad it rains around here in the summer, in Arizona we don't get much rain and the ground is harder. Here it was soft. I dug a hole, really deep, like four feet down, and went back to the car. I couldn't get the car in that field, cause of the fence, so I drug him out of the trunk and all the way over, under the fence, and to the hole. I was so tired by now. When I looked at his face, I got mad all over again and just pushed him in. He tumbled down, and I threw the dirt on top of him. I packed it down some. I guess not good enough, on account of the cow went through and all…"

All of a sudden Donna burst into tears. "I didn't mean for any of this to happen. I only wanted to be happy. I wanted the fairy tale."

She leaned over and laid her head down on the couch. Between the sobs and the mumbling, I couldn't understand her anymore. She was about to go to sleep, so I quickly went in and pulled down the bedspread and sheets in the spare room and went back out for her.

"It's going to be okay, Donna. You need to get some sleep, and we can talk some more tomorrow."

"Okay," she sighed, without moving an inch.

"The bed is this way. You'll be more comfortable in there." I touched her arm, and she moved with me, standing and following like a rag doll.

After I'd helped her take her shoes off and tucked her in, I picked up the bottles from the living room and tucked myself into my own bed.

It was a while before I was able to fall asleep. I kept thinking, *what do we do now?*

~~*~*~*

I awoke shortly after seven o'clock the next morning. We'd stayed up late talking, but that didn't change my internal clock. Silently cursing, I rolled out of bed and padded into the kitchen. I would definitely need some coffee this morning.

Once the pot was started, I grabbed some clothes and took a quick shower, trying to be quiet so as not to wake Donna. The door to the spare bedroom was still closed.

When I'd finished, I wrapped my hair in a towel and headed back for the kitchen. Donna was there, searching through the kitchen cabinets.

"Morning." I yawned.

She jumped and spun around, hand to her heart. "Oh, goodness, you scared me. Where do you keep your coffee cups?"

Covering my mouth with one hand, I pointed with the other. She turned back and reached for the next cabinet over; she would have found them momentarily.

"Thanks."

"No problem. How did you sleep?" I opened the refrigerator and pulled out the creamer.

"Good. Better than I've slept in weeks. You?"

"Like the dead." My face colored when I realized what I'd said. "Sorry. Unintentional. My brain doesn't kick in until after the first cup."

"That's okay. I'm the same way." Donna smiled and leaned back against the counter, blowing the steam from her coffee.

I poured some for myself, adding creamer and offering the container. She shook her head.

"Listen…" I began.

She looked at me over the rim, waiting.

My thought had been to offer to let her stay with me though I wasn't sure what was going on yet with this whole writing thing, and the pen, not to mention the books. As much as I liked her and wanted to help, I couldn't bring myself to say it.

"Today's my day off. I can take you to Miss Claire's, and if you don't like that, I can run you around until we find you a place. What time did Darrell say he would be calling, morning or afternoon?"

"I appreciate it. He didn't say, but he's got my cell number. He can reach me whenever. I work the dinner shift, so hopefully before then."

Nodding, I blew on my own coffee. Subconsciously, I leaned back against the counter, mirroring her pose.

"My turn," she started. "I don't normally trust people I've just met—especially women. Last night you reassured me that my secret wouldn't go any further than you. I really hope that's true. I want to believe you; I do, it's just, well… I have these trust issues. Please don't take it the wrong way."

"Secret? What secret? That your snores sound like a freight train? Somehow, I don't think you're doing a very good job of keeping that under wraps. My neighbors probably know."

The relief was evident on her face. "Hey, now."

Donna hit it off with Miss Claire, so I ran her back by Crazy Mary's to clean out her room and move her stuff over. We finished that chore with half an hour to spare before her shift started, so I took her by Darrell's and made sure her car was ready for her to drive before I drove away.

The incessant beeping of the alarm clock was like ice picks to my brain. Reaching out to hit the snooze, I miscalculated and caught the edge of the lamp with my hand, knocking both it and the clock to the floor. The light bulb broke. On the good side, the clock shut up. The cost was worth the price, in my mind.

I tossed some aspirin back with a glass of water and struggled through my morning routine. When I arrived at the diner, I saw Jerry wasn't alone. Roxie was already halfway through pulling the chairs down from on top of the tables.

Sliding out of my car, I approached the diner. I watched through the window as she practically bounced between tables, executing a pirouette with the last chair still in her hands.

A thought niggled at the back of my brain; I shoved it out of my thoughts. Just then she turned and saw me through the front window. Her face lit up, from her oversized smile to the shine in her eyes. She positively glowed. The pit of my stomach formed a knot. Reaching out, I pulled the door open and stepped inside.

Roxie clapped her hands together and bounded over to me as if she had springs in her shoes.

"Oh, Beth, you'll never guess!" she gushed. I swear I could see cartoon bluebirds flying in circles over her head, carrying strings of construction paper hearts in a decoration dance.

"They brought back reruns of Fantasy Island?" I deadpanned. Her laugh was light and airy. I wanted to run away before she could confirm my fears.

"No, silly!" Remember I was going to visit granny in Tulsa for her ninetieth birthday? Well, the nurse that's taking care of her came in while I was there. You'll never guess who it was!" She giggled, a girl with news too good not to share. "Remember Sebastian Darian from high school? He was always quiet but cute in a geeky sort of way. But now…"

If she swooned, I was going to throw up. "He's cute in a grown-up sort of way?" I guessed.

"Oh, Beth, he's so much more than cute. We sat and talked at granny's house, and then he asked me out for dinner. I couldn't believe it! So we went to eat and talked until they closed. Neither one of us wanted the date to end yet, so we went back to his apartment and talked until three in the morning."

The look on her face was unmistakable, and her story was exactly what I'd written. Stars exploded in front of my eyes. I reached out and grabbed the back of a chair to steady myself.

Her face clouded over. "Are you okay?" She pulled another chair out for me to sit.

"I'm fine. Just felt a little lightheaded is all." I sank into the chair.

"You're not still sick, are you? I thought you were getting better when we talked, or I would never have left. Here, sit, let me get you some water."

"Thank you."

Roxie came back with a glass, and I drained it.

"Better?" She asked, her happiness on hold at the thought of a friend being in distress.

She was one of the most genuinely nice people I'd ever met. If anyone deserved love, it was Roxie. With that one thought, the weight lifted from my psyche and was replaced with an epiphany. Everything was as it should be.

"Yes, better. I didn't sleep well, maybe that's it. This headache I woke up with isn't helping. I took aspirin before I came in. It should start working any time." I offered a wan smile.

Roxie smiled in return, looking relieved.

"Okay, you stay here. I'll go help Jerry chop vegetables." Sproing, sproing, sproing, and she was gone.

Jerry popped his head out of the kitchen. "You okay?"

I nodded. "I will be." And I knew it was the truth. Suddenly, I had this opportunity in front of me, a way to help the people I care about, and I was scared, elated, and hesitant all at the same time. My brain skipped ahead. If I can help people with my pen, can I make them pay, as well? I mulled this over through my shift, operating on autopilot.

When I arrived home, there was another paper-wrapped volume, identical to the last two, on my doorstep. I took it in the house and unwrapped it, sure of what I would find. I was not disappointed. Volume III in the Mamie Addlemeier series. Cradling it in my arm, I fingered the string tie; it was almost as though I could feel the worn leather through the wrapping. I took it to the bookshelf and cleared a space for it and its predecessors. Moving back to the desk, I opened the drawer and lifted the first two volumes out, then I carried them carefully to the bookcase and placed them in order. I would read them later; right now, I had a theory to test. Settling into my armchair, pad of paper in hand, I picked up my pen and began to write.

I dotted the last "I"and crossed the last "T." Watching the ink soak into the page, I felt... vindicated. Knowing that the first and second story had come true, I was more than confident that my stepfather would finally have to answer for his addiction. The year I turned thirteen I'd been the one to find the hidden camera in my bathroom, and not knowing what it was or why it was there, I took it to my mom and asked her. I'd never in my short life seen mom cry that way; it scared me. That night she confronted him with it after I'd gone to bed, when he'd come home from work. She tried to keep her voice down so I wouldn't hear, but pressing an empty glass to the hollow door helped, and I made out most of their conversation. She made him leave that night, and filed for divorce the next morning. He needs to be stopped from his criminal activity. Who knows how many other girls he's watched that way, before or since, or to what level he's advanced. I had the power in my hand to change his future, and I fully believe that I've done just that.

~~*~*~*

I've written seventeen stories since that day, and each one of them has come true. I've thought about the marks on my soul, whether the stories that pay people back for the sins they've committed are counted against me or if they're under the karma umbrella, and I'm still not sure. I'll probably not know until it's time to meet my maker.

What I am sure about is this: being perfectly honest, the feeling I get when I use the pen, hold it in my hand, touch the nib to paper, is as close to euphoria as I've ever been. It feels like all is right with the world. That may sound corny, but that's the only way I can describe it that comes even close to what I was feel.

It turned out that the man from the antique store had been right; I hadn't chosen the pen; the pen had chosen me.

THE PAINTING ON THE WALL

There were four of us seated around the grey, standard institutional table in a drab, windowless room, each of us with a water bottle on the table in front of us. The chair was standard issue, as well, complete with the padding long gone and permanently indented by the multitude of butt cheeks that had flattened it over the many years. I tried to get comfortable. It wasn't happening. The fluorescent rectangular light fixtures hung down, swaying as if a train were passing nearby. What appeared to be water pipes ran above them along the entire length of the room with metal straps attaching them to the ten foot high ceiling.

We all sat waiting for whatever was supposed to happen next. I'd answered an online ad to join a focus group and was given a questionnaire to fill out and return. There were an even one thousand questions on it. I know this because they were numbered, asking everything from favorite color to time of birth. The ad offered twenty-five dollars per hour. The thought of eating something besides bologna sandwiches appealed to me. Finding a job, any job, had turned out to be more difficult than I'd anticipated after being a professional housewife for twenty years. Bob's life insurance helped, but after paying off the house and the car, the money was dwindling fast, so I filled out their paperwork and sent it back in. The next day an email arrived with instructions on where to show up and when.

The instructions didn't mention a dress code or even what the focus group was focusing on, so I erred on the side of caution and wore a business suit and comfortable flats. As I looked around now at the three other people, I felt overdressed.

When I arrived they asked me to sign in and lock my purse and all personal belongings in a locker. I did so, pocketing the key. They also informed me that I was not to speak with any of the other participants, and we would all be identified by a temporary number until the focus group had concluded. My name tag said I would be 1113.

There was a young man in the chair next to mine, probably in his early twenties, wearing dark pants with holes in the knees and an old stained t-shirt with a yellow happy face on it that had a bullet hole in its head. His black hair was slicked back with some sort of gel and gave an unobstructed view of his face with its thick black eyeliner. He slumped in his chair and picked at the edges of the black nail polish coating most of his fingernails. His name tag dubbed him 1294. Since I was no good with numbers, I would think of him as Goth Boy.

Fidgeting in the chair across the table from him was a woman who appeared to be in her thirties, judging by the crow's feet that were just beginning to show next to her eyes. Her straight blond hair was loose, and she wore a shift dress with large flowers all over it. They appeared to be crashing into each other each time she moved and were so garish it almost hurt the eyes. She looked at her watch every couple of minutes as if she needed to be somewhere else. Meet participant 1077, or as I dubbed her, Nervous Girl.

Across the table from me, and the fourth in the group, was an elderly lady. Her grey hair was cut short, and the spectacles hanging from a chain around her neck rested on her chest. Her name tag identified her as 1673. She reminded me of my grandmother. She smiled at me, and it crinkled her whole face. I couldn't help but smile back. She would be Grandma. It was nice to connect with someone else here; I felt so out of place.

For twenty-five dollars an hour I didn't mind sitting here, though a more comfortable seat would have been appreciated. Grandmother shifted in her chair as I thought this. We were both having the same trouble. The two younger people didn't seem to have a problem. Not with the chairs, anyway.

The door opened and a man wearing a lab coat entered the room carrying a clipboard. He wore glasses that made his eyes look owlish, and he had crumbs dusting his large round belly. The white coat gave him the outward appearance of a jumbo marshmallow. He crossed the room to the table and stopped about five feet away. He waited until we'd all looked up at him before he began.

"Good morning ladies and gentleman, I am Dr. Andrews. Thank you for coming. As you know, this is a focus group. Now that you're here we will outline what we're studying and what your role will be in the group. Once your task has been completed you'll be paid for your time. I would like to take this opportunity to remind you that the information packet with the questionnaire you each filled out, signed, and returned contained a non-disclosure form. That means you will not be able to tell anyone about what happens here today or anything you learn while in the confines of this program. Are there any questions so far?"

His double chin was coated with sweat, and it jiggled as he talked. I tried hard not to stare at it and instead concentrated on his eyes. No one raised their hand or spoke up. We were off to a good start.

"Good. Dr. Phillips will explain the process. Dr. Phillips?" Dr. Andrews stepped to the side and revealed a second person who had, until now, been hidden behind his girth.

"Thank you, Dr. Andrews." Her voice was high-pitched and reminded me of the sound a mosquito makes as it buzzes near your ear. She was as thin as he was fat and had light brown hair scraped back and held firm with a banana clip on the back of her head.

"Today we're going to ask you to paint. We are testing a new product and will be giving each of you a can and a selection of brushes to paint a picture of whatever you wish. Your choice of subject is entirely yours. The only requirement is that you are to paint one thing, and only one thing, you wish to become real. That is, whatever you paint will become real." She held up her finger to make sure we understood that only one item could be painted, and she looked at each of us in turn. "Are there any questions?"

Nervous Girl raised her hand. "What do you mean, it becomes real? Paintings can't do that."

She made a notation on her clipboard before answering. "This is a new formula. We are relatively certain that whatever you paint will become three-dimensional and will become a useful object."

"Well, how long does it take?" she asked, her voice raising an octave as she held up her arm and tapped her watch with her index finger. "Does it happen right away? We just paint whatever, and it pops off the wall, or are we going to be here awhile? I have to be home in time to make dinner, Roy's bringing his boss and his wife, and I need to be there, it has to be perfect, he needs this promotion..." Her leg bounced up and down.

Dr. Phillips made another notation on the clipboard. "Go with Dr. Andrews, he'll make sure that happens."

Nervous Girl shot out of her chair as if she'd been electrocuted and beat Dr. Andrews to the door. He waddled his way over and showed her out, closing the door solidly behind them.

Grandma and I looked at each other. Raising her hand, she said, "What if we aren't artistic?"

Another clipboard notation was made. "The paint is special. As long as you can make your painting look somewhat like what you're thinking, the blanks will be filled in."

My mind was reeling. Had they really invented a formula for paint that could make a picture become real? Paint with the ability to pull details out of my imagination, pieces of a whole that I am unable to bring to light yet this... this... paint, can read my mind and actually fill in blanks as if it were alive? How is this possible? If what she's saying is true, this is the breakthrough of the century! No wonder we'd been asked to sign a non-disclosure form.

"Any other questions before we get started?" The only question I could think of was for me. What was I going to paint?

No one spoke up or raised their hands. "Excellent. Let's move on to Phase Two, then. Follow me, please, one at a time."

Goth Boy wasted no time. He shoved his chair back and strode toward the door. Once again Grandma and I exchanged a look of mild disgust. This one said, "No manners."

Dr. Phillips opened the door and walked out with him, closing the door behind them.

We waited patiently. Dr. Phillips returned a couple of minutes later. I motioned for Grandma to go ahead while I waited. She smiled and nodded her thanks. Getting up, she took her water and her cane and followed the doctor.

~~*~*~*

When it was my turn I was escorted down a long hallway, around the corner, into another hallway. About halfway down the second hall we stopped. Apparently this would be my room. Dr.

Phillips opened the door and ushered me in. She told me to make myself comfortable, she'd be back shortly to get me situated.

The first thing I noticed was that this room was nearly identical to the first meeting room; the only differences between the two were the one-way mirror running across the far wall and only one chair instead of four. I pulled the chair out and sat down, immediately noticing one more difference. This chair had actual padding left in the seat. I set my water bottle down on the table.

The question still remained: what should I paint? I went over what I knew. The paint was supposed to be able to bring something to a solid state and make it usable. Would it then be in the room with me, or would it concentrate whenever I'd thought about it being useful? Would it need to be small enough to carry out in a pocket or did size matter? I didn't know the answer to any of these questions. I had trouble coming up with anything at all... the whole concept was blowing my mind.

As I pondered, the door opened and Dr. Phillips returned, followed by a gentleman in a grey jumpsuit. He carried a plastic bin over to the table in front of me and set it down, then stepped back, clasped his hands behind his back and waited. His stance reminded me of a soldier at parade rest, his bald head so shiny it reflected the overhead light.

Dr. Phillips, still carrying her clipboard, pointed to the bin and said, "Here are your supplies—paint, brushes, and a smock. Please put the smock on before you open the paint, we don't reimburse for personal items damaged during the process. There will be people behind that mirror on the wall from time to time, just to check and make sure everything is alright in here and that you don't require anything. If something arises where you need to get our attention, for any reason, flip the switch on the wall and it will light a bulb, alerting us. Do you have any final questions for me before we begin?"

I glanced in the bin and then back at the doctor. "What am I supposed to paint on? There isn't any paper or canvas."

"You'll paint on this wall right here." She pointed to the wall opposite the mirror and made a notation on her clipboard.

"What am I allowed to paint? Animal, mineral, vegetable, any help would be appreciated. Just a place to start is all I'm asking. I want to do the best job for you that I can."

She scribbled another notation, longer this time. "I can't help you with that; the decision on what to paint must be yours entirely, without outside stimuli or ideas. That's the only way we can keep the trial untainted."

I nodded. That made sense I guess. "So, I can paint anything at all, no restrictions. Okay. How long do I have? I wasn't prepared to come up with something like this on the spot; it might take me a few minutes."

"Take as much time as you need. We'll be here until you're through, no matter how long you'd like to take."

I thought about it. "I guess that's all the questions I have, then."

She looked at Jumpsuit Guy and tilted her head toward the door. He took his cue and opened the door, holding it for her. The doctor motioned once more toward the mirror and the switch on the wall next to it. "If you need anything," she hesitated, looking intently at me for the first time, "flip the switch." With that, she turned and left, closing the door decisively behind her.

The tiniest inkling of unrest settled between my shoulder blades. I looked hard at the closed door, my forehead creasing with worry. There was something I was missing, some question I should have asked, a piece of information I hadn't fettered out, and nobody had offered it. Except Dr. Phillips with her veiled warning. What the hell had I signed up for and what was going to happen that I didn't expect?

~~*~*~*

By my watch, forty-five minutes had passed, and I still couldn't decide what to paint. Maybe the best way to figure it out would be to empty the bin. Getting everything set might help spark an idea.

Standing up, I reached in and pulled out the smock first. I'd expected it to be splashed with paint spatters from previous participants and was surprised by the fact that it was crisp and new, still carrying the creases from the packaging. No one had worn this before. Did that mean this was the first focus group? I shook my head. That line of thinking didn't help me get creative, and it didn't matter anyway. Giving it a quick snap, I slipped it on. The material was a little bit scratchy but it fit nicely over my clothing. I tied it and gave myself the once over in the mirror; knowing they could see me didn't stop me from smiling at the visual. The last time I'd worn a smock had been in high school art class. As I'd done back then, I took my watch off and slipped it into my pants pocket, alongside the key to my locker. No sense taking a chance on paint getting on it. I ran my finger back and forth across my wedding ring before sliding it off and placing it in my pocket, as well.

Turning back to the table, I picked up the paint can and studied it, turning it to see it better in the light. There were no markings on it, nothing to tell me anything about it except one tan drip of color down the side. An opener was taped to the side. Good, I hadn't thought about how I was going to open it until just now.

Setting it on the table, I reached in again and pulled the brushes from the bin. They were also new. Running my hand along the bristles felt good; their texture brought back more memories from high school. I smiled again. That was where I'd met Bob. We'd both had a passion for art and found ourselves paired up by the teacher for a project. I don't even remember what the project was that we were given. I just remember mentally thanking the teacher for putting me with the boy I'd secretly longed to meet. My smile turned to melancholy. I wished he was here with me now. "I miss you so much, Bob," I whispered. If only that truck driver hadn't fallen asleep at the wheel and plowed his eighteen-wheeler across the barrier and into oncoming traffic... If only we'd have been able to have children, I'd still have a piece of you.

Now was not the time for a trip down memory lane, especially if it were going to take me down a sad alley. Sniffling once, I wiped the tears that had formed in my eyes and focused on the task at hand. Wandering around the room, I concentrated. What in the world was I going to paint?

~~*~*~*

The sound of an alarm blaring sounded in the distance, interrupting my pacing. I heard several sets of feet pounding past my room. Voices called out to each other, tension evident in the tone. I went to the door to see what was going on. Grasping the knob, I tried to turn it but it wouldn't move. Was I locked in? That was strange. I guess they didn't want us wandering around the building by ourselves.

What if I had to pee? Flip the switch, I suppose.

The alarm stopped, and everything went back to being quiet. I drew in a deep breath and puffed up my cheeks before blowing it back out. Think, what to paint...

My thoughts wandered back through the disappointments of not being able to conceive. We'd wanted a child so badly but without the means to pay for medical help to make that happen, we resigned ourselves to our barrenness. Even adoption was out; we didn't have the money to do that, either. We'd briefly thought about fostering, but were turned away at the county desk where we'd asked about applying to become foster parents, as well. They even charged a hefty fee to get a copy of the paperwork to fill out, not to mention the costs associated with home visits. Those were to verify your house was ready and able to handle children, and then there was a series of psychological exams with a professional trained to detect our worthiness to help foster children. All of this out of our pockets before we could help children in need. Who'd ever heard of that? There were always children who needed love, and the children shouldn't be the ones to pay with their time and their lives while adults who wanted to love and help them navigated the red tape.

That's it! I could paint a program that helped couples who were in the same situation as Bob and I had been! A facility where they could go to get low cost or even free help conceiving, or at least answers as to why they weren't able. The means to help with the red tape and the costs of adoption. A place where people who cared about families could bring loving parents-to-be together with children who desperately needed them!

I scrabbled at the paint key, trying to remove it from the side of the can. I needed to get to the paint as quickly as possible. I wanted to get this on the wall immediately! So many details flowing in my brain, I wanted it out there right now, wanted it more desperately than I'd wanted anything in a long time. If this paint really works, I want this program to be real for the children! Thank you, Bob, you *are* here with me! I love you so much!

As I dipped the brush in the paint, the ideas flowed. The building would be beautiful and welcoming, everyone wearing smiles, the doctors and nurses garbed in bright scrubs and lab coats, and flowers blooming outside. The children would know by looking at it that this was where they would find their new families, and the hopeful parents would feel the positive vibes all around them, giving them hope and knowing someone else believed, as well.

The table was too far away from the wall. I dragged it closer so the paint would be nearby as I created.

Losing myself in the painting, I had no idea how much time had passed before I backed up and took a look at the big picture. The details created with just one color amazed me. I could see the faces of the people and the hope emanating from them. Either this paint really was magical, or I was better at painting than I remembered. The peaceful feeling inside reminded me how much I'd enjoyed it. When I was through here today maybe I could turn the empty spare room or the garage into a studio. Maybe I could sell my paintings, and that could be my job.

Rolling my shoulders, I felt the familiar aches of muscles gone too long unused. Picking up my bottle of water, I drank deep. I must have been at it awhile; I was really thirsty. Studying the painting, I saw it as almost perfect. One or two more trees and it would be finished. I only hope the program I envisioned would come through for the viewers as well as it had in my head for me. Dipping the brush back in, I added the extra trees and then laid the paint brush down across the top of the can. My hands went to my lower back and rubbed before I clasped them together and stretched my arms above my head, leaning from side to side to relieve the tension. I gave one more long studied look at the painting on the wall before calling it finished.

Walking over to the light switch, I flipped it to let them know I was done. The door unlocked when I did. Making my way back toward the door, I slipped off the smock and laid it across the back of the chair as I passed.

This time when I grasped the doorknob it turned easily. I opened the door and leaned out.

"Hello?" I called into the quiet. "Is anyone there?" My voice echoed down the hall. Nobody answered. Looking left and right I didn't see anyone.

"I'm finished with my painting, what's next?" I called out.

I walked down the hall the way we'd come and saw the door to the room next to mine was ajar. Curiosity took over and I peeked in. The room had been evacuated and emptied of supplies, only containing the chair and table. The painting looked to be an armory of some sort. There were weapons easily identifiable as guns and knives, even what appeared to be hand grenades. Others within the painting were unfamiliar to me though very ominous-looking. I stepped closer and studied the crude design. This was heavy duty firepower. As I stood there, one of the painted guns finished creating itself and dropped off the wall, landing with a clang on the floor below. Another was expanding as I stood there. I remembered that Goth Boy had looked like trouble; apparently I'd been right.

As I turned to go, I saw a smear of something dark red on the inside of the door jamb. Leaning closer, I caught a whiff of something metallic. Blood? No way could that be blood! Could it? What happened in here? I looked back at the wall and then at the mark on the door jamb again.

My body stiffened; every fiber of my being on high alert. There was an armory on the wall and blood on the jamb. The paint worked! Oh my God. If that were true, I had to get out of here, right now. Someone had painted this and was probably running loose in the building. That could have been what set the alarm off earlier.

With one last look at the wall I turned and made my way out of the room, quieter now. As I crossed the threshold, I saw a small drop of blood on the floor to the right. Great, just great... of course it would be in the direction I have to travel.

I strode quickly and quietly down the hall to the connecting hallway. Before turning the corner, I listened hard for a few seconds. Hearing nothing but my own heartbeat, I took a deep breath and peeked around the corner. The hallway was empty.

The need to get out of this place was getting stronger by the second. No stronger than the need to do it quietly, though. I came upon another door. This one was closed and latched. I stopped to listen and heard nothing; not feeling the need to open it, I continued on.

There was one more room to pass before the main meeting room and on through to the locker room where my purse and keys had been stowed. The door was open. I slowed to a stop at the edge of the doorway and listened. Not hearing anything, I looked in. The table was pulled close as I'd done in my own room, and the painting covered the entire wall. It was of the largest pile of money I'd ever seen. American dollars, Euros, Pesos, Francs, Pounds, and several other currencies I couldn't readily identify. I stepped in closer to get a better look. The details were impressive. Apparently Grandma wanted to travel.

Then I realized I wasn't alone. Dr. Andrews was here as well, sprawled face down on the far side of the table. Only his face wasn't down; it was looking toward the doorway, tipped at an unnatural angle. It took me a moment to identify why; his head had been almost completely severed from his body. The only thing keeping his head from rolling away was the spinal cord. His double chin was sitting in a pool of blood, the ragged edges of his open wound creating a garish sight for whoever was unlucky enough to come upon it. Unlucky me, I thought as I stumbled back and retched in the corner.

Thankfully, for him, he was already dead. The pain he would have endured had he lived through the brutality would have been horrific. I wiped the back of my hand across my mouth. Turning toward the door, I couldn't help but see him again. The blood was still draining out, the pool growing larger while I watched.

Tearing my eyes from the gruesome sight, I looked around for something, anything, to take my mind off of the scene until my legs stopped shaking enough to trust them to walk me out of here. I hadn't noticed until now that the paint can had been knocked over. It, too, spilled and pooled, acting like regular paint until it touched Dr. Andrews' shoe. From there it was creating its own picture right before my eyes. From the point of contact, the paint splotch was turning itself into an outline of a tiger. That must have been what he would have painted had he been given the option, or it was the last thing he'd been thinking when he died.

Oh, crap, a tiger... from what I was learning, I only had a short amount of time to get out of here before it became a living, breathing carnivore. Pushing myself off the wall, I stumbled into the hallway. I couldn't possibly outrun a tiger, but I could close it in the room.

Turning back, I grabbed the doorknob. It was slick with blood. My fingers slid around on it. My stomach lurched, threatening to heave again. Swallowing hard, I gripped tight and yanked the door shut. The last thing I saw through the crack was the tiger's head lifting off of the concrete floor.

Shuddering, I backed away from the now closed door, putting distance between me and that room. I needed to put distance between me and everything in this building. I wished I'd kept my smock on. At least I'd have something to use to wipe off my hand.

I stumbled down the hall toward the locker room. Another open door was coming up on my right. I slowed down and listened. Hearing nothing, I inched forward. Not really wanting to look but needing to make sure there was nothing in there that would come after me, I peeked around the doorway. This room was empty except for one woman's high heel shoe lying on its side. There was nothing painted on the walls, or nothing I could see from the doorway anyway.

Continuing past I held my stomach with my clean hand. I didn't know how much more pounding my chest could take before my heart beat its way out. At the rate it was thumping, it could happen any time. My stomach was still churning and couldn't be trusted at this point, either.

The door to what should be the main meeting room was ahead on my left. Still several steps away, I heard something slam against the door behind me. I jumped and turned. The door held. Another slam against the door shook it in its frame and was followed by a bone-chilling roar. I'd heard that sound once before when Bob and I had visited the wild animal sanctuary on our trip to the Arbuckles. The involuntary shiver started at my scalp and raced down to my toes, fear following close behind. The third crash cracked the wood of the door. I turned and ran the last few feet to the door ahead, slamming my own body against it as I turned the knob with my clean hand and shoved through, slamming it behind me.

Wasting no time I ran through the next doorway and out into that hall, sliding around the corner into the locker room. There was a lab coat hanging on a hook next to the first set of lockers. I made use of it to clean the blood off of my hand as best I could. Fumbling in my pocket, I found the key and opened my locker. Grabbing my purse, I headed for the entrance. The last locker had a piece of material sticking out of it, carelessly left flapping when the door was closed. Material covered in huge flowers. Nervous Girl had been wearing a dress with flowers.

I reached out with trembling fingers and hovered, not sure whether I wanted to see what was in there or not. Before I could think myself out of it, I opened the door. Nervous Girl was stuffed tightly into the small space, her head twisted completely around, facing backwards. Her tongue lolled out of her mouth. Stuck to the inside of the door was a name tag that read 909. *That hadn't been her number*, I thought. We'd all had four-digit numbers.

With absolute certainty I knew we were not the first focus group, not by a long shot. Even with the non-disclosure form signed I knew people couldn't help but talk about things like this. Word would have leaked long before the thousandth participant. My stomach churned. Also with absolute certainty I knew we weren't meant to live long enough to honor the non-disclosure. I had to get out of here.

Knowing the tiger would break free eventually, I gently closed the locker door against Nervous Girl. The least I could do was to protect her body for as long as possible.

Digging through my purse as I ran, I fumbled around and found my car keys. As I rounded the corner, I came face to face with Jumpsuit Guy. He must have heard me coming; his eyes were wide and he held up his hand for me to stop. I was startled enough at seeing him there in the first place that I already had.

Unsure of what to do, I shrugged my shoulders at him. He pointed toward his ear and then the office near the outside door.

There was a window with a sliding glass pane where we'd checked in and been instructed about our belongings and the lockers.

I listened. There was someone or something moving around in there. Belatedly I realized I should have grabbed one of the weapons from the wall with the armory painting.

Before we even had time to whisper a plan, a shadow crossed the doorway ahead and Grandma stepped out.

"Oh, thank goodness you're alright!" I said, turning toward her. As I did, she raised a powerful looking weapon that required the use of both hands to hold it up. Still, it wavered as she tried to point it toward me. She tilted her head back and maniacal laughter filled the hall. Of all the things I could have expected, this was not even in the same universe. My brain screamed, "RUN!" My body didn't listen.

I froze.

Jumpsuit Guy didn't.

Before she could get off a shot, he raised his hand and squeezed off two shots; both hit her dead center. Her body jerked, falling back against the wall and sliding down.

"Oh, my God, what did you *do* that for?" I hollered. Oh, my God, what did I *say* that for? She was going to shoot me! The thought slammed home. She really *was* going to kill me, if she could have. I'd have put money on it being Goth Guy that was the painter of the armory. Jumpsuit Guy had just saved my life, and I was yelling at him for it.

My head swam. I'd never fainted before, but it sure felt like I was about to do just that. Jumpsuit Guy grabbed my arm and lowered me to the floor. Squatting down next to me, he pushed the back of my head down until my face was between my knees.

"Breathe. Don't pass out now, there's no time."

I breathed deeply. When that danger had passed, I raised my head and looked at him.

"I'm sorry. I'm not reacting correctly right now. I don't know why I yelled at you. I just… thank you for saving my life."

"Are you okay now? Can you stand without fainting? We really have to get out of here."

The tiger let loose a roar that could be heard through the door I'd closed behind me. The sound startled Jumpsuit Guy. He straightened up, pointing his gun in the direction of the sound.

"What the hell was that?" he whispered.

"A tiger. Bengal, I think," I said. "There was a spilled paint can in one of the rooms, a dead Dr. Andrews, and a tiger forming out of the paint. I closed the door. He busted through it. We've got to get out of here; there's only one more door between him and us."

"Oh, *HELL* no!" He grabbed my hand and yanked me to my feet, pulling me along behind him. "If you pass out now, you're on your own."

I wasn't interested in tangling with a tiger, either. I held tight to his hand and followed at a full run down the hall. We jumped over Grandma's legs and into the office. As we rounded the end of the counter I slid in a puddle of blood. There, behind the counter, was Goth Boy. His hand was clutching an airline ticket in its blue and white paper folder, and his cell phone was lit up with a call in progress. The tinny voice issuing forth was calling out, "Jimmie? Jimmie? Hello? I can't hear you! Was that gunfire?" A duffel bag was on its side next to his still form, the zipper partially open and a bundle of one hundred dollar bills poked out through the opening.

Jumpsuit Guy let go of my hand and fumbled a set of keys out of one of his pockets. Finding the right key, he unlocked the door to the outside. He slammed it hard behind us. We ran across the parking lot.

"Listen. I know you don't know me, but I need a ride."

Without a thought, I said, "Get in." He'd saved my life. If that wasn't ride-giving material, I don't know what was.

"I have to get the gate. Pick me up there." He ran toward the fence, sorting through keys as he went.

I jumped in and started the car, wasting no time in pulling out of the parking lot. When I'd pulled clear, I stopped and waited while he closed the gate and relocked it behind us. He hopped in.

"Go, let's get out of here." He leaned his head back against the headrest and closed his eyes.

I drove toward town. This place had been hard to find, not located on any map, and now I knew why. The long dirt road wound around and through a wooded area before opening onto a one-lane paved road. I followed that back to the main road.

When I reached the stop sign, I idled for a minute. The adrenaline was wearing off, and I was bone tired.

"Where can I take you?" I asked.

Without lifting his head or opening his eyes, he said, "I don't know. Is there a gas station or truck stop nearby?"

Putting the car in park, I shifted in my seat to face him. "Why do you need a gas station or truck stop?"

He sighed, resigned. "I'm not from around here. I'm not from any one place. I've been all over, and this is just the latest stop in a really bizarre life. Today tops the cake, though. I can honestly say nothing before that whole experience was half as off the charts."

I waited. My brain wasn't firing on all cylinders at the moment and I wasn't sure what he was trying to tell me, or not tell me.

When I didn't respond, he turned his head and opened his eyes. He looked as tired as I felt.

"I've got a spare room if you want to get some sleep before you continue on to wherever you're going," I offered without hesitation.

Confusion crowded his features. "You don't know me from Adam. It's not smart to invite strangers into your house.,You know that, right?"

Lifting my hand, I waved his concerns off. "You saved my life. You didn't know me from Adam, either, and could have easily left me back there. You didn't. Do you want to rest or would you rather I leave you at the truck stop? There's one off the interstate about five miles down. It's your call."

Facing forward again, I buckled my seatbelt and put the car in drive.

"Thank you. I would appreciate the use of your spare room," he said, his words becoming heavy. Leaning the seat back, he was asleep before we'd driven a mile.

~~*~*~*

I awoke to the aroma of coffee. The sun was streaming in through the window. I'd slept through the night without waking once. That was unusual for me. Inhaling deeply, I wondered idly how long Bob had been up. Then I remembered. Bob was dead. A tear tracked down the side of my face, unbidden. One of the hazards of getting a good night's sleep was remembering in the morning that nothing was the same.

Wait a minute. Bob's not here. Then who made the coffee? I sat straight up in bed. The details of yesterday's focus group came back to me in a rushed jumble. I flopped back down. *That whole experience was insane*, I thought. Then I remembered about Jumpsuit Guy using the spare room. He must have made the coffee.

Climbing out of bed I realized I was still wearing my suit from yesterday, minus the shoes. Grabbing my robe, I made my way to the bathroom for a quick shower.

Once I'd gotten through with that routine and slipped into a pair of comfortable stretch pants and an oversized t-shirt, I went downstairs and found Jumpsuit Guy sitting at the kitchen table, mug of steaming coffee in one hand and the newspaper in the other.

"Good morning," he said, laying the paper down on the table.

"Hi. How did you sleep?" I asked, pulling a mug out of the cabinet and pouring coffee for myself.

"Fantastic. Thank you for the use of your room. I hope you don't mind that I made myself at home, fixing the coffee. It's been a long time since I've had a good cup."

"I don't mind at all. It was nice waking up to the smell again. It's been a long time since that has happened, too." I joined him at the table. Blowing across the top of my cup, I took a test sip and sighed. "Mmmmm. Hello, coffee."

He laughed at my conversation with my cup. He had a nice laugh, and his smile traveled all the way up to his eyes.

"How is it you can make a great cup of coffee yet you haven't had a good one in a while?" I asked, watching him over the top of the mug.

His smile left as quickly as it came. "I'll be out of your way in no time. Just let me get my shoes on and …"

I reached out touched his hand. "I'm sorry if I offended you. That wasn't my intention. I was curious. It's none of my business; I understand. Tell you what, let me make it up to you. I make a mean omelet. Please, stay for breakfast. If you're as hungry as I am, you'll need to eat."

A slight hesitation on his part was the only encouragement I needed. I went into the kitchen and started gathering supplies from the fridge. To keep the morning moving in a positive direction, I rattled on while I worked.

"So that was something, yesterday, wasn't it? I'm still not sure it was all real. I mean that would have been easier to accept if I'd have woken from a dream, but for that to happen you wouldn't be here, and I wouldn't have slept in my suit. I guess it will be back to the drawing board for creating income for me."

Mixing and chopping, I kept up the one-sided conversation. "Something I'm wondering. What should I call you? I mean, what's your name? I'm Suze. Not Susie, Suzanne, or Suzette, just Suze."

He was quiet for a few seconds, probably wondering if I were going to stop talking and give him a chance to answer. "Jake. It's nice to meet you, Suze."

"Nice to meet you, too, Jake. You look like a Jake. What I mean is, your name fits you. Sometimes people look exactly as you would expect them to once you've heard their name, and other times not so much. You know? Hand me that loaf of bread, please. I hope wheat is alright with you."

Jake picked up the bread and brought it to me.

"Thank you. Would you mind dropping a couple of slices in the toaster, there? Great, thanks."

Continuing on with the random dialogue, I finished fixing the omelet, cut it in half, slid it onto two plates, added the toast and brought them to the table. "Would you like juice, or is coffee good? I've got orange and apple."

"Orange juice would be nice, thank you."

"Then orange juice it is." I poured us each a glass and brought them to the table, too.

We ate in silence, the tension not as thick as it had been but still there. When we'd finished, Jake took both of our plates to the sink, rinsed them off and stacked them in the dishwasher.

"I should be going. Thank you for the hospitality, Suze." Jake gave me a nervous smile.

"Where?" I said.

"Excuse me?"

"Where are you going?"

Jake didn't answer right away and looked everywhere but at me. "I don't know. I haven't had time to formulate a plan. I will."

"Look, I've been thinking," I started. "You need a place to stay, and I need a boarder."

Before I could say any more than that, he started shaking his head. "You don't understand."

"What don't I understand? Am I mistaken? Do you have somewhere to go, a place to stay?"

He sat back down, clasped his hands tightly together on the table and stared at his white knuckles. "Okay. I'm just going to put this out there, and then I'm gone. What you don't understand is that I was in prison. I got released three days ago, and outside the fence where I would have caught the bus to town was Dr. Andrews. He asked if I needed a job and offered me twenty-five dollars an hour to work at the compound. Where else was I going to make that kind of money straight out of prison? I would have been a fool to say "no." So, I said "yes," and he gave me a ride to that place we were yesterday."

"What did you do?" I asked.

Jake looked up at me, confused. "I got in the car with the doctor, rode out to the compound, was issued a jumpsuit and told I would be carrying supplies, doing general maintenance, whatever they needed."

"No, I meant, did you murder someone? Rob a bank? Pee on a police car? What landed you in prison?" I rested my elbows on the table and my chin on my hands.

A ghost of a smile passed across his face. "I hitched a ride with a stranger. A cop tried to pull him over, and he ran. When we were finally stopped by police, that guy jumped out of the car and put a bullet in a cop and killed him. His brothers in blue opened fire and put seventeen bullets in that guy. I stayed in the car, folded as flat as I could so I wouldn't be hit. The cops dragged me out of the car, and when they opened the trunk they found it was loaded with marijuana and firearms that had the serial numbers filed off. Since that guy was deader than a doornail, I went down for the drugs and guns. Now, I don't expect you to believe me, nobody else ever has, but that's why it's not safe to get in a car with a stranger or let one in your house, by the way. I'm a convicted felon."

His eyes lit up and he sat up straight. Quickly he unbuttoned the top two buttons on his jumpsuit and reached inside, pulling out an envelope. His hand shook as he opened it and smoothed the paper out on the table. When he looked back up at me, his eyes were shining.

"I forgot. When that kid with the slicked back hair finished with his painting, I was told to clean out the room. I was gathering the supplies when the alarm sounded. I knew everyone would be paying attention to that and I had a small window of opportunity. So I picked up a paintbrush that was still new and added my own painting to the wall. It didn't take long to dry, and I took my time cleaning out that room while I waited. When I heard this hit the floor, I picked it up and pocketed it on my way out the door."

"What is it?" I asked, getting up and coming around behind him to where I could read it over his shoulder.

He smoothed the wrinkles out carefully. "It's a full pardon from the governor, with a promise that my record would be erased. Not sealed, just gone. With this letter, it is as if the arrest and prison sentence never existed. Well, not for anyone else. I'll never forget it, but it won't affect the rest of my life. I can go anywhere and do anything I want without fear of recrimination."

"That was quick thinking on your part. How did you come up with something so fast?" I asked, curious. "It took me almost an hour to come up with an inkling of an idea on what to…"

The doorbell rang. We looked at each other. "I'm not expecting anyone, are you?" I said.

Jake laughed. "No, I'm not either."

I went through the living room and opened the door. A courier stood there with his clipboard and a large manila envelope. "I have a delivery for a Suze McIntyre."

"That's me."

"Sign here, please."

Popping his earphones back into his ears, he jumped on his bicycle and pushed off, pedaling down the driveway and out into the street. I took the envelope back into the kitchen, opening it as I went.

"Curiouser and curiouser…" I muttered under my breath.

Sitting back down, I slid the contents from the envelope out onto the table. A thick stack of documents fell out, including trifold color flyers announcing the opening of "Bob's Hope."

The letter on top was from, apparently, my attorney, instructing me to sign everywhere that had been tabbed and giving details on the date and time of the opening of my new non-profit business. It was a good thing that I was already sitting down because all the blood drained out of my head, leaving me feeling woozy.

"Are you okay, Suze?" Jake's voice brought me back to the here and now.

"I'm more than okay. I'm fantastic!" The excitement bubbled up. I let out a whoop.

"Jake, this is our lucky day. These papers, right here, are for the business I created with my painting on the wall. It will help couples that cannot, for whatever reason, conceive and have children of their own, who are in the same position that Bob and I were in. Bob, my husband, was killed in an accident at the beginning of the year. We weren't able to have our own children. The adoption process is so expensive, and the red tape involved is massive and so intricate. I painted a facility where couples can become a family, where they can go for help in making that happen, for treatment from fertility specialists or weaving their way through the legalities of adoption. All of this is that dream coming true, becoming a reality. I had no idea it would really work."

"That's terrific! This IS our lucky day!" Jake seemed as genuinely happy for me, as I was for him when we read his letter.

An idea sparked to life. "You know, I'm going to need help. You wouldn't know anyone who is looking for a job, would you?" I smiled at Jake.

He looked at me for a minute, thoughtfully. A slow smile spread across his face. "As a matter of fact, I do."

Six months later:

My thoughts returned to my own painting on the wall. How could we have known what would cost us and what would kill us? We didn't. Looking down at the smiling face of the cherub-like child before me, I thanked my lucky stars that I'd painted something to help others, not something selfish that would come back on me.

Jake opened the door to my office and led a young couple in, chatting with them about daycares in the area. He smiled at me as he let himself back out, closing the door softly behind him.

Unseen, outside the office window, hidden behind a large holly bush was a thin man in a white lab coat. He watched the scene unfold, scribbling notes on a clipboard. Lowering his clipboard, he watched intently for a few moments before disappearing into the black, nondescript car, behind darkly tinted windows, and being silently carried away.

CAR WASH

The bubbles squirt out of the automatic bubbler and trace lines through the tiny bits of dirt down the side of the Mercedes. The bubble path changes with every car. The water follows closely behind, chasing the bubbles like children chase each other at the park across the street. I watch the kids, too.

Sometimes I wish I was over there, playing with them. Today it's a blonde boy pushing his little brother on the swing, three girls with pigtails and girly dresses huddled up and giggling under the tree, and a redheaded kid with freckles off by himself, reading a book in the gazebo. I wonder if it's the same book I've seen him reading before, or if he reads different ones. I can't tell from here. Every day when the weather is warm, there are kids there. Sometimes the big kids bring their football or Frisbee. One day I want to play football.

I'm not allowed to go over there, though. My dad prefers to keep an eye on me. So, I'm somewhat of an expert, I'd say, on bubbles. I've been watching the cars roll slowly through on the conveyor belt in their unending line for three years tomorrow and haven't missed a day yet. This window in the office, where I sit, is my own portal into another world - the world of others where anything is possible and everyone is happy.

My name is Thomas. I'm twelve years old, and that's my dad over there, the one cleaning the tires. His name is Greer. He's worked here ever since my mom died. We're all we have left. But it's okay because we take care of each other.

Dad works two jobs. He's a janitor at my school during the day, and then we come here and he works cleaning cars until bedtime. Mr. Bandy lets me sit here and watch because I'm quiet and don't cause nobody no trouble. That's what he says. I think it's because my dad can't afford to pay someone to stay with me while he works. So he comes here and cleans other people's cars, and I stay at this table and do my homework. I stay by this window so I can see him, and he can see me. He looks over at me sometimes and we wave. Other times, when he's having a hard day and his eyes are sad, I pretend I don't see him looking so he won't have to pretend he's happy. That's when I watch the bubbles instead.

The cars pull in; they get in line, and when it's their turn on the conveyor belt the people pull up until their car hooks on, and then they get out and go to the waiting room. Sometimes the kids like to ride through in the car, and Mr. Bandy lets them. I've done that. It's fun. The car gets pulled through and washed, then out the end where my dad and Marco wait to dry them off, wash the windows and clean the tires. Sometimes the people watch their cars, sometimes they talk to Mr. Bandy. He's owned this car wash on this corner for thirty years, and everybody knows him. Small towns are like that. They say Aspen Grove isn't real big... the big town is Oklahoma City, twenty miles away or something like that.

That car that just turned in the drive, the yellow one, that's a Saturn Sky. I like those. They look like they go really fast. This car comes through every week. I know it's the same one because it has the paint scratched off the back corner bumper. You'll see it when it comes through. I don't think that guy even knows it's there, or he'd probably fix it. He has to go around and get in line, there are a few cars waiting today.

My mom was the best mom ever. I remember she made chocolate chip pancakes on my birthday, sang to me when I was sick, and helped me with my homework. We didn't even know she was sick until she was really sick. Sometimes cancer does that, the doctor says. We took a vacation right after mom and dad told me. We made a great adventure for her and went to the ocean. Mom always wanted to put her toes in the surf, and walk on the sand with her shoes in her hand. We all did it, mom, dad, and me, and it was warm, and the sand was scratchy on my bare feet but I liked it. I found a shell and gave it to mom. She had dad put it on a necklace for her, and she wore it all the time.

I don't think this car has been through before. I don't remember the red handprint sticker in the back window. That sticker must be on the inside because the bubbles raced right across it. See? If that was a sticker, the bubbles would have gone around first, then across. Oh, that's not a handprint, that's a hand. Can you see the top of his head at the bottom of that window, too? Black curly hair and big brown eyes and he's peeking up over the edge of the door. He's holding a lollipop in his other hand. See it?

Sometimes I'm afraid because I can't remember her face very well. I don't want to forget her. Somehow dad always knows when I'm having trouble remembering because he brings out the photo albums and we spend Saturday morning looking through pictures and telling the stories that go with them. My favorite picture is the one from Mother's Day when I was five, and I made her the macaroni necklace that she wore for a whole week until it rained and the noodles got wet.

He's waving. I wave back when kids are in the cars and they see me. He's waving pretty hard and shaking his head. Why are his eyes so big? He looks scared. I try to tell him it's okay, they're just bubbles. He's still shaking his head. He's only like five or six, probably, and maybe has never gone through a car wash before.

She used to tell me not to be scared, that I would do great things one day and that growing up strong and wise and good would serve me well. I'm still not sure what she meant by that. Sometimes I feel her in my heart and hear her in my head, reminding me to be good and stay true. I think my dad still feels her sometimes, too; once in awhile I can hear him at night, talking to her in his low voice. I think she must tell him the same thing as she tells me because the mornings after I hear him talking to her, he's strong again.

Can you hear the swish, swish sound of the brushes going around and around, rubbing the grime off the cars? Dad says they're not really brushes; that they're more like rags, so they don't scratch the paint, but they look like brushes to me.

He waves again and then points at his lollipop. I look hard to see what he's pointing at; it has writing on it. HELP ME. Help me? On a lollipop? That's weird. He's pointing at it again, really hard. I try to let him know I'm going to go get his dad. He keeps shaking his head really hard, and he's crying. Why's he crying? He taps the lollipop against the window and then holds it there, staring hard at me, tears streaming down his face. He looks quickly at the window to the waiting room and drops down out of sight.

I look over and see his dad looking out the window at his car. He doesn't see me. The window between the office and the waiting room has one-way glass. People think it's just a mirror. Sometimes they pick their teeth or comb their hair in it, especially the moms. His dad turns back around and answers Mrs. Talkington. She's the one who owns the Mercedes.

It feels like there's something wrong here. Even being little and being scared, that's not right. The kid peeks back up and looks around. He must have seen his dad turn away. He slaps the lollipop with its HELP ME sign back up on the window. I motion that I'll get help. I don't know his dad, and I don't talk to strangers, so I'm not going to him. He looks scary anyway.

I give the kid a 'thumbs up,' get out of my chair and go for the door. Looking back, I see he's dropped back down out of sight again. His car is almost finished, so I hurry.

When I get outside, my dad sees me and stands up. He's tall and wide like a linebacker, mostly muscle from the physical work he does every day. I tell him what I've seen and that the boy looks real scared, not like a normal kid going through a car wash. He asks me what the kid looks like, and I tell him, then he looks at me for a long minute and nods. He leans down and whispers to me to walk calmly inside, go into the office and close the door, then call the police. I nod, too. My heart thumps hard in my chest; he pats me on the shoulder, and I walk back like he told me.

I do exactly what he told me and go back normal, like nothing's wrong. I make sure not to look at that kid's dad. It feels like the longest walk of my life. It's taking forever. When I finally get inside and close the door after me, I run the last few steps to the phone and dial quickly. When the 911 operator answers I tell her what my dad said. She says to stay on the line, they're on their way. She asks me all sorts of details about the kid, the car, the dad. I tell her everything.

While I'm talking to her I watch through the window, waiting for the kid to peek back up. I want to tell him we're helping him, but he doesn't look again.

My dad stands at the end of the conveyor belt with Mr. Bandy, motioning toward the car. It rolls through the last of the rinse cycle and to the drying tube. In a minute it will be out the other side and ready for windows and tires.

The man sees it's almost done and walks out of the waiting room to where it will stop, by my dad and Mr. Bandy. I can't hear them from here, but it looks like he's telling Mr. Bandy and my dad that he doesn't want anything else done to the car, just the wash. His hands are going like he's an umpire calling the runner safe.

All of a sudden the conveyor belt stops and the emergency bell sounds, letting the workers know there's a problem with the belt. The car jerks to a halt and the kid's head pops up at the bottom of the window. He looks straight at me; I point at the phone. He's still crying, but he must understand because he nods.

The 911 operator must have heard it, too, because she asks me what that sound was and what's going on now. I tell her what it means, and that I don't know what's happening, but I'm looking. She tells me to stay on the line, they're almost here.

Marco strolls out of the back of the car wash and goes around to the front. He must have been the one to hit the manual stop; he doesn't say much, but he's pretty smart. I wish I'd have thought of that. But my job was to call the police, and that's what I did.

Mr. Bandy throws his hands up in the air and stalks around like it's the end of the world. It's strange to see because he doesn't normally act like that. He's a laid back kind of guy.

The people in line get out of their cars to see what's happening, and they walk over to where Mr. Bandy and the dads are standing. The guy in the yellow Saturn Sky takes off his ball cap and scratches his head, then shakes Mr. Bandy's hand and goes back to his car. He starts up and drives out, probably coming back later or tomorrow. He never misses a week.

I feel like one of those commentators at the ball game the way I'm telling the operator everything I'm seeing. She asks if the kid is still looking. I tell her "no." She asks if I see the officer arriving yet, I look around as far as I can see and I tell her "no." I tell her that my dad is crawling around on the ground, looking to see why the belt is stuck, like he can fix it from there. They never fix it from there; they always go to the maintenance room for that. She tells me we're doing a good job, and that it was fast thinking.

The police car drives in and stops in front of the group of people, blocking the car, and the officer gets out.

The dad of the kid is very animated and wants the officer to move his car and my dad to get his car unstuck. He's sweating, and his face is red; I can see it from here.

I tell the operator that the officer has arrived. She asks me to stay on the line and keep telling her what's going on, so I do. I think she just wants to keep me out of the way, but that's okay, it's safer in here.

That dad is mad now; I can tell, because he almost runs over to the car and yanks open the back door, reaching inside toward the kid. The kid scrambles backwards across the seat, as far away as he can get, and the police officer shouts at him to stop. The kid stops; the dad doesn't. The police officer pulls his gun and yells again for the man to stop. This time he freezes.

The officer comes closer, telling the dad to back up and put his hands on the hood of the car. The dad doesn't listen; instead, he tries to grab the kid again. The kid squashes himself as flat as he can against the far door, shaking his head and screaming. I can hear him even through the glass, and I tell the operator what's going on.

All of a sudden there was a flurry of activity. The officer yells one more time that the dad guy needs to stop, or he'll shoot. The dad guy doesn't stop; he abandons his kid and the car and tries to run out the back of the car wash where people pull in. The officer shoots him with his Taser gun, and the dad guy goes down, all floppy on the soapy rails of the conveyor.

The kid is still flat against the far door, but he's stopped screaming. He's just looking at me and holding the stick of his red lollipop tight with both hands, his knuckles turning white from squeezing them so tight. I don't know what's going on for sure yet, but I try to make the kid feel better by nodding and smiling, and motioning that everything is going to be okay. He nods, and a big fat tear falls out of his eye and slides down his already wet cheek.

Once everything calms down, my dad comes into the office and tells me I did a great job of being aware and acting when something looked wrong. Then he tells me what just happened out there.

The kid had been kidnapped from Missouri a couple days ago, and his story had been all over the news, in the newspapers and on the internet. His parents have been looking for him, and for the guy they thought had taken him. They said that not-dad guy had family here in Oklahoma, and they thought he might travel this way. The guy was a maintenance man at the apartments where the kid and his real parents lived, and he'd made friends with the parents, but then stole the boy out of his bed in the middle of the night and ran away with him. It's very scary to think about, people you thought were friends who go and do something like that.

Mr. Bandy and my dad are very proud of me, and after the bad guy was handcuffed and taken away in a second police car, the first officer brought a police badge into the office for me. Not a real one, I'll have to work for that if I want to be a police officer when I grow up, but it's still shiny and new, and I can wear it if I want to. It has a pin on the back. Maybe it's childish but I like it and I want to wear it, so the officer pins it to my shirt and pats me on the back, telling me again what a great job I did.

The kid is sitting in the back of the police car, still looking scared. I can see him through the window. I ask my dad if I can go talk to him. He looks at the police officer, and they say it's okay, so I do.

He's sitting still, backed up into the corner of the back seat, and I ask him if I can sit with him. He nods "yes." We talk for a few minutes, and he tells me his name is Ben, and that he misses his mommy. I tell him she's coming. He hugs me tight, and tells me thank you for helping him. I ask him how he got his lollipop to say 'help me' and he tells me he found a marker in the back seat, and the not-dad had given him the sucker to keep him quiet while they were on the road. This wasn't the first sucker he'd been told to eat, and he knew it would make him tired, so he only pretended to lick it and pretended to go to sleep. The not-dad thought he really was sleeping and it would be okay to leave him in the car while it got washed. When he peeked out and saw me he had the idea to write on it instead.

He said the car was red when he first was in it, and now it's blue, so I think the not-dad was washing a fake color off of it so he wouldn't be found. The kid hugs me even harder. I hug him back and tell him how smart that was, writing on it like that. I found out he wasn't five or six. He was eight. He only looked younger.

That man, the not-dad, will be in jail for a really long time, my dad tells me. I'm glad. Nobody should steal kids. The kid's mom and dad were called, and they are coming to get him. I'm glad about that, too.

My dad tells me everything happens for a reason, and that it was a good thing I stay at the car wash with him and that I saw Ben. My dad hugs me so hard I can barely breathe, but it feels good to make him so happy.

I agree with my dad. Everything happens for a reason. I hear my mom's voice in my head telling me she's proud of me, too; her voice says I stayed strong and true, and I did a good thing. I keep thinking about it, and I rub my fingers over my badge. I like the way it feels under my hand. It feels strong and right and good. Helping people feels right and good, too. I know now. I'm going to be a policeman when I grow up. It just feels right.

The car wash is running again, and the bubbles run down the side of a minivan full of kids. They are all waving at me and smiling. I wave back. I watch the bubbles make their path, and I see them trace a picture of my mom. I blink hard and rub my eyes. When I look again, she's still there, and she's smiling at me. I smile with my face and with my heart, just to make sure she sees me too.

DEAD COEDS

"Are there any questions so far?" Sometimes you could tell if they were paying attention by the look on their faces, other times not. This class was extremely introverted; he couldn't tell at all.

One hand rose from the middle of the group. It belonged to a twenty-something blonde cheerleader type. He searched his memory, coming up with a name.

"Yes, Ms. Anderson?"

"Professor Winters, can we be let out early tonight?" Her voice was quiet, her words tentative. Several murmurs were heard throughout the group.

He looked at the clock above the door. Eight-thirty. He frowned, absently stroking his five o'clock shadow. Theo had been a professor at this college for two years and another two before that at his alma mater in Washington. "Why, Ms. Anderson, would I want to dismiss class an hour and a half before the scheduled end time?"

She scooted around in her seat, a bundle of nervous energy. "Did you hear about John Peterson, the student who was killed over by Munroney Hall a few weeks ago? The police said that it looked like cause of death was from a dog attack."

He tilted his head and speared her with his almost-black eyes. "What, pray tell, does that have to do with my class, Ms. Anderson?" He clasped his hands behind his back and paced the full width of the classroom, never losing eye contact with her.

She shook her head. "He doesn't have anything to do with your class, it's just ..." She fell silent.

It appeared she didn't have an answer for him. Another hand shot up. This one belonged to Josh Pearson, star quarterback of the football team. "Prof? I think what Violet is trying to say is that he was killed by a dog, on the night of a full moon. There's been talk that it's a werewolf." Several voices murmured again, apparently agreeing with the two.

He tried hard not to roll his eyes, barely managing. He wasn't that much older chronologically than his students, but in experience he was light years ahead. As such, his tolerance level was much less than it could have been on ridiculous topics such as this one.

"And do you, Mr. Pearson, believe in werewolves?" He smirked. There was no controlling that; it was absurd, the fairy tales kids today carried with them, and believed, well into adulthood.

Scratching his head, a blank look on his face spoke before Josh did. "Well, yeah, what else could it be? There aren't any dogs on campus, and nobody's seen one around in the last month. Tonight's a full moon again and, well, the girls are nervous."

Several of the girls nodded, and the guys slumped down in their chairs, either to affect a no-fear attitude or to avoid being looked at because they were just as scared as the girls.

"First of all, ladies and gentlemen," he addressed the group as a whole. "Tonight is not a full moon. That will happen on Friday. Second, we do not let class out early for anything less than a full-blown fire or a rogue gunman. Third, and lastly, there's no such thing as werewolves. There are no vampires, ghosts, or tooth fairies either."

Several hands shot up. He held up his to stop them. "No amount of arguing or attempts to convince me differently will change my mind, so I suggest you get your pencils ready. We've got work to do. To get through the full curriculum, we'll need every minute of class time we can get. If you've forgotten, English is a mandatory credit, and I do not give credit where it is not due."

Turning his back to the class, he began writing their assignment on the chalkboard behind his podium. Hearing the whispered voices, he allowed himself the eye roll he'd controlled earlier. These individuals are a sampling of the future of our country. We are in serious trouble.

~~*~*~*

At exactly ten o'clock p.m., he closed his book and dismissed his class. The students wasted no time picking up their backpacks and rushing the door; the majority of them didn't wait for the end of class to gather their belongings. Several of them glared at him on their way out, thinking he wasn't paying attention. He made a mental note of which ones.

The last of the students were filing out while he packed up his own materials for the trip home. He read and studied as much, if not more, than they did, but he preferred to stay ahead of them and be ready for their questions. There weren't many students in this particular class who he expected would challenge his knowledge.

One lone female remained behind her peers. "Excuse me, Professor?"

He turned. The voice belonged to Cadence McPherson. She was one of the few who chose to sit in the front row and take notes. Her blond hair was pulled back into a ponytail, a small section escaping confinement and curling near her jaw. Her arms were loaded down with books that wouldn't have fit in the overflowing book bag she carried by a strap slung across her body. Though she was a little bit plump, the extra weight didn't look bad on her; she carried it well.

"Yes, Ms. McPherson?"

"I wanted to talk with you about the assignment, if you have a minute."

"Certainly. What can I help you with?" He took off his reading glasses and cleaned them with the hem of his polo shirt before slipping them into their protective case.

"We can walk and talk, if you don't mind." She motioned toward the door with a nod of her head, shifting the load of books in her arms. The loose hair brushed her cheek as she moved.

It seemed that she was staring straight through him, her eyes the most fascinating shade of blue he'd ever seen. Funny he hadn't noticed that before now, he thought, since she chose to sit in the front row. He made a mental note to make more eye contact with his students that were closer towards the front of the classroom.

"Alright." He gathered his last pile of papers and stashed them in his briefcase. Clicking it shut he picked it up and motioned for her to go first.

"Which section of the assignment is giving you trouble?" He turned the lock on the inside of the classroom door and pulled it closed after them. They walked together toward the exit doors.

"You gave us instructions to write an interview we would like to conduct with a specific author and to name that individual as well as to answer the questions we were asking. We weren't told whether they had to be well-known or if we could choose an independent or newly-published author."

"Right." The lights in the hallway were turned down; only every other one was lit. Just one of the university's many ways of trying to save money after hours. They walked behind three other students who were also on their way out from late classes.

"First question, is the author we're choosing limited to those that are well-known? Second question, does the person have to be alive today? Last question, is this more of a research-based interview or relaxed and open to questions we'd personally like to ask?"

He listened to her breathing, and swore he could hear the breath whispering past her lips. It was seductive, erotic somehow, though he wasn't sure she had meant it to be. He felt a familiar stirring below the belt.

The other students were laughing and talking as they moved swiftly down the hall and out into the night. As the door clicked shut behind them, he realized he was completely alone with Ms. McPherson . His heart thudded hard in his chest.

"Professor?" Her voice, like silk, interrupted his thoughts.

He quickly rewound his mental tape and reviewed what he should have been paying attention to. The questions she'd asked were impressive. He hadn't expected anyone to come back for clarification on this project.

Clearing his throat, he said, "Yes, I'm sorry. Those are very good questions. I've given this assignment to prior classes, and you're the first to ask them. I didn't specify the authors you could choose because I want you to decide whom *you* would like to interview, not whom you think *I* would like you to interview. The questions you decide on can be whatever you like, as long as they're properly written and answered as if the author were in the room with you, the one providing the answers."

They'd made their way outside. The halogen lights over the parking lot 300 yards in front of them were misty behind the cool evening air. Bats flew aimlessly around the farthest lamp, feasting on insects that had been attracted to the light. The expanse of well-tended grounds between the building and parking lot was broken into pieces by the sidewalks leading out and down. Voices could be heard talking and laughing, and then car doors slammed, an engine gunned and, once again, they were alone.

"Okay. What about the other question?"

"What was that again?" The parking lot was on the other side of the hedgerow. They followed the sidewalk toward it.

"Does the author we choose have to be alive today?"

"Not unless you plan to actually interview them." He chuckled at his own joke. She didn't; she stopped and looked at him, waiting for something. He wasn't sure what.

He stopped as well. They'd almost reached the curb and stood between the two box hedges. From where they stood, anyone walking by would be less than likely to see them unless they turned down this particular eight feet of sidewalk. The feeling that it was a whole different world inside their world wasn't lost on him.

"Was there something else?"

Her eyes reflected the light. The iridescence was disconcerting. He wondered if his eyes were giving the same effect. His internal fire flared.

She smiled. Nervously she asked, "Would you mind watching until I get in my car? This section of the campus has always creeped me out a little bit, especially after dark."

"Why didn't you take the earlier class, then?"

"I tried. It was full."

He nodded. That roster had filled up rather quickly. "Where did you park?"

She pointed at a gold Camry near the back row of the parking spaces. "Right there, that's me."

"Go ahead, I'll wait right here."

"Thank you. I know it may seem silly to you, but ..." She looked at the ground and then back up at him.

Her eyes really were the most interesting shade.... "It's alright. Really."

As she shuffled her stack of books, her keys slipped from her grasp, hitting the sidewalk with a tinkle of metal on metal. He bent down to retrieve them for her. As he stood up, she was close enough for him to detect a subtle perfume. Without thinking, he leaned in and inhaled. She did too. A soft hum escaped her lips. His body responded in arousal. He realized what he'd just done, smelling her that way; his face flushed and he pulled as far back as he could without stepping into the hedge.

Holding her keys at arms length, he croaked, "Here you go."

She smiled at him, a knowing smile. What she knew, well, he had no idea. "Thank you," she purred, in a tone that told him she was thanking him for more than retrieving her keys. When she broke eye contact and turned away, relief flooded over him.

Sighing inwardly, he was watching her power-walk toward her car, juggling the armload of books. If he were a betting man, he'd have laid money on her not wanting to walk out alone as being the reason for her questions. Had it been just that, she could have walked out with the rest of the class, though. Most of the students who attended here lived off-campus as well and would have had cars parked in this same lot. Who knew what was in the mind of a young girl. He snorted at himself. She wasn't that young, probably three years his junior.

He waited as he'd said he would until she was safely in her car and backed out of the parking space. Transferring his briefcase to the other hand, he searched his pocket for his own car keys.

As he climbed in and pulled the door closed behind him, he heard a dog howl in the distance.

His mind went back to the conversation about werewolves and how the kids were all buying into it, even the jocks. Well, that probably wasn't a stretch of the imagination, the jocks believing things like that. He shook his head. Once again he reflected on these kids being the future of our country. If that thought all by itself didn't scare the hell out of the older generations, nothing would.

Generally he enjoyed going over his recent class in his mind on the drive home; tonight, however, he couldn't stop thinking about Cadence. Why, really, didn't she walk out with the class and instead chose to wait for him? Her questions were good, but that wasn't the problem. Not entirely anyway. Most students preferred to log on to the school's website and send him a message through the class bulletin board if they needed clarification. He couldn't put a finger on what, exactly, he had trouble with other than the general discomfort he felt any time he was alone with a female student. The discomfort he'd felt tonight wasn't general. It was highly specific and concentrated in one portion of his anatomy.

Though he had high standards of moral conduct, not everyone did. Some professors took advantage of coeds, and vice versa, for grades. He did not, and didn't want to be put in any position where the topic could be brought up at all.

Twenty minutes later he pulled into his driveway. When he'd accepted the position he'd purposely chosen a house in a small town that was a decent drive away from campus; he didn't want to encourage students to drop by unannounced and, in fact, preferred they didn't even know where he lived.

He turned off the engine, got out and went around the back of the car to the passenger side to retrieve his briefcase. The unexpected tickle running up his spine, like fingers on piano keys, caused him to whirl around. He fully expected to see someone standing there, staring at him, as certain as he was that he was being watched. Squinting, he looked out into the darkness, concentrating on discerning the causes of different shadows. He couldn't make out anything that shouldn't be there. Listening hard, he thought he heard a twig snap. Whipping his head around toward the sound, he scanned the fence line between his and the neighbor's house. Still, he saw nothing out of place.

He shook his head at himself. The kids' stories were getting to him. It was entirely unlike him to go with the crowd mentality and follow along like a sheep. He was more interested in the science side of things than the fantasy. He turned back to the car and picked up his briefcase. Clicking the remote he locked his car and covered the distance between the driveway and the front door in quick steps.

As he took the steps two at a time, his motion detector porch light came on. He should change the settings on it so that it came on when he pulled in, instead of waiting for his arrival on the porch. He'd deal with that tomorrow.

He opened the front door and stepped across the threshold, closing the door and locking it behind him, setting his briefcase down next to the wall. Then he did something he would never admit to anyone: he turned off the porch light and looked out the small, diamond-shaped window set high in his front door, scanning the narrow view. The lack of anything visibly sinister didn't help dispel the feeling of dread that still crawled across his nerves.

Double-checking the deadbolt, he rubbed the back of his neck and headed for the kitchen. For some reason, he wanted a beer.

Thursday was his free day. He spent the morning puttering around the house, throwing a load of laundry in and giving the kitchen a once-over while he waited for the washer to finish. He took a few minutes to look through the file cabinet in his office, searching for the instructions on the porch light. He found them and set the adjustment. It was as easy as turning a screw.

He finished picking up and cleaning the house. Not that it got that dirty with just him there. Still, it didn't hurt to run the vacuum cleaner once a week and scrub down the stove top. He liked a tidy area at home as well as in the classroom.

The afternoon was usually reserved for errands. Grocery store, gas station, anything else he needed to combine into one trip.

When he arrived back home, he pulled down the longer portion of the driveway and around to the back door. He unloaded the groceries, taking them straight into the kitchen. As he brought the last two bags out of the trunk and slammed it closed, he heard his trash can bang against the side of the house. Still carrying the two plastic bags by their handles, he walked back around the corner to see what was going on.

A dog, probably a stray judging by its lackluster coat and the ribs evident through his fur, had tipped the can over and was head and shoulders inside, digging through a trash bag. Papers and envelopes were being shoved out of the way; the breeze rustling them and sending them skittering down the drive.

"Hey!" he shouted. "Get out of there!"

The dog backed out of the can; teeth bared at him. A low growl issued forth. It looked like a German Shepard from the markings and the size. A big German Shepard. Its fur was dull; its muzzle splattered with dirt or dried ketchup, or blood, he couldn't tell from here and wasn't going to get any closer to verify. Apparently this one had been on the streets for awhile.

He backed up, grocery bags in hand, calmly talking to the agitated animal. "You go on now. I'm going in the house and calling animal control. You don't want to be here when they arrive, so go on. Shoo."

The dog hunkered down, gave a look at the trash can and another back at him before turning tail and slinking off. One more look over its shoulder and it was gone, jumping over the white picket fence and into the neighbor's yard.

He took the grocery bags into the house and set them down. He put the produce and dairy away before going out to clean up the mess. He didn't want to think about the fact that he was giving that dog time to skedaddle before he went back out and turned his back on the direction it had gone.

Why do people drop dogs off in the country? It was almost always a death sentence. Giving them to the pound at least gave them a chance to be adopted by a family that would love and care for them. Though he lived on the outskirts of Aspen Grove, it was considered "the country" by a lot of people. This wasn't the place to drop off dogs; there were farmers who put poison in the cattle feed, not enough to kill the cows but damn sure enough to kill a dog. People drove down these roads at ten plus miles per hour over the limit and dogs were hit and killed every day along the stretch of road in front of his house. Packs of wild dogs were shot on sight by the local law enforcement as well as the sheriff's department. The lucky dogs were picked up by the animal control officer and taken to the pound. One of his pet peeves was people who thought they were doing unwanted pets a favor by dumping animals and thinking they would be taken care of or adopted by country folk. Most times that just didn't happen.

He gave the dog a good half hour before he went out and cleaned up the trash. Even so, he kept his eyes and ears open.

~~*~*~*

As he finished drying the pan he'd cooked his spaghetti in, the phone rang. He looked at the clock. *Who would be calling me at almost nine o'clock?* He set the pan aside and wiped his hands, picking up the phone on the third ring.

"Hello?"

"Hey, Theo!"

His face broke into a smile. "Lily! Hey! When did you get back?"

The voice on the other end was melodic and happy; her voice had always reminded him of a fairy, ever since they were young, and their mother had read a book to him and his sister about a fairy that saved the day. That was one of the books that had gotten him interested in reading, really. Pumkiniah the Brave. That was the fairy's name.

"The plane landed an hour ago. I'm beat."

"So, how was Ireland? Scotland? Where else did you go?" He took the cordless phone into the living room and got comfortable. This could be a long call.

Her laughter tinkled over the line. "Oh, Theo, you should make time for a trip to Ireland. The landscape is gorgeous, and the people…"

She went on telling him all about her trip. The company she works for sent her all over the globe for research purposes. They stayed on top of technological advances wherever they were reported to be advancing. Great job for her; she was the most outgoing and intuitive person he knew.

"Well, it sounds like you've had an amazing time. Where are you now?"

"L.A. I'll be checking in with headquarters tomorrow and then falling flat on my face for the weekend. My body clock is all out of whack. That's one of the few downfalls of all the traveling!"

"Thanks for calling, Lily. It's good to hear your voice. Listen, Christmas break is coming up, why don't we plan to meet somewhere?"

"That sounds like a great idea! I've got some vacation time built up. Tell me where you want to go, and we'll do it."

"Oh, no you don't, it's your turn to decide."

Her laughter infected him, and he laughed, too. "It was worth a shot! You know I hate deciding; I've been almost everywhere. I'll think about it, and we'll talk again in a couple of weeks."

"Sounds great. Glad you had fun! Sleep well, talk to you soon. Love you."

"Love you too, Theo."

They had been close growing up, and had grown even closer after their parents passed away. Their parents had been high school sweethearts and enjoyed their life together, not having children until late in life. When their dad passed away in his sleep, their mom followed the same way within a week's time. Theo had been twenty, Lily eighteen, at the time. Legally they were adults but nowhere near ready to lose their parents. They'd clung to each other and had grown closer for it. Now, they were best friends.

He went back into the kitchen and heard a rustling noise outside his back door. He set the phone on its cradle and flipped on the backyard light. There were three dogs milling in a group, alert and watching the back door. It seemed they were locking gazes with him; each that he looked at seemed to be staring back. Maybe it was a trick of the light.

Grabbing the broom, he opened the door and stepped out on the back stoop. The door swung shut behind him. "Get OUT of here! Go!"

Waving the broom around and yelling, he hoped he was making himself bigger, not a target. From around the side of the house, he could hear his trash can being knocked around and two dogs snarling. He made the mistake of taking his eyes off the dogs in front of him and glancing toward the side of his house; when he looked back, the three dogs had aligned themselves and were advancing on him, teeth bared, throaty growls emanating.

Fear flooded his veins. He reached behind himself with his free hand and grappled with the knob. It wasn't turning. Warm adrenaline and the knowledge that he'd screwed up enveloped him.

Suddenly, from out of nowhere, a larger dog appeared between him and the pack. It turned its back on him and snarled at the other dogs, haunches tense and quivering, fur on its back standing on end.

The pack stopped their advance. The middle dog took another tentative step and let out a growl of its own, saliva on its canine teeth reflecting the light. The newest dog launched, snapping its powerful jaws an inch from the face of the advancing dog. The three turned tail and ran, disappearing around the side of the house. The trash cans quit rattling; those dogs must have fled, too.

He watched the remaining dog, not wanting to bring attention to himself, utterly positive this dog could kill him in an instant.

It turned and looked at him. Iridescent eyes shone the most intense shade of blue. He'd seen that shade before. Cadence McPherson. How odd to see it twice in one day on two different...

The dog turned and trotted across the backyard, effortlessly clearing the five foot fence.

His heart thudded hard against his ribcage. The doorknob turned easily this time, admitting him. Slipping through, he closed the door and collapsed back against it. He hadn't been that scared in a very long time, maybe ever. Not something he wanted to admit even to himself.

Waking before the alarm, he laid in bed feeling lethargic. He'd gone to bed around midnight and had still been awake to see three o'clock a.m. When he finally drifted off, he slept fitfully, dreaming of Cadence McPherson shifting into the dog and back again, the shared eyes staying locked on him the entire time. What was it about this girl...?

He rolled out of bed and hit the shower. *Shake it off,* he told himself. *She's a student; you're an idiot, and there's no such thing as werewolves.*

His first class didn't start until one o'clock p.m. It was eleven thirty; he had time yet. He sat down at the kitchen table and opened his lesson planner. As it was already predetermined for the year, he only had to refresh his memory as to what section they would be covering in each class. He kept the classes on the same schedule, teaching the same section to each, making his life a lot easier, though occasionally one class was a day ahead or behind the rest.

Going through the motions of his day, Theo floated on lack of sleep until just before the start of the last class. Finally beginning to wake up, he watched as the students filed in. The minute hand ticked to eight thirty, and he looked around the room. There were only about half of his normal number of students present. A frown creased his brow.

Among the missing were Violet Anderson and Josh Pearson, two of the students from Wednesday's class who'd made a big deal about the moon being full. More than the rest of the missing students combined, he was irritated that Cadence McPherson wasn't in attendance. He was forced to admit to himself that he'd looked forward to seeing her here, and had been thinking about her off and on since Wednesday.

"Is there a football game tonight that I'm unaware of?" He started his session with a general question.

The students looked at each other and back at him, quizzical, shaking their heads.

"I can't help but notice there are quite a few empty chairs this evening. Any of you have an idea as to why?"

A hand near the middle of the room went up.

"Mr. Oxford."

"It's a full moon," he said, as if that should explain everything.

"Yes, it's the full moon. What does that have to do with attendance of my class, or anything for that matter?" His frustration echoed throughout the room.

The only sound was the ticking of the clock. He raked his hand through his hair and turned to the blackboard. He picked up the chalk and dragged it across the board hard enough to make it screech. Even he shuddered at the sound.

Motion from the corner of his eye caught his attention. The door slowly opened, and a lone girl slipped through. She looked at him and stopped in her tracks; he was watching her. *At least she had the decency to look guilty*, he thought, as he pinned her with his intense stare.

"Ms. Anderson, it's nice that you could join us this evening."

"There was a car accident on I-40," she offered as her excuse as she dipped her head and moved quickly to her seat.

"Get out your textbooks and turn to Chapter Seven."

~~*~*~*

With the small number of students in class, the discussion he'd planned for tonight had finished earlier than anticipated.

Throughout the evening, most, if not all, of the students had become increasingly edgy; their surreptitious glances at the clock, legs bouncing up and down, and fingers tapping out cryptic messages on desktops. There remained fifteen minutes of their scheduled class time. He had a choice—make them stay as was his rule, or let them out and free everyone from the nervous energy that had become almost unbearable.

Slipping his bookmark into place, he snapped his teacher's volume closed.

"Remember, your assignment on author interviews is due next Wednesday. There will be no extensions given, so be here on time, homework in hand. Good night."

It took a full five seconds of silence before they processed and realized they'd been let go early. As if operating as one, they grabbed their belongings and hit the door without a word. The tension drained out of the room almost as quickly as they did.

Gathering up his own books and notes, he snapped his briefcase shut and took an extra minute to give them time to be gone from the parking lot before he left. He'd just as soon not have to see anyone else tonight if he could help it. A headache had formed behind his eyes sometime during the evening and had all the makings of a migraine.

Turning off the lights on his way out, he locked the door and closed it tightly. Looking up and down the hall, he noticed that his classroom wasn't the only one dark; it seemed the other professors had let their classes out early, as well.

His footfalls echoed too loudly in his ears as he made his way toward the exit door. As he passed through, the difference in temperature caused him to shiver. The night had grown cooler, and the air had a snap to it that hadn't been present when he'd arrived earlier in the day. It wasn't that far to his car, so he didn't bother stopping to put on the coat he carried.

As he neared his car, he glanced up at the sky. The moon was indeed full, and clouds were heavy and thick as they passed overhead, playing peek-a-boo. Now you see me, now you don't. He couldn't be sure if the howl he heard was real, imagined, or the wind. The hair on the back of his neck stood up moments before he heard a blood-curdling scream.

Quickly, he unlocked his car and tossed his briefcase and coat inside before taking off at a run toward the source. It sounded as if it had come from the commons area around the back side of his building. The area was central to three different halls, one on each of three sides, the fourth edged with woods.

Rounding the corner he pulled up short, almost running into Violet. Her hands were balled up to her face, and she was near hysteria when she backed into him. He grasped her upper arms, and she jerked away, whipping her body around, her eyes searching for an escape. Recognition dawned; she realized who he was and stepped forward, burying her face into his chest, grasping handfuls of his shirt and holding tight.

Not knowing what else to do, he awkwardly patted her back.

"No, no, no!" she cried, over and over, shaking her head as if her actions could make whatever it was disappear. Tears streamed down her face, wetting his shirt, as she went into shock.

He looked over her head at the surrounding area, past the picnic tables and the fountain, searching for the cause of her grief. A reflection from the woods looked like eyes; he squinted, trying to bring it into better focus. As quick as he blinked, the reflection was gone. *If it had been there at all,* he thought. *You're cracking up, man.*

He scanned the rest of the commons, and spotted what looked like a pair of legs barely visible from where they stood, near the far end of the hedgerow that lined the back of his building.

Sitting her down on the grass, he told her to stay right there, he'd be right back. She pulled her legs up and wrapped her arms around them and began to rock. He wasn't sure if she'd understood, or even if she'd registered that he had talked to her. He quietly called her name, and her only response was a nod.

Moving cautiously, Theo went over to where he could see who it was. Josh Pearson, the quarterback and one of the missing students. The light by the picnic table nearby cast an eerie glow on the gruesome scene; Josh lay face up, glassy-eyed, his mouth open in an unvoiced scream. His torso was ripped open from collarbone to groin, and his right arm was positioned above his body with what could only be teeth marks from being drug to his final resting place on campus.

Theo tore his gaze away and swallowed hard once, and then again, before pulling his cell phone out of his pocket and dialing 911.

Red and blue lights revolved on top of the parking lot full of cop cars that had pulled haphazardly in, some left running, each with lights flashing. This included the nondescript mud-colored sedan with its portable red light stuck to the roof near the driver's door. He hadn't seen one of those since watching cop shows with his dad when he was young. The effect now reminded Theo of a carnival. *All that's missing is a big top, a few trapeze artists, and a lion tamer*, he thought.

It was now after one o'clock in the morning, and he was bone weary. He'd given his statement to the police, multiple times, and stayed long enough to see Violet's parents take her home. They'd arrived within thirty minutes or so of being called, so they must live relatively close. That was good for her. She would need the support of her family after making the discovery tonight.

Theo walked slowly toward his car, noting the sudden interest taken in him by the loitering news reporters. Luckily his car wasn't blocked in by the police cars, and he would be able to get it out without much trouble as long as the reporters stepped out of the drive and let him pass.

The crime scene tape surrounded the entire commons area and would likely be there for a few days; at least until they figured out what happened to Josh.

He drove home in a mental fog, not remembering the trip. Next thing he knew he was sitting in his driveway in a cold car.

Climbing out, he looked around warily. The feeling of being watched hadn't gone away, even though he couldn't see anyone around.

Stepping up on his porch, he searched his pockets for his keys. They weren't there. He strode back to his car and was in the process of checking under his seat when a car pulled into his driveway and parked behind his.

The headlights extinguished, and the driver's door opened. A shadowy figure stepped out.

"Professor?"

"Ms. McPherson? What are you doing here?" His heart raced at the sound of her voice. He hated himself for it.

"I found your keys in my book bag. I hope they're yours. I don't know whose they could be if they aren't." She stepped closer, holding the keys out by the keychain with his picture of Lily on it.

"She's beautiful. Who is she?" Her eyes reflected a myriad of shades in the porch light.

"Lily. My sister."

"Good. For a minute I thought you were going to say she was your wife." She continued to advance slowly.

Adrenaline flared, warming every inch of him. He shook his head slowly.

"No. Not married."

The next thing he knew, they were wrapped in an embrace that would embarrass anyone who stumbled upon them. Her scent surrounded him; he couldn't get enough of it, or her.

His resolve shattered completely. The night flew by in a flash of images for him: carrying her into the house, the ripping and shredding of clothes discarded in a trail between the front door and the bedroom, the frantic lovemaking, the round two of much slower, more intimate bonding, the shared shower and third bout of incredibly intense intercourse.

When he awoke Saturday morning, she was gone. He could almost make himself believe it had been a dream, except for the fact that her scent permeated the air.

He rolled onto his side and groaned. The pillow where she'd laid her head was intoxicating. He groaned again, this time because she was a student. The one thing he'd been sure of when he'd begun teaching at college level was that he wouldn't be one of "those" professors. He could control himself. *So* sure he was above being seduced, he hadn't paid heed to the warning signs that were crystal clear in retrospect.

"Damn it," he growled, throwing the covers back and stalking into the bathroom. He turned the shower on full blast, climbed under the sharp spray, letting the stinging icicles pelt him, punish him, cleanse her smell off his body and out of his mind.

The shower did nothing to relieve his frustration with himself, so he dried off, dressed in sweats and an old t-shirt, and headed for the gym. Maybe he could work it out that way.

When he arrived, he set himself up on one of the treadmills. The television was tuned to a news station. As he ran, getting into his rhythm, the station broke with a news story that caught his attention and almost made him trip over his own feet.

"Following closely on the heels of last night's murder, another co-ed has been found dead on the grounds of the community college in southeast Oklahoma City. As you can see behind me, the police tape is still up, and the crime scene unit is working on the north side of that building. The name of the victim has not yet been released, and we have limited details as to what happened. The body was found by a security guard during his rounds at approximately four-thirty this morning. He's asked not to be identified on camera, though has told us that he saw a huge dog, possibly a German Shepherd, hovering near the body, which focused his attention on the crime scene. He scared it off, and went over to investigate what had held its attention. That was when he made the discovery. We'll be back with more details as we have them. This is Karen Fielding, Channel 9 news."

"Hey, buddy, are you done?" A male voice asked from behind him.

"What? Yeah. Sorry." Theo realized he'd been standing still on the treadmill. He stepped off. Clearly, exercise wasn't going to work, either.

~~*~*~*

As he made the short drive home, his thoughts sifted through the last few days. Could the dog in his yard be the same as the one on campus? How many rogue German Shepherds were running around?

He turned onto his road. There was a car parked by the curb in front of his house. He was sure he already knew who was in it. As much as he didn't want to, he had to let her down easy. With any luck, he would be able to do that and still retain his career.

As he parked in his driveway, she stepped out of her car. *Damn my hormones,* he thought, as his body began to respond to her proximity.

She raised her hands, palm out, as she crossed his yard. "I want to apologize for…"

"No, I need to apologize. I have no idea what came over me. Wait, that's not right. It's simple biology. What I meant to say is I shouldn't have taken advantage of you. It was wrong; I'm your professor, and…" a thought occurred to him.

"How did you know where I live?"

She lowered her hands and continued to move toward him: slowly, methodically, in an almost predatory manner.

"You're not that hard to find, Theo."

It wasn't only the use of his first name that took it to another level; it was the *way* she said it—her tongue darting out between her lips on the "T," the "H," and "E" rolling along behind, and the way she pursed her lips into a perfect "O." He knew he was losing control. Not something he wanted in this situation.

Scrambling to regain it, he tried again.

"We cannot be more than professor and student. Anything else would be against the code, and not only could I be fired, you could be expelled."

"Then we won't let them find out." She was within arm's reach. Taking one more step forward, she entered his personal space, and he was inexplicably aroused by it.

Her eyes were doing that iridescent thing again, which brought to mind the dogs.

"Do you have a dog?"

She smiled a humorous, sideways smile, cocking her head. "Why do you ask?"

"I've never seen eyes like yours before, and there has been a dog hanging around my house lately… and this sounds ridiculous now that I'm saying it out loud."

Then, she kissed him.

~~*~*~*

Christmas break signified the end of the semester. Theo had given the final exams, and all he had to do over the break was grade them. He collected the tests as the students filed out, each one as glad as the next for the upcoming holiday. Several students wished him a Merry Christmas as they moved past his lectern; he returned the sentiment, wishing them luck in their career if they were through with their English requirements, or letting the holiday greeting stand alone if he knew they weren't quite there yet.

The parking lot was empty. As he crossed to his car, the hair on the back of his neck stood at attention. A flutter in his chest had him quickening his speed and tugging keys from his pocket as he power-walked the last fifteen yards.

As he rounded the front of his car toward the driver's door, his progress was halted. His sharp intake of breath was the only sound. There, near the back wheel well of his car stood the wolf. He would recognize those eyes anywhere. His blood froze, and his heart skipped a beat.

Her fur cast a silky shine as her eyes reflected the glow from the sodium lamps. She tilted her head slightly, as if she'd been presented with an unforeseen opportunity, then lifted her muzzle toward the sky and howled. The sound chilled him to the bone.

An answering howl from the distance perked her ears. Returning her attention to him, she padded closer and sniffed his hand, inhaling deeply. *This is it. I'll die in the parking lot of the college, ripped to shreds like Josh Pearson.* His heart broke loose with a triple-time rat-a-tat-tat. It sounded like a hard rock drummer to his ears.

With that, she continued on by, brushing his leg with her side before breaking into a run toward the side of the building. She disappeared around the corner and continued, he was sure, into the woods beyond.

Stars exploded before his eyes. The relief was complete; his legs buckled. He reached out and braced his hand on the hood of the car to keep from sliding to the ground. Now that the danger had passed, he felt lucky… luckier than he'd ever felt in his life, and yet, at the same time, safe. As he stood there waiting for his body to steady, he tilted his head back and looked up at the stars, silently thanking whatever being might be up there. A cloud shifted, and the moon peeked through. The *full* moon, he noted wryly. H didn't want to believe the kids could be right. Seriously, there's no such thing as werewolves.

He didn't know what the hell was going on, but there was no way it was a supernatural creature. Whatever it was, he thought it best to get inside the car where there was at least something protecting him from the night.

The door handle didn't want to cooperate; it had taken three tries before his fingers found purchase and he was able to pull it up. He tossed his briefcase across the center console and slid in after, pulling the door closed behind.

The windows wasted no time fogging from his warm breath. All he wanted at this very moment was to get the hell out of this parking lot and off campus altogether.

As he stuck the key in the ignition, a knock on the passenger window caused him to jump and whip his head around. The hand that knocked was attached to a recognizable body. "Damn it, get a hold of yourself," he muttered under his breath. He reached over, popped the lock, and moved his briefcase to the back seat.

"Jesus, you scared me," he uttered and she climbed in.

"Brr, it's cold tonight." It would appear she hadn't heard either his muttered curse or his statement.

"What are you still doing here? Where's your car?" He scanned the parking lot again to be sure he hadn't missed it.

"It's a quarter of a mile down Juniper. Damn thing just quit. No warning, nothing." Blowing into her hands, she looked over at him. "I'm glad I caught you."

He started the car and turned the heater on full blast. "This will warm you up in a minute. Did you call a tow truck?"

"No, it's too late. I'll deal with it tomorrow." Settling back in the seat, she tucked her hands underneath her thighs to warm them quicker.

It was her call; he let her make it. Without having to talk about it, he drove them to his house. They'd been seeing each other on the sly for the last two months. He was glad she'd been out of town visiting her family when Lily had come in from California to surprise him with an impromptu visit. Theo wasn't ready to explain what was going on to anyone yet. Hell, he wasn't entirely sure what was happening, himself.

"Did you talk to your advisor and confirm your credits today?"

"Yeah. I'm good. As long as I pass your class, I'll graduate. Am I going to pass your class, Professor?" She walked her fingers up his leg.

"I don't know yet. I haven't read your final exam." He tried to keep a straight face. It didn't work.

"Oh, you!" she exclaimed, feigning indignation.

Cadence had been an A student from day one. Even if she failed the exam entirely, she had enough points to earn a passing grade. Once she graduated they wouldn't have to be nearly as careful to keep their relationship a secret.

The house was quiet when she went out to dinner that one night per month with her girlfriends. They ate, drank, and Cadence would come home giggly and worry-free. It seemed her eyes sparkled for days after the "girls' night out." Theo wasn't worried about her spending time with her friends; they stopped by the house from time to time, and occasionally a random card game would spring up. He was happy she'd kept in contact with her friends. It was important to have a life outside of the one she shared with him. This arrangement worked out well when she had to work, and he had a chance to fly somewhere and visit Lily. Their relationship was good; better than good, it was fantastic.

He walked over to the wall and swung the photo frame out. The hinges gave their tiny squeak. As he turned the dial, he listened for the sound of tumblers falling into place. The last one clicked home; he turned the handle and swung the door open.

Inside, among his important papers and silver coins, sat a velvet box. He reached for the box and opened it. The large, clear diamond refracted and reflected the light from the fire blazing in the fireplace behind him. The gold band had been his mother's, and he'd had it melted down and used for a design he had created.

Theo was waiting for the right time to ask her to marry him. He was sure he would know the time when it came, and wanted to be ready.

Closing the box, then the safe, he adjusted the picture back in place. The thought of making Cadence his wife gave him a warm feeling that spread throughout his entire body. She was his best friend.

The trash cans against the side of the house clanged, announcing his monthly visitor. He tugged on his coat and picked up the to-go container from the counter and pulled the baseball bat from behind the door, purely for protection should anything vary from their usual encounter. Stepping out the back door, his exhaled breath became a plume of white before dissipating. As he rounded the corner, the dog was sitting, waiting. The same dog, the same knowing look, though now he had a healthier coat than he had the first time he'd shown up. Theo believed he'd been adopted by a nearby family since his eyes were healthy and his muzzle was clean. He'd taken to only rattling the cans against the house, not tipping them over or scattering the contents. They'd come to a silent understanding.

"Hello, boy, nice to see you. Here for your monthly check-in?" He moved slowly, closer by a step than the last time before setting the food container on the ground and opening it up. Inside rested a few chunks of steak and a raw bone he'd picked up at the meat counter on his way home this evening.

"Here you go. I got you one of the bigger bones. Maybe it will last a little longer this time," he said with a smile in his voice.

The dog thumped his tail three times in acknowledgment. As soon as Theo backed away, the dog stood and took the remaining three steps to the container. He ate the chunks of meat and picked up the bone. It hung out both sides of his mouth. He looked at Theo, wagged his tail once more and turned around, disappearing over the picket fence with grace.

He picked up the empty container and tossed it in the trash can, taking care to fit the lid back on tightly.

Cadence had never seen the dog; he only came on nights when she wasn't home. He showed up once a month, on the full moon, and disappeared again until the next. For some reason, Theo didn't see the need to mention it to her. This was his treat, and the dog's, on that one night a month when she was out having fun with her friends.

His thoughts turned back to Cadence. He felt the familiar warmth envelope his body again. He loved her with all of his heart, and though it might sound strange, he never felt more protected than he did when he was with her. Moving back inside, he latched the back door and flipped the deadbolt lock. Had he turned, he would have seen the other huge dog, the one with love shining in her iridescent blue eyes, staring at him from the dark, watching over him. When he was safely locked back inside, she tilted her head back and howled at the full moon before turning and disappearing into the night, in search of her friends and their meal.

EMPTY HOUSE

It was after three o'clock in the morning and traffic had dwindled to almost nothing. I'd been getting ready to call it a night when a stealthy-looking car turned the corner and slowed down near where I was standing.

"Are you looking for a date, Honey?" I drawled in my best southern belle impersonation.

"Get in." His voice was deep and rich. He'd pulled up to the curb between the street lights, and all I could see through the shadows was a portion of his lower arm, his hand on the steering wheel, and his watch. A Rolex.

The price of the car and the watch alone had me mentally raising my prices. I opened the door and sank in. The seat was leather and cradled me in a way that had me outwardly sighing. He pulled back out onto the street and the engine all but purred.

"Put on your seat belt." He glanced at me, then back at the road. His eyes were dark; I guessed brown, and his round face void of any remarkable characteristics. I did as I was asked, trying not to wrinkle the silk camisole I wore in place of a shirt. It was dry clean only, and I hated to have to take it in more often than necessary. All of a sudden it struck me as funny... a hooker wearing a dry clean only shirt, when it was more than likely going to get some guy's stuff on it at some point. It was so silky soft, though, and had only been a dollar at the thrift store. A girl needs a little something to make her feel better about her life, right?

"What are you looking for, Darlin'?" I continued with the drawl after buckling in. His arm was lightly scattered with hair, visible below the rolled up sleeve of his button-down dress shirt. His collar was loose; the top button undone. I couldn't tell if there had been a tie around his neck before he'd picked me up or not. Reaching out to touch his arm, he surprised me by pulling away.

"Don't touch me," he ordered.

I pulled my hand back. Not sure what the deal was; I smoothed my mini skirt, tugging it a bit lower, before interlacing my fingers and laying my hands in my lap.

Adding as an afterthought, in a gentler tone, he said, "Not while I'm driving."

"No problem, Doll." If that was supposed to take the tension out of his first statement, it failed miserably. Pushing the discomfort to the back of my brain I sat still and kept quiet, letting him take the lead. This was his date, not mine. We'd do it any way he wanted.

He drove towards the highway and merged on. We were going west, out of Oklahoma City. Most guys wanted it quick and dirty, either in their car in a dark parking lot or at a nearby no-tell motel. This was a first, and I wasn't entirely comfortable with it.

After about ten miles of silence, I couldn't help myself. "Where are we headed? I've got a place a few miles back." I motioned with my thumb over my shoulder.

"I've got a place. It's close." The silence closed over us again, pressing on me.

He drummed his fingers on the wheel, tapping out a tune only he could hear. My anxiety ratcheted up a notch. My scalp began to sweat under my wig, but I didn't want to scratch it when I couldn't see a mirror to readjust it afterward.

I tried again. "What's your name?"

He didn't answer. The quiet was unnerving. Maybe he'd rather break the ice with mundane matters. "This is a nice car. What kind is it?"

He turned the heater up. The sigh could have been a whisper of air, or it could have been his. I couldn't tell.

My head grew warmer. A bead of sweat trickled down my temple. I looked toward the side window and surreptitiously wiped it away. My scalp was itching like crazy; I tried to think of something else, anything else, to take my mind off it.

"It's warmer than usual for November, don't you think?" I turned my head and smiled at him. My intention was to get him to turn the heater back down. Instead, he turned and looked at me.

As warm as I'd been a moment ago, chills traveled across my core like cockroaches running from sunlight. His eyes were black, bottomless, and empty. I recoiled, bumping into the door. Without answering, he turned his attention back to the road.

I was officially in fear for my life. The girls who had taken me under their wing when I'd first found myself on the street had warned me about men with eyes like his. They'd told me to always look them in the eyes and make sure someone's home before getting in the car. The threat of disappearing at the hands of an 'empty house' were as great as catching VD. At the time, I'd nodded, tucking that piece of advice to the back of my brain. It didn't seem important; I mean, come on, how many of them were out there? I hadn't planned to be a hooker for long... just until I got on my feet. I was almost there. Another two weeks, max, and I'd have enough money for a decent apartment. My closet already contained five outfits appropriate for office work. All I lacked there was a good pair of shoes.

The further out of town we drove, the higher my anxiety rose. Any time now I would start to hyperventilate, I could feel it coming on.

He took the next exit. There wasn't much here besides a gas station and an abandoned restaurant with boards over the windows. As he slid to a stop at the sign, I lifted my right knee to block his view of my hand which was gripping the door handle. As soon as we stopped, I pulled on it, ready to tuck, duck and roll. Nothing happened. I tried again. Nothing.

Turning to face me, he tilted his head. Whether he knew what I'd been doing or not, I couldn't tell.

"I apologize for my earlier harshness. I've never done this before, and I'm nervous."

The boyishness lent to his face by his smile did nothing to relieve my tension. I forced myself to look into his eyes, prepared this time. The lights were on. Had I been mistaken earlier? Was it a trick of the night, the lack of stars and moon, or was this, now, the trick?

He hesitantly brushed his hand down my arm, an imitation of a gentle caress. A hint of his cologne tickled my nose. The combination was musky and woodsy. It smelled nice. With that one touch, I knew this was a trick, that my earlier glimpse into the abyss had been the real thing.

I could get out of this if I were smart about it. My mind unfroze, kicking straight into high gear. Play the game. You're good at that. I lowered my eyelids, looking at him through my lashes. My mouth curved into a semi-smile, something I hoped would convince him I was buying his act.

"No problem, Doll. Everyone is new at the beginning."

His smile widened, extinguishing the light again for one instant, long enough to let me know I was out of my league.

"Great. Let's start over. I'm Boggs, this fine piece of machinery is a Ferrari, and you're right about the heat being unusual for this time of year." He reached over and turned the heat down, then flipped a switch turning off the seat warmer.

"So, where are we headed?"

He settled back in his seat and dropped the car in gear, making a left turn before answering. "I've got a cabin not far from here. I'm more comfortable in my own bed. Surely you understand."

I didn't, but nodded anyway since he seemed to expect it. With the heat off, the temperature inside the car began to cool. Goose bumps rose on my arms and legs. Shivering, I rubbed my arms to try and warm them.

His cell phone rang. Lifting it from the center console, he checked the readout before pulling to the side of the road.

"I have to take this. You're shivering; stay inside, warm up, I'll be right back." He flipped the seat warmer back on and touched a switch on the dash before opening the door to climb out. He put his phone to his ear and said, "Go," then closed the door, leaning his back against the car.

The seat re-warmed almost instantly as the heater hissed. The air took on a slight odor; there must be something wrong with it. I wrinkled my nose. The smell was almost electrical.

I looked out the passenger side window, then the windshield, for any clue as to where we were. The world could have ended where the headlights left off; that's how dark it was. Even if I could make the door handle work, it was pitch black, getting chillier all the time, and for the Trifecta I really had no idea where I was, except that we'd turned north when we'd exited the highway after heading west out of Oklahoma City. I turned my attention to sound. I concentrated on trying to hear what he was saying. Something about being ready Saturday.

My eyelids grew heavy. Could be the warmth of the seat, or

the utter darkness and quiet. Whatever the cause, I sighed contentedly and sank deeper into the seat, completely relaxed for the first time in longer than I could remember. Time didn't matter; right now, the only thing that was important was sleep. I drifted off.

~~*~*~*

The feeling of weightlessness and cold air across my body brought me back enough to register that I was being carried. My eyes didn't want to open. To be honest, I didn't want them to, either. I'd been so comfortable in my warm place… where was that, anyway? My thoughts were scattered, and I had a hard time focusing on any one thing. The sudden flip-flop my stomach performed woke me further. A moan escaped, and whoever was carrying me shifted their hold just in time. When I threw up, it missed him entirely.

When I was done, I felt him stepping up several stairs, and the squeak of hinges told me we were going through a door. I still couldn't open my eyes without the nausea returning, so I opted to leave them closed. Hopefully we were at a doctor's office or hospital. Had I been in a wreck? My memory was foggy. The doctor would tell me what happened.

My hero laid me on what felt like a couch. He covered me with a blanket and everything returned to quiet. I drifted back off while I waited for the nurse or doctor to come in.

~~*~*~*

I came to, chilled and nauseated again. When I tried to sit up, my head spun and throbbed. Leaning over as far as I could, I dry heaved. When I was reasonably sure my stomach was finished, I lay back down on the cold floor.

Wait, cold floor? Where am I? Prying one eye open a slit, I waited while my head cleared and my stomach settled. In front of me was a steel-barred door. The floor I lay on, cold grey cement. One bare light bulb was attached to a fixture high up on the cement block wall outside my cell. Across the hall from me I could see another cell, and a girl with stringy brown hair watching me with her huge brown eyes. Squatting down in front of the bars on the front of her enclosure, her arms were wrapped around her knees and she was clutching the bars. Raw fear was etched in her features. Seeing her fear intensified my own.

I opened my mouth to ask her where we were, but before I could form the sentence in my brain she shook her head, placing her index finger to her lips.

Cautiously, I turned my head to the other side. There was a rectangular mat along the cement block wall, and a coffee can with a red plastic lid. The mat had to be softer than the floor. With more effort than it should have taken, I rolled over onto my side and managed to move myself onto the mat. It wasn't much softer, but it wasn't as cold as the cement.

The little bit of moving I'd just done had my stomach roiling again, and my head spinning. Maybe if I lay still, I would be okay. When did I get so sick? I thought back. I'd slept until seven o'clock or so this evening, when the sun was starting to go down, then showered, put on my favorite camisole and little black skirt, strapped on the heels and went to work. I remember walking the street, it was slow. Then the car pulled up, and he said to get in.

Memory clips after that were random. I tried to open the door and couldn't. Then I was sitting in his car, feeling tired. From there, my brain skipped to waiting for a doctor... that doesn't make any sense. Then it's blank until waking up here, in a cell, trapped like a circus animal.

I wasn't sure how much time had passed before I felt reasonably sure I could sit up without the world spinning. Testing the theory, I carefully inched up, resting on my elbows. My stomach turned, but didn't do anything more than argue.

The light gave eerie shadows to everything from the bars to the face of my new co-habitant. It looked as if she hadn't left her post. She continued to watch over me.

I felt the need to whisper. "Where are we?"

She shrugged her shoulders as if to say she didn't know. She shook her head again, harder this time, and replaced her finger to her lips.

Okay, so she isn't going to talk at all. Maybe if I formed my questions for yes or no answers…

So many questions spun through my mind. Like a slot machine, I waited until my still-foggy brain landed on one. "Did Boggs bring you here, too?"

Tilting her head to the side as if the question didn't make sense, she took a minute before something clicked. Shaking her head, she drew an S and then another S in the air.

"S S?"

Nod of affirmation.

"S S. What is S S? Oh, I get it. His name is Boss, not Boggs, right?"

She nodded again, and brought her finger to her lips, then pointed at the ceiling. I looked up. There were wooden beams running across the ceiling with either plumbing or electrical pipes between them. I didn't know enough about that sort of thing to tell the difference.

"He's upstairs?" I lowered my voice even further, barely above a whisper now.

Another nod. I was batting a thousand. She shifted her position. The charm on her necklace shone as it twisted.

The meaning of what she was telling me began to come through. I tried to put the pieces together, but the drugs weren't completely clear yet. I pulled the handle again.

Ching, ching, ching. While the wheels turned, I realized I was naked, except for something around my neck. My fingers gently moved over the collar. It was cold, smooth, and about an inch wide. I could only assume that it looked like the one she was wearing. I felt the latch, but, without being able to see it, I couldn't figure out how it clasped. As my fingers moved around the front, I found there was also a charm on my necklace, with an indentation of some sort.

"Is this a dog collar?" Whispering was becoming more difficult as I began to realize the depth of trouble I'd found myself in.

What does this tag say?"

She must have seen the reaction coming even as I felt the anxiety take hold. Lifting her finger to her lips once again, she reminded me to keep my voice down.

The sound of a heavy wooden door closing came from overhead and scared her. She scrambled back into the corner of her cell and shoved her hands out as if telling me to get back. Then she wrapped her arms around her knees and pulled in on herself, as if she could make herself smaller.

Another sound, closer, more like rusty hinges, and then a beam of light shone through the ceiling at the far end of the hall. It rather reminded me of an alien ship, though, for the life of me, I have no idea why that particular visual came to mind.

A wooden ladder on the wall became visible in the light. First one foot, then another, appeared through the opening. Whoever it was began their descent.

He reached the bottom of the ladder and turned, planting fisted hands on hips.

"Did I hear voices?" His own voice carried through the cave, bouncing off the walls, giving the illusion that he was everywhere at once.

I glanced across at the other girl. She'd buried her face in her arms, furthering her effort to disappear.

As quick as I'd looked away and back, he appeared to have covered half the distance without making a sound. His eyes locked on mine. The soulless pits had returned with a vengeance.

"I asked a question." His voice was conversational; I wasn't buying it.

Feeling the need to protect her, I answered. "I asked a question, she didn't answer. I'm not sure she can talk."

His smile chilled me to the bone. "Oh, she can talk. She just knows the rules. Since you're new, I'll let this one pass, and tell you what is expected. There will be no talking or noise of any kind. Any sound you make, I will hear. No one else will, of course. We're in the middle of nowhere."

The thought of being at the mercy of this… man, with no one to help us, was too much.

"Why are you doing this?" My voice cracked.

He moved closer to the bars. "What is rule number one?"

Before I could answer, he reached into his pocket and withdrew a Taser. I wasn't moving quickly enough yet. A jolt ran through me, followed immediately by excruciating pain. I screamed, folded like a rag doll, and dropped to the floor, flopping like a fish out of water.

"No talking," he said, releasing me from the Taser's control.

My body continued to spasm, and I lost my bladder.

By the time I regained control of my body, he'd gone back up the ladder, brought trays down with our dinner, and left again. I heard the squeaky hinges, the heavy door slamming, and then another door, even further away.

It was a full five minutes of complete silence before she came out of the corner and reached for the tray.

I used the napkin provided with my dinner to clean myself up the best I could. If I were going to be living in a cage, I didn't want it to stink like urine any more than it had to. Once I was reasonably dry, I moved closer to my tray and tried to eat something as well, though my stomach wasn't happy at the moment.

When we'd both finished eating the meager portions delivered to us, she spoke for the first time.

"What's your name?" she whispered.

"Kelsey. What's yours?" I followed her lead and whispered too.

"April. How did he catch you?"

"I was a runaway. I left home as soon as I turned eighteen because things were hard for me there. I made it as far as Tulsa, only to find out my friend, the girl I was going to stay with, had moved to Oklahoma City, and I didn't get the message if she sent one. A neighbor of hers from the apartment complex, the one who told me where she had gone, said he was driving down that weekend and offered me a ride. I took it. We stopped for gas: I got the key for the restroom from the attendant; jerk face neighbor followed me around the side of the building and tried to rape me. I kneed him as hard as I could in the nuts and ran."

It occurred to me that I was rambling, but it might be my only chance to tell someone my story, so I started again.

"Then I found the apartments he'd said she had moved to, but the manager hadn't heard of her. I needed a place to live, and managed to get a bed at a shelter. I didn't know how scary those places were at night until I had to sleep with one eye open. The lady there referred me to an apartment that was free for thirty days.

I couldn't find a job, so I started hooking. Told myself it was just for a few weeks, until I could get everything in order. I'm getting close; almost have enough money to rent my own place, if I can get a decent job to put on the application. Boggs—Boss picked me up tonight. The car and the Rolex sucked me in. I thought he was good for the last push I needed to quit the night life."

"That sucks."

"Yeah, I know. How did he get you?" I asked.

"I'm also a runaway, of sorts. Got on the next bus out of Dallas, and that happened to be the one going to Oklahoma City. I only had enough money for that ticket and a couple of meals, so that's where I landed. Boss was in the bus station, said he was waiting for his sister, and asked if I'd seen her on the bus. I said no. He bought me a hamburger and listened to me. Offered his couch for the night, no strings attached. I thought it was too good to be true, to run into someone nice like that. Turns out I was right."

"He's a real piece of work." We continued to whisper, even though we had heard him leave.

"You don't know the half of it." She pulled her mat closer to the bars and used it like a chair, so she wasn't leaning directly on the cement blocks. I did the same.

April didn't seem the least bit uncomfortable with the fact that we were both naked, except for the collars. Our state of undress didn't bother me, either. Not after my recent choice of employment.

My hand went to the charm. Without my having to ask, she answered.

"We all get them. I can't read yours from here, but it probably has the number seventeen on it. We don't have names, us girls under the kitchen. He calls us by our numbers. Don't ever say my name out loud, he'll know we've been talking, and the punishment gets worse from what you got earlier."

My fingers scrabbled at the collar, trying to find a way to get it off my neck. What I first thought of as a charm, and now knew to be an identification tag, jingled against the collar as I moved.

"It won't come off. He has a special key to unlock it." Her words were hollow, as if she were used to saying them and they lacked meaning for her.

My fingers slowed. They somehow already knew what she said was true. I scooted close to the bars and wrapped my hands around them. Pressing my face closer, I looked out between the bars, trying to see more than what was directly in front of me. Once again, as if she knew what I was thinking, she filled in the blanks.

"There are eight cages. We are at the far end, away from the stairs. It's just you and me right now. Six other places for girls are ready and waiting for him to fill them. When they're full, he'll schedule a hunt. This is how he works. At least it is since I've been here. The stairs at the end of the hall have a trap door at the top. I hear him lock it after he closes it, when he leaves. Then there's another thud after the locking noise. I think it's the door that closes off the area under the sink so no one can see there's a trap door there."

"There are cages for more girls." I was still having trouble wrapping my brain around this whole scenario. Then something else became clear in my mind, and I was horrified.

"How do you know all this?" I whispered past the lump in my throat.

She just looked at me, watched the answer come to me unspoken.

"Oh, God, no." I shook my head slowly and never took my eyes off of her. My body broke out into a hot sweat; my pulse raced through my veins and darkness encroached on my vision. I held on, willing myself not to pass out. Hot tears poured from my eyes; sobs choked off before they could make a sound.

There had to be a way out of here. Wiping the tears from my eyes, I stood and started at the top left corner, yanking and twisting each bar in an effort to find some semblance of hope.

After I tested each and every section of bar for movement, and found none, I dropped back down onto my mat/chair.

"How many?" I wondered aloud. She understood what I was asking.

"Seven hunts so far."

So far?

"What number are you?" referring to the number imprinted on

her dog tag.

"Ten." She held up all ten fingers. The light reflected off her tag, drawing my attention to it again with its hypnotic swaying. I watched it while I processed the information.

I was speechless as my brain tried to catch up. Like a bomb going off, my thoughts exploded in a ball of fire, and it all came together. I did not want to believe it.

"He's treating us like wild animals... as game for hunters? You're telling me... oh, my god, you're saying men pay him money for the opportunity to run down a human being and shoot them like prey? What the hell kind of sick game is he playing?"

Another piece of memory snapped into view. He was leaning with his back against the car, talking on his cell phone. All I'd caught of that conversation was something about being ready by Saturday.

I looked at April, slack jawed. "Saturday."

"What about Saturday?"

"He took a call while we were on our way here, and all I caught of the conversation was that he would be ready Saturday. I think that's when the next hunt will be. He's probably gone to get more girls now."

"What day is it?" She had been down here in this hell hole without windows for an extended period of time, and her days had most likely run together.

"Today is Thursday. Or it was when I got into his car. How long was I out cold?"

"Not that long. It hasn't been long enough to be Friday yet."

We fell silent, thinking our own thoughts. Mine wondered where he was going to get six more girls in the next twenty-four hours. Hers must have been running along the same lines.

"Is there a college west of Oklahoma City? That's the only way I can think of that he can possibly come up with six more girls in that short a time span."

"Seems there is, though I don't know where exactly or what it's called. There were college guys last weekend, or the weekend before, talking about it while we were on our 'date.'"

"You did two of them at once?"

"No, another girl and I went together. They paid for both of us.

It was separate, but we all drank and smoked together first. They were new, needed to relax." I hadn't known April before tonight, but for some reason I wasn't uncomfortable talking to her about what I did. Not surprising, I suppose, considering we were sitting in cages without clothes and expected to be running from hunters before the weekend was over.

"I'm going to try to get some sleep. The drugs are finally wearing off so the dreams won't be so weird. I'm exhausted."

"Move your pallet back against the back wall. You don't want to be awakened by his Taser or, worse, the cattle prod." She stood up and moved her mat back to the wall as she said it.

"A cattle prod? Jesus." I tried to get comfortable, knowing full well it wasn't going to happen.

I don't know how long I'd been asleep when a cage door rattling woke me. I started to sit up, but looked across at April and thought better of it. She was unmoving on her mat with her back flat against the farthest wall. Her finger moved slowly to her lips. I nodded, just as slowly.

He must have brought another girl. I heard him moving around in the cell next to mine. It sounded as though he were taking her clothes. I hadn't thought about how mine had actually come off of my body, and now wondered if he took pleasure in the act, took advantage of us once our clothes were removed, or if that was just part of the job for him. There wasn't much time between his opening the cell door and what I was now hearing and believed to be his closing of it, so I ventured a guess that if he were going to do anything to us while we were passed out, he'd done it upstairs. If that were the case, it would have been just as easy to take our clothes off before we were brought down here.

As the door clanged shut, and the lock hammered home, I heard his breathing. Not labored, exactly, but heavier than it had been earlier. As sure as I was that there was another girl down here now, I was sure he was listening to our breathing as we were listening to his. We must have passed inspection, because he finally turned and left without checking on us visibly.

The hinges shrieked like fingernails on the chalkboard as he lowered the trap door. With a resounding thud, the wooden door blocking the entry followed.

April's posture relaxed slightly at the sound of the second door. I held my breath and listened for movement of any sort from our newest member.

The only noise was a raspy-rattle to her breathing from time to time. When I looked over at April, she seemed to be hearing the same thing I was, and shook her head sadly. The new girl had asthma. My heart went out to her, knowing she would be the first of the three of us to fall, and at the same time I was horrified that I was elated. I wouldn't be the weakest member of the group.

With conflicting emotions swirling through me, I lapsed into a semi-sleep—the plain between the worlds of the conscious and the subconscious. Knowing I couldn't do anything else, I rested while I could, to be as ready as I could be for what was to come.

~~*~*~*

When breakfast arrived, I was already awake and had used the coffee can. There was a small roll of toilet paper on the floor behind it, something I was glad to see.

Yesterday's lesson was not forgotten, and I kept my mouth shut as Boss brought our meals down and left them by our doors. My goal now was to mimic April and stay as far away from the Taser and as-yet unseen cattle prod as possible. He stood in front of my cell for a few extra beats, giving me the chance to say something if I was going to, but I had nothing to say. His ghost of a smile confirmed his suspicion—I was a smart girl, only having to be told one time. Well, no shit, Sherlock, electricity running rampant through a body has a way of driving that lesson home.

I'd been afraid the new girl would be awake and have to learn the lesson this morning; her luck and ours held until he was gone from the dungeon and what I could only assume was the front door had opened and closed.

When she stirred, she freaked out even more than I had when I first awoke in this place. I couldn't imagine finding myself here, like this, and having asthma on top of that. I would have been in a world of hurt, too.

Her breathing became labored as she stumbled to the door and rattled the bars.

"Help me, somebody, please..." her words came out in a wheeze.

I moved toward the corner of my cage that was closest to hers, and held my hand out between the bars.

"Here, calm down, you're not alone," I whispered. I was worried about her lungs closing off, at the rate she struggled to breathe.

She clamped onto my hand with both of hers, a drowning woman clinging to a life preserver.

"What's happening?"

I looked at April. She was looking at me; she shrugged her shoulders then pointed at me as if to say, your turn. Before I could say anything, new girl let go of my hand.

"Oh, thank you," she said to no one in particular, and within a couple of seconds the sound of her inhaler being compressed; as she took a breath to draw it in, I took a breath with her and felt my own anxiety lift.

After several minutes her breathing regulated. I saw her hand waving in front of my bars, so I stood back up and moved to where I could reach mine out, too. I took her hand to let her know I was here.

"Thank you." She'd calmed down well past the point where she should have. I wasn't sure what to expect, but total acceptance of an unknown and unanticipated situation was not anywhere near the list, let alone in the top ten.

"You're welcome. Are you okay now?" That was a rather stupid question, considering where we happened to be at the moment.

"I can breathe, that's the most important thing. I'm almost afraid to ask where we are and why we're... here, like this."

By the time I'd finished explaining, her hand was shaking. Whether it was fear or disbelief, I wasn't sure.

Her voice wavered, and I strained to hear her. "My name is Lisa Sharp. My parents passed away last year, and while going through their personal papers I found a note written to me by my mom. It was dated twenty years ago. The letter told me the story of my adoption, and every detail she had in her possession regarding my birth mother. She said I was born in Oklahoma City to a seventeen-year-old girl named Jessica Martin."

Lisa became quiet. I could tell she was trying to regain composure.

"I just want someone to know who I am, in the event I am the one who is killed during the hunt tomorrow. Being asthmatic has never been easy; very soon it could cost me my life."

The emotion was evident in her voice. She held on to my hand for another minute; when she loosened her grip and slid her fingers away, she became very quiet.

"This is kinda cute," she said as she flipped the dog tag with her manicured fingernail. "Mine looks like yours, right?"

I nodded, unsure what to think about this girl.

"The whole not being dressed thing, though... they should totally turn up the heat." The newest girl was in the cage next to April's. She thought this was a tryout for a commercial. I wondered how she would react when the reality of what was happening finally sunk in. She wandered back and forth, running her fingers across the bars.

"What's your name?" I whispered. She didn't take the hint. Her voice remained at conversation level.

"Peyton Cashmere. That's my stage name, anyway. So, there were, like, at least a hundred of us, all wanting the same part. Most of them were bottle blondes, and their boobs totally weren't real. I mean, you can tell implants, obviously. They don't look anything like mine." Cupping her breasts, she held them like trophies.

I glanced at April. She rolled her eyes. I nodded. "How did you get here?"

"The guy brought me. He was the judge, or whatever, that we all had to audition for. So, he told us to fill out this stack of papers, and they had all sorts of questions about where we were from, about our parents and family, hobbies, school, work, all sorts of stuff that didn't have anything to do with the commercial. I *really* wanted the role; a national commercial would be, like, amazing. So, I did it, I answered them all, even though it was totally unnecessary. When he called my name the second time he said to get in the limo out back, he was taking me to do a run-through in front of the big bosses. I must've fell asleep, because I woke up here."

Did he drug her, or was she really stupid enough to get in a car with a total stranger and not be scared? The irony hit me. I was a hooker and did the same thing, but at least I had the wits to realize I'd screwed up long before I woke up in the cage. Too late to get out of it, but still, I *knew.*

"So, where are we? This is kinda kinky and totally wasn't in the commercial. Is this for some other part for, like, porn or something? I've never done that before, but I'm not, like, grossed out by it or anything. I'll try anything once. The big bosses are here, right?"

The heavy door above us opened, and the sound from the hinges scraped down my spine. April and I scrambled back to the corners of our cells. Lisa didn't move; I was pretty sure she was still in the corner from earlier. I hadn't heard her move at all, even when Boss brought Peyton down the stairs and locked her in.

Peyton was so clueless she didn't pay any attention to the reactions around her. From where I was pressed into my corner I could see her leaned against the door, hands wrapped around the bars, hot pink nails advertising her front and center presence.

"Hey, I wondered when you were coming back. When's the audition? And about that, where'd you put my clothes? That purse is my roommate's, and it cost her three hundred bucks; I hope you put it somewhere safe. She'll kill me if I come back without it."

Boss stopped in front of her. I studied his profile while his attention was focused on her. He had a square jaw, freshly shaved, and the angle of his nose hinted at having been broken at least once. He was handsome in a bad boy sort of way; the type I might have been attracted to had it not been for the lack of soul. Even from where I sat I could see he was wearing the empty eyes. Peyton either didn't see them or had no idea what it meant.

"Rule number one, no talking. You have nothing to say that I want to hear, and I hear everything. So shut your mouth, and keep it shut."

She jerked back as if he'd hit her. "You can't talk to me like that."

I cringed as the Taser came out. She took a jolt, dropping like a bag of rocks.

"*NO* talking," he said, putting the Taser back in his pocket as if it were nothing important, and he strolled down the walkway, stopping to look in April's cage. He must have approved of what he saw, as he turned to face mine and his smug smile stayed in place as he went on to Lisa's.

Withdrawing the keys, he opened her door. I couldn't see what was happening, but by the look on April's face, she could. I only heard rustling and movement, then a grunt. The door clanged shut, and I heard him climbing the stairs. Shortly thereafter the hinges made their lovely noise, I shivered involuntarily, and the thud of the heavy door rang out. Finally, the outside door signaling his leaving the house was heard.

I didn't wait long. Crawling to the bars, I whispered, "What the hell just happened?"

"He took Lisa. She was unconscious, and her lips looked blue." April scooted close to her bars and whispered, as well. "I think she's dead."

Tears welled in my eyes. Even in the situation we were in, I was sad that Lisa gave up and chose to take her own life by refusing to use her inhaler.

"There has to be a way out of here. If just one of us could get out, and somehow get that Taser away from him, or find the cattle prod, we could..." I felt my mental stability slipping. The analytical side of my brain knew I'd already tried the bars, and there wasn't a way out or I would have thought of it already, but my creative side had us out and running for freedom.

"Almost every one of us who has been in a cage down here has tried, and no one has figured a way out yet. I worked on it for weeks and finally came to the conclusion there isn't a way out, not while we're locked inside the house anyway."

My blood pressure was rising. I could feel it in the way my heart jackhammered against my chest. *Not while we're locked inside the house...*

"Okay. Tell me *exactly* what happens when he opens the cages."

"He links our collars together with a long cord, then we climb the ladder into the house. We'll come out from under the kitchen sink; that's where the trap door is located. Once we're all through, he'll close the trap door and the door that hides the entrance. Then he'll put a hood and handcuffs on each of us before he leads us outside. There's a walkway, takes about four hundred and fifty steps to get to the large cage. He walks us to it, positions us inside with our hands through a hole in the side. He removes the cord and steps outside, locking the cage door behind him. He'll remove the handcuffs, and tell us to take off the hoods."

I studied the details in her words, but remained quiet as she continued.

"From there, we wait while he goes to get the hunters. When they arrive, they'll look us over. Try not to cringe or cover your body in any way; that excites them and makes them want to choose you. They decide which girl they want to hunt, and once that happens, Boss opens the door and pokes the cattle prod at any girl who tries to stay in the cage. We run. They have a certain amount of time they wait, to make it 'fair.'"

April made air quotes with her fingers.

"We run as far and as fast as we can to get away from them. The hunt continues until a hunter bags one of us."

"He lets us loose? Why haven't you escaped while you're running away?"

"As far as I can tell, we're in the middle of more acres of wooded land than any one of us can run across or find our way out of in the time allotted. I've tried to find the edge. All but once I've tried and haven't been successful, obviously." She waved her hands to encompass our surroundings.

"What did you do that once, when you weren't searching for the property line?"

"I had to find a hiding place. A hunter was getting close. I could hear him crashing through the brush like a bull moose."

"It's over when one of them 'bags' one of us?" My stomach turned over. I hadn't truly believed the horror story my mind had created. I didn't want to believe any of it. My brain had made the leap to the correct destination the first time.

"The hunters carry a walkie talkie, and as soon as one of them shoots a girl, and the kill is verified by Boss, the announcement goes out over the air and the game is over. They play for a *chance* to win, not for a guaranteed kill."

My mind was racing a hundred miles an hour.

"What stops us from continuing to run after the hunt is called off?"

"That bastard tased me," Peyton was coming around, and she was pissed. "I'm gonna kick his ass when I get out of here." She continued to rant and rave. I tried to block her out so I could think.

"If we can keep running after the game ends, we might be able to find the edge, or a fence, or some way out of this. It's worth a try, right?"

"You can try, but he's got some way that he tracks where we are so he can locate us and pick us up after it's over. I don't know how."

The sound of the outside door alerted us to his return. Soon after, both the inside door and the trap door sounded, as well. Scrambling, April and I assumed our positions.

He brought our trays down. Dinner was served. I wanted to ask what happened to Lisa, but didn't dare. I wasn't going to incur the wrath again. Being tased wasn't a walk in the park the first time; I didn't want to get it again.

Peyton, however, let her emotions run away from her. When he set her tray down, she let out a snarl as she reached out and tried to grab his arm, scratching him in the process. "You bastard!"

"You don't learn easily, do you?" He touched the drop of blood seeping out of the end of one of the scratches. He walked toward the ladder and just as I thought he was going back up I heard a rattle, and he returned with the cattle prod.

She tried to get as far back as she could, but the cage wasn't deep enough for her to be able to stay out of his reach. I couldn't watch. My eyes were closed, but even covering my ears wasn't enough to keep her wail out. It seemed to go on for a long time before she passed out. The sound the prod made quit when she did.

Boss picked up her tray and took it away with him. A few minutes later, he brought her a bowl of something mushy instead, apparently another form of punishment for her disobedience.

With him in the house, we weren't talking any more. Neither of us was willing to take a chance. Peyton groaned a few times before crawling to the front and spooning the oatmeal-like substance into her mouth.

There must have been some sort of sleep aid in our meals. Not long after I finished eating, the grogginess I normally felt after taking a sleeping pill came over me. The last sound I heard was one of the other girls begin to snore.

When I awoke, the end of the cord April had told me about was already looped through the ring on my collar, and my hands were already cuffed. Boss was squatting next to me, tapping my cheek.

"Wake up, sleepy head, it's time to play a game. There you are. Stand up."

I did as I was told. Even groggy, I knew better than to talk back. If today were the day, I would need all the strength I could get to try and escape.

"Good girl," he cooed, apparently happy I wasn't going to give him trouble. "Stand here, please." He stood in the hallway, pointing at an X on the floor. I hadn't noticed it before.

Clipping my lead to the bars, he went in and woke April the same way, tying her to the end behind me. Then, it was Peyton's turn. She must have lost some of her fight after the cattle prod incident. She didn't give him any trouble at all. I wondered if she was broken, or if her mind was finally connecting the dots.

The same steps April had outlined the night before were taken this morning, and before I knew it we were standing in the cage outside, waiting for the hunters.

Peyton began mewling like a tiny kitten, low and sad. I took that to mean that she'd finally figured out that we were in serious trouble, and she had no idea what to do. Since she was next to me in the cage, I tried to calm her.

"Shhh, we can't make noise out here, either."

"What's happening? I thought it was all a joke or something, until he used that, that, thing on me."

"In a few minutes he's going to let us go…"

"He's letting us go? Thank God!"

"No, listen. There are hunters. He's going to bring them out here, and they're going to open the cage and let us out. You need to run. The hunters are going to hunt *us*."

"You're shitting me. That's like, illegal or something, right? They can't do that."

"Yes, it's illegal. They're still going to do it, though."

She began mewling again. Calming her wasn't going to work. I had to stop her.

"Shut *up*," I hissed, putting as much power into those two words as I could muster quietly.

Peyton jerked back from me the way she had from Boss.

"You have to be quiet or he'll hurt you again. Rule number one, no noise."

Her noises stopped, and she nodded.

"When he opens this cage, you have to run."

She nodded again.

A male laugh echoed. "Here they come. Remember, no noise."

They trudged through the woods, up and over the rise. There were four men, walking in pairs, three of them dressed to hunt. The hunters carried rifles slung over their shoulders like they didn't have a care in the world, and one had binoculars dangling around his neck. The fourth man was Boss.

I'd expected to see men that were physically fit, active outdoorsy types. I couldn't have been more wrong. They were all of medium height, overweight, and I was sure that if I could see their faces, which were hidden behind handkerchiefs, they would be pasty white like their hands. These men didn't spend any time at all outside; it shouldn't be difficult to outrun them at all. One of them was currently handing out cigars for afterwards, as if they were at a high society club meeting instead of getting ready to gun down innocent girls for sport.

Tuning out their conversation, I tried instead to form a plan. I should have been doing that instead of calming down Peyton earlier. I'd lost precious time. The woods on the three sides away from the area we entered were thick. They were all large trees with underbrush around them, and the leaves that had begun to fall, coated the majority of the ground. I could see several footpaths leading off into the woods; I would take the one on the left to begin, and then go off path and through the uncut vegetation. Hopefully there wasn't any poison ivy, oak, or sumac out here. That would be just my luck. Well, I couldn't be too worried about that right now, not with my life on the line.

My thought process was interrupted when Boss clapped his hands together. "Alright then, let's get down to business. The rules are simple: we'll let the girls go, and the hunters will give them a two-minute head start. Once those two minutes have expired, the hunt will begin, and will continue until one of the girls is bagged. You each have a two-way radio. Please turn it to channel four. The first person to find and bag a girl will key the mic and announce their success. At that time, the game will go on hold. No one else shoots until I, the gamekeeper," he laughed at his own double entendre, "have arrived at the site of the bagging and verified one way or the other whether the game is over or to continue."

He held up his index finger. "IF the girl is *not* bagged, and you call it in as such, you will be disqualified and forfeit your cigar." They all laughed. I didn't know how this was supposed to be funny.

"Please, check over the girls, decide which one you'd like to pursue, and get ready to start. Be careful, though, there's a live one in there. I won't tell you which one." They all snickered again at his witty sense of humor.

The hunters swaggered up to the cage, staying just out of arms reach. I tuned out again. I wasn't interested in hearing which of us had the better attributes or more desirable figure. It came down to who would be the one to shoot one of us; I highly doubted it mattered which one of us they found first.

Once they were finished ogling us, the hunters turned and walked back to where Boss was lounging against a tree.

"Ready, then?" All three nodded.

Boss pushed off the tree, walked down to the cage and opened the padlock on the door. Looking at his watch, he waited several seconds before opening the cage.

"Ladies, off you go now."

With that, April pushed my back insistently. I was in her way, and Peyton was in mine. I pushed Peyton to get her started. She took off, stumbling on a rock in her path. I didn't stick around to see if she fell or not; time was ticking, and I wasn't going to be the one.

The path was worn at first, though that didn't last long. Soon it began to fray, as previous runners took off in different directions. Apparently I wasn't the first to think to run off the actual path and make myself more difficult to find. The branches from bushes scraped my skin, occasionally drawing blood. I didn't feel them, not now; later, I'm sure I would be surprised to see how many times I'd been scraped and scratched. If I lived to find out, that is.

Survival was my only thought. I found myself wondering if any of the previous runners had circled back and tried to boost one of the hunters' cars. It was worth a thought, and probably a better idea than running aimlessly, not knowing the territory or the pitfalls that were sure to arise without warning.

Veering slowly left, I continued on, running and occasionally stopping to listen for anyone pursuing me. I didn't hear so much as a twig snap. Good news for me, not such good news for April or Peyton.

I took as much time as I dared, making my circle big and wide on my way back toward the cabin. Hopefully I would come out near a road this way and be able to flag someone down. If we weren't in the actual middle of miles and miles of woods.

A whining sound began in my ears. Not in my ears, really, more as a sound issuing from my collar. Ignoring it, I pressed on. The sound grew louder, more insistent, and a vibrating began in it. I slowed to a stop, waiting for the noise and the buzzing to go away. They continued steady.

Taking several steps backward, both noise and vibration lessened. What was this? I'd never had an outside dog growing up, but I'd heard about invisible fencing, wires buried underground that were as good as a real fence to keep pets in the yard by shocking them if they got too close to the wire. There was something about a transponder in the collar, if I remembered the commercial correctly. That would explain why he wasn't worried about us running off.

He'd never met me before. I took off at a flat out run, hoping against all hope that the shock I fully expected to receive wasn't as intense as that from the Taser I'd received recently.

The whining and vibration grew louder and stronger. Putting my head down, I barreled through, ducking and dodging, making my way around the trees. When I thought I couldn't take any more, I leapt and rolled. The jolt when I reached what must have been the fencing was intense, indeed, and took my breath away. I continued rolling until my momentum stopped, then pushed my way back up to my feet, forcing myself to go on. When I thought I was going to pass out, the whining began to decrease, and the vibration didn't hurt at all anymore.

Yes! I'd made it out of his enclosure. Now, if only I could find either a vehicle or a road.

The further I got from the fence, the less the collar bothered me. Finally, it was back to being just a collar. I tried to take a deep breath, instead ended up with a stitch in my side. Well, now was better than two minutes ago, I told myself, and walked for a bit, until the stitch loosened.

As I climbed up a short rise, I found myself on a road. It was paved, so I must have been close to a city or a town, somewhere civilized. Which way to go? Both directions looked about the same, woods on both sides of the road and a curve not far from me on each side, so no idea which way was closer to people.

When I ran, we'd been behind the cabin. I'd run left, and veered around to the left, which meant the cabin was to my left if I'd made it past that location. I should go to the right, and get as far away from that cabin as possible.

My feet were cut and bleeding. Pine needles were merciless on bare skin, and there were plenty of them out there in those woods. Who knew there were so many pine trees in Oklahoma? The cedar trees were just as sharp, and their needles were still fully green.

The sound of an engine approached from behind me, from the direction of the cabin. I ran about ten feet off the side of the road and hid behind a large tree, in case it was Boss or one of the hunters. The car that rounded the curve and came toward me was a sheriff's department car. Adrenaline poured into my system.

Quickly, I moved around the tree and ran back to the road,

waving my arms to flag him down. He slowed, pulling up near me and turning on the red and blue lights on top of the car.

I'd done it; I'd escaped! My breathing was slowly coming back to normal. I hadn't run this hard or this far in a long time. I knew now I needed to get back to the gym, as soon as I had a better place to live and a job. Hopefully I could land a job somewhere that included a gym within their building. That would be awesome.

The officer stepped out of his car, pulling his hat down onto his head as he approached me. He was tall with wide shoulders and slender waist, and probably in his mid-thirties. I'd never seen a man wear the uniform better.

"Ma'am, are you okay? What are you doing out here like this?"

"Officer, there's a cabin over that way somewhere, and a man named Boss. He kidnaps women and hosts hunts where men come out with their rifles and they chase the women and shoot them. I escaped from his enclosure a few minutes ago. There's a hunt going on right now, and two other women are still out there running for their lives. Please, you have to call it in and get some backup out here, save them. Arrest him. Arrest all of the men."

"Calm down, let's go over here." He led the way toward his car, opened the trunk and pulled a blanket out, which he wrapped around me.

"You say there's a man named Boss who has men come out and hunt humans?" He opened the back door of his car and helped me sit down. He pulled a first aid kit out of his trunk and began doctoring my feet.

"Yes. We don't have time for this right now, if he figures out somehow that I'm gone, you'll never catch him."

"Do you know where this cabin is?" His eyes were hazel. I wanted to disappear into them.

"It's back that way somewhere."

"Slide in, let's see if you can show me where."

He closed the door behind me and slipped into the driver's seat. As he turned the car around, we drove slowly, looking for the driveway. I couldn't be sure where, exactly, it was, since I'd been drugged when he took me in.

"There, that may be the road; we haven't seen any others and that one has tire tracks coming out of it from the dirt onto the pavement."

He turned down the road, driving even slower, keeping the dust to a minimum.

We'd gone about half a mile down the road when a cabin appeared off to the right. "That's it."

"Are you sure?" He said, watching me in the rear view mirror.

"Yes, that's his car there, the black one. Those pick up trucks must belong to the hunters."

"Wait here." He opened the car door as a gunshot rang out. Pulling his gun from the holster, he walked up onto the porch and looked in the windows. Apparently not seeing anybody, he went around the back of the house.

Several minutes had gone by before he came back around with Boss. Someone must have just said something funny, because they were both laughing. The officer was tucking a cigar into his upper shirt pocket, his gun already back in its holster.

They approached the car, and the officer opened the back door nearest me.

"You're a naughty girl," Boss said, resting his arms on top of the car door.

The officer reached in and took my arm, pulling gently. "I like this one. I hope she's still around by the time my name comes up in the lottery."

"I'll put you in twice, for bringing her back."

They both laughed.

THE END...OR IS IT?

The price of gas just keeps going up. I was irritated by the thought. Looking down at my fuel gauge, I calculated how long the less-than half a tank I currently had would last. Not until payday, that's for sure. Twenty dollars will probably get me through the weekend and past the price hikes... if we stay home and out of the holiday traffic. Not like I'd made any plans anyway.

It was Monday, May 20, 2013, and the average price of gas was edging up toward four dollars per gallon. With Memorial Day weekend coming up, the price was sure to continue to climb for at least a few more days. It happens every time a holiday rolls around. I only wish I'd thought about it last week and filled the tank then. Gasoline was sixty-six cents cheaper per gallon seven days ago.

I kept one eye on the red stoplight as I ran my hands through my hair and pulled it up into a ponytail. I pulled down the sun visor and looked at myself in the mirror to make sure my lion's mane was at least relatively tamed. It was difficult to get all these natural curls into one hair tie. They were all corralled, more or less, for the moment anyway. My eyes looked tired; hell, I was surprised there weren't bags under them, with as little as I'm sleeping lately. I pulled the skin back on the sides of my eyes, gently, like I'd seen my mother do so many times when I was younger. *When did I get these wrinkles? I'm pretty sure they weren't here yesterday.*

The windshield wipers kept up a rhythmic staccato beat—swish thump, swish thump, swish thump—as they chased each other rapidly back and forth, trying to keep up with the increasing rainfall. *I hope these things hold out until the rain quits. Just one more thing that needs to be replaced on payday... damn wiper blades.* The light turned green. I kept enough distance between me and the car cruising along in front of me so spray thrown up off the road by their tires wasn't adding to the poor visibility; between the spotty wipers and the wind-whipped rain I don't need any more distractions. As if on cue, lightning seared across the distant sky. Out of a habit borne in childhood, I counted the seconds between lightning and the rumble of thunder… one one thousand, two one thousand, three one thousand, four one thousand, five one thousand, si—boom! The portion of the storm that produced that bolt of lightning is five miles away.

With a sigh of resignation, I put on my turn signal and pulled into the Zippy Mart parking lot. A white SUV was the only other vehicle currently parked at a gas pump. I was happy to see an open space underneath the overhang where I could get gas without getting soaked. The rain, which had started shortly after I'd left work, had steadily gained intensity and didn't look like it would let up anytime soon. The wind bursts spit the rain under the overhang, but wasn't strong enough to fling it all the way to the middle, directly in front of the gas pump. There was a two-foot wide stretch of concrete that wasn't wet. This was not an unusual sight; it was springtime in Oklahoma after all.

I turned off the key and dug through my purse for my credit card while I waited for the engine to complete its sputtering noise routine in protest. I needed to have a mechanic figure out what the problem was. Yet one more thing I couldn't afford right now. When the engine quit with a sigh of its own, I climbed out and inserted the card into the reader on the pump. The readout on the screen promptly requested that I take my card inside to the cashier.

Freakin' figures. I don't even have my umbrella. I reached back into my car for my purse. They would probably want to see my driver's license before they ran my card through in there. Mentally congratulating myself on thinking ahead, I snagged the newspaper from the passenger seat and held it on top of my head while I made a mad dash for the door. Within two steps of reaching the door, the wind whipped up and snatched the newspaper from my hand, pelting my face with rain. *I hadn't read that yet!* I made it to the covered sidewalk in front of the store and looked back, wiping the rain off of my face with my hands and drying my glasses with the hem of my shirt. *Probably wouldn't have been able to read it, anyway, after using it as a hat in this weather.* The paper disassembled in the air, performing a ballet of sorts. Separating out and flying different directions, it made me think of the trip to Texas the year I took the kids to see hundreds of bats fly out from their cave at sunset. *That was a fun trip for all of us*, I thought wistfully.

I opened the door and walked in, pulling the door shut behind me. That wind was really picking up. Taking my place in line, I waited behind a woman with a toddler on her hip. I wiggled my fingers at the boy peeking at me over her shoulder. He stuck his thumb in his mouth and smiled at me around it, wiggling the rest of his fingers in response. He lowered his head to her shoulder, apparently shy. I looked around absently. The sky continued to darken, and for the first time I noticed that the clouds were looking particularly ominous. As if on cue, thunder rumbled deep, low and loud. It seemed to come from all sides at once. *Fast moving storm,* I thought.

The cashier finished the transaction. The woman hiked her child up into the air and wrestled him into a football carry position. His infectious giggle made me smile. She asked him if he was ready to go, and he clapped his hands and kicked his little feet in response. She carried him that way out of the store and ran toward their car, calling out the run as if it was a football play. "Mom gets the Bryan and makes a beeline for the door, dodging left, stepping right, jumping clear over the puddle..." The wind closed the door with a forceful slam, cutting off her recitation and his belly laugh. Enamored, I watched her cross the parking lot at a serpentine run, dodging imaginary opponents, entertaining her son the whole way. She got to her SUV and lifted him in the air, doing what could only be interpreted as a touchdown victory dance. The lights flickered, breaking my trance.

I was still smiling as I stepped up to the counter. Before I could say anything, the cashier, who couldn't have been older than high school age, apologized for the inconvenience. "I know it's a rough day for the pumps to act up, I'm sorry you had to come inside."

"Not a problem. I'm glad I did. I might not have seen her play with her son like that." I motioned over my shoulder, toward the parking lot. "That was fun to watch, took me back to when mine were little. Have the gas pumps been giving that message to everyone?"

He blinked at me as if I was from a different world. The generation gap loomed large between us. Apparently he didn't have any memories like that one from his own childhood. "Since the rain started, yes. How much gas did you need?"

As I opened my mouth to answer, the tornado sirens sounded. We both looked out the window immediately, as Oklahomans do, and saw nothing except more rain. The woman at the SUV looked at the sky, startled by the sirens, and quickly hung up her gas nozzle before jumping behind the wheel.

Apparently not one to take a chance, the clerk reached over and clicked the remote control, turning the television to a news station and un-muting the volume. "Take cover immediately, tornado on the ground, I repeat, tornado on the ground!" The excited voice of the storm chaser filled the store. "If you're in the Moore area, you need to be in your storm shelter or safe room NOW!" called out the weather man. "The tornado is on the ground on Fourth Street, about half a mile from Tuxahawney Road, heading east. Oh! It just took out the strip mall! Oh, my God, look at that. Oh, my God... Get underground immediately, right now, RIGHT NOW, it's gaining intensity!"

We looked at each other, both of our mouths hanging open. The Zippy Mart was on the corner of Tuxahawney Road and Fourth Street! "This way, hurry!" He yelled over his shoulder as he turned toward the back of the store and the door to the cooler, not waiting to see if I was going to follow. He knew what to do in this situation; it must have been part of his training because he didn't waste time.

I ran to keep up. The floor trembled, and the power went off with a loud pop. The light fixtures and television exploded, raining shards of glass down all over the store. I ducked and dodged, covering my head with my arms.

Thunder and what looked like lightning, but could have been street lights exploding, filled the air around me, crushing in from all sides, reflecting off overhead security mirrors used by the cashier to watch customers throughout the store. The inside of the store was completely black except for the erratic bursts of light from outside, and the sound of the rain was drowned out by the unmistakable and increasingly loud sound of an oncoming train.

The tornado was almost upon us! The air pressure changed; I felt like I was being crushed. Breathing became a chore, and the last few steps before reaching the cooler and the outstretched hand of the teenaged cashier were like running through mud. The ground shook and rolled, coming apart underneath my feet.

I gripped his hand and he pulled me off my feet and into the cooler, slamming the door behind us to the shrieking sound of ripping sheet metal. The roof of the Zippy Mart creaked and groaned under the pressure and strain before being torn loose with an exaggerated fingernails-on-the-chalkboard shriek. I cringed as I heard it go. The walls of the cooler shuddered and shifted, twisting, ripping. We shoved some boxes out of the way and crammed ourselves underneath the bottom shelf, away from the cans and bottles that were toppling and falling from the creaking and tilting shelves. I prayed the tornado would lift; our shelter wouldn't be able to take much more. We held onto each other and the shelf above us. I was crying. Someone was screaming; I don't know how I could hear it except... it was me.

The ceiling of the cooler suddenly and completely let go without much fanfare; I watched it disappear into the sky like the house in The Wizard of Oz. I don't know what made me think of that. This whole situation was surreal, and it was so much worse than any movie. Unidentifiable debris poured in, swirling and whirling, slamming down all around us before being picked back up and thrown somewhere else. The walls of the cooler collapsed in, held off us by the only shelf left, the one we'd crawled under. I don't know how long it was there, couldn't have been more than a second or two, before it was ripped from the last of its moorings and lifted out of sight. It happened faster than I'd ever seen anything move. The cashier was torn away with it. He'd been holding onto my hand, but he was gone before I knew he was moving. The shelf above me was twirling, like some macabre dance, before whistling back down and lodging itself in the concrete floor inches from my head.

With no walls left between me and the outside, I guess I was outside now too, I watched my car flip end over end and bounce several times before being sucked up and out of my line of sight. I didn't see the SUV with the lady and her son. I sincerely hoped they'd seen the tornado coming, and she'd been able to drive them safely out of the area. Lying as flat as I could, I pressed my body hard onto the concrete, trying to become one with it. I prayed that the tornado wouldn't pick me to throw around like a rag doll as it had the clerk. Pieces of metal, shards of glass and fragmented wooden beams danced and dipped, shuddered and disappeared only to reappear and rain down from the sky. I couldn't watch it anymore; I squeezed my eyes shut and burrowed my face into the crook of my arm, and I prayed over and over that it would end soon. I knew I was still screaming but there was nothing I could do to stop it. I had no control over anything, including myself.

As quickly as the tornado came, it left. The ensuing stillness was palpable; though there wasn't any wind at all, the air was pressing in on me as I stood surveying the damage. *Why can't I hear the sirens? Surely they're still going off,* I wondered idly. *Maybe I'm temporarily deaf. That would totally make sense.* There wasn't anything standing between me and the rain—no roof, no walls, nothing. In fact, there wasn't anything between where I stood and the tornado. I could see it clearly and I watched it as it moved away, swaying like a drunken sailor, creating a path of destruction, and leaving devastation behind in its wake.

Where my car had been was a twisted hulk of metal. The overhang I'd parked under a few minutes ago was now wrapped around and through an old red pickup truck that hadn't been there when we'd run for the cooler. I was pretty sure it didn't drive itself in, either, as it was upside down and crushed to half its normal height. It was still raining. *Why can't I feel the rain?* My car was nowhere to be seen. *I hope it didn't hit anyone or hurt anybody during its short career as a plane.* Paper, leaves, and other lightweight debris floated calmly down, seesawing their way back to earth. The entire scene was surreal; so much destruction in such little time. I'd never seen anything like this before in my life and hoped never to see anything remotely similar again. I watched the tornado continue its trek, and I thought about the people it had yet to encounter.

A man in a worn pair of jeans, an old t-shirt, and well-worn work boots stepped out of his front door across the street. The tornado had missed his house by about four feet. His neighbor's home was a memory, along with every home behind theirs. He scanned the area and started running toward the store, or where the store used to be, where I stood. I could see his mouth moving, but I couldn't hear a word. He ran past me without slowing down and dropped to the ground, hastily pulling boards off a pile and flinging them to a relatively clear space next to him.

That's when I saw what he was digging for; there was an arm protruding from underneath the edge of the pile. I tried to move toward him, to help. *My ears don't work; I can't feel the rain, and now I can't walk either? Jesus. What else could go wrong?*

Another man, dressed in what was probably once an expensive suit and tie, climbed out of the sunroof of a car that had obviously been expensive too. The vehicle was crushed like a tin can, and partially wrapped around a telephone pole. Lucky for him, it was the passenger side that had taken the hit. Except for the blue plastic slide from a child's swing set that was currently lodged in the rear door, the driver's side of the car looked fine if you didn't notice the deployed airbags visible through the windows. Suit man hopped down off of his car unsteadily and loped toward worker man and the wreckage. *Suit man, worker man, and the wreckage. Sounds like the name of a heavy metal or punk rock band.* He didn't seem to notice the trickle of blood tracing a path of its own down the side of his face. He was intent on getting to worker man and helping pull the bricks and debris off the person underneath.

The rain slowed to a little more than a drizzle as the clouds began to disperse. The sky grew lighter as the storm passed. From here it appeared that the clouds were rubberneckers following the tornado, jockeying for position and watching to see what other horrors it was going to deliver. *Wow, my thoughts sure turned macabre. I guess being attacked by a tornado will do that to you. Who knew?*

As suit man continued to unearth the top portion of the woman's body, worker man held his fingers to the wrist for several seconds and then tried to find a pulse in her neck. His eyes suddenly became sad as he shook his head once at suit man. Worker man reached into the purse near her body and pulled out her wallet, opening it and laying it on the ground near her head. They moved on, continuing to clear detritus, moving it to the side, searching for survivors. I could have told them the only other person in the store besides me was the cashier, and he was lying over there in front of what used to be a pickup truck, but even from here I could tell he was dead.

Wait. There were only two of us in the store. If he's over there, and I'm right here, then who is she? Where did she come from, and when did she get here? Was she tossed in with the debris by the tornado? I didn't see anything like that, never saw another person. Was it while I had my head buried in my arm? All of a sudden I felt lightheaded. I sat down on the ground, dropping my head between my knees. *Well, no wonder, with what I've just been through. Why aren't they asking me if I'm okay? It's almost as if they can't see me.*

The lack of hearing, of feeling, of control over my body, it all fell into place with one last click and realization struck as quick as lightning. *They can't see me.* I jerked my head back up, not wanting to know what I now knew to be true, fighting it every step of the way. *That's not another lady; that's me. It can't be! I'm not there, I'm here. I'm NOT dead!! Am I? I'm not... I'm not... I'm not...*

In the blink of an eye, without feeling as if I'd moved at all, I was next to the men, looking down at the unmoving lady. She was me alright. As sure as I squatted here she had my hair in my ponytail holder, and that was my shirt and my watch and those were my eyeglasses broken in half and twisted around what appeared to be a door handle. Without a door, it was hard to tell for sure if that's what it used to be. Somehow my purse strap had stayed on my shoulder—something that never seemed to happen when I wanted it to. I found it very funny considering a tornado had blown a building on top of me, and there was the strap finally staying where I put it—and my wallet was lying next to my hand, open to my driver's license. No doubt that was me.

I can't be dead; I'm not ready. Carrie's coming home for the weekend after her last class tonight, Bill should be home from Iraq any time, and I promised to bake him a cake. Mom can't drive herself to her doctors' appointments. I need to live long enough to pay off my damn house and meet my grandchildren, and they're not even conceived yet. I have so much to do. I don't have time for this. I realized I was trying to pep talk myself out of this situation as I'd done for so many others. *Somehow I don't think it's gonna work this time.*

What am I supposed to do now? I tilted my head back and howled my frustration as loud as I could, with everything I had, until I was empty. Neither of the men turned to look, they continued moving bricks and wood and large clumps of grass, looking for people who weren't in that mess. It wouldn't do any good for me to tell them. They can't hear me. Nobody can hear me anymore. *Wait… if I'm dead, and I'm here, then I was right, there IS life after death. If I'm in my death after life, what the hell am I supposed to do now?*

# # # #

Turn the page to read an excerpt from

THE BOOMERANG EFFECT

PROLOGUE

"It would be so much easier if real life mimicked the movies and ominous music played by itself when bad things were about to happen. It doesn't, though, so if you aren't sure you're going to be ready, practice on your own. See you tomorrow."

With the concert fast approaching, Mr. Baxter, the band teacher, expected everyone to stay for the extra practice sessions held after school. The students grabbed their various belongings and made their way toward the doors, out of the auditorium, and into the parking lot where parents waited or students' cars were parked. The buses were long gone, along with the rest of the students and teachers. The only other person left at this time of the day was the janitor.

Glad practice was finally over, Katy stowed her music in her backpack, disassembled her flute, wiped it down, and put the pieces carefully away in a custom case she'd bought with her allowance. Waiting for Andrea to finish talking with Mr. Baxter, Katy stood up on her chair and looked out the thin row of windows halfway up the wall. "Oh, look, it snowed," she squealed to her best friend. "They keep promising, and it finally did."

She grabbed her book bag, instrument case, coat, gloves and hat, jumped down off the stage where they'd been practicing, and sprinted up the aisle. The low stairs led her past the rows of well worn, red velvet-covered auditorium seats where all of the parents and guests would sit next Saturday night for the concert. Right now all she could think about was getting outside. "Come on, let's go," she hollered over her shoulder.

"Thanks, Mr. Baxter, see you tomorrow." Andrea finished her conversation and scrambled to gather her things. Squinting at the clock on the wall, she could hear it tick, tick, ticking, but couldn't read the time. Pushing her glasses back up her nose, the clock came into focus, and she saw it was only 5:15 p.m. "Wait, Katy, hold up. We're done early. My mom won't be here for a few more minutes."

Andrea took the time to use the stairs instead of jumping off the stage. Katy was out the door before she even got near the aisle. Hurrying, she broke into a lopsided run, slinging her backpack onto one shoulder and bumping the saxophone case into her thigh to avoid crashing it into the rows of seats as she hurried by. Her mom would kill her if she banged this case up. The last one hit the seats one too many times and wouldn't close and latch anymore. Short of breath, she mumbled, "You'd think it was the first time it ever snowed here."

As long as they'd been friends, it was still a wonder to Andrea how Katy could show so much enthusiasm and pure joy over the changing seasons. Summer was fun, with the swimming and bike riding, but winter was definitely Katy's favorite. Snowmen, sledding, and, just as she'd been expecting, a snowball flew at Andrea as she pushed through the door. Ducking, she laughed and called out, "I knew it. You're so predictable."

Scanning the parking lot and the road, she didn't see her mom's white minivan yet. Dropping her book bag on the steps and balancing her saxophone case on top of that, Andrea darted to the bottom and around the side of the stairs where there was undisturbed snow, grabbed a handful and packed it together.

Laughter bubbled out from behind the huge old oak tree on the school's front lawn. Popping out from behind, Katy launched another snowball just as Andrea's snowball burst against her shoulder, causing Katy to squeal with delight.

Even without the electric blue hat and hot pink gloves, Katy was hard to miss. She was a stunning girl, already five foot six, weighed 110 pounds, and only fifteen years old, with ice blue eyes, an explosion of cascading curly red hair, and pixie-like features. That in itself was enough to turn the boys' heads and make the girls jealous, but when she smiled, everyone around her smiled, too.

As far as Andrea was concerned, they made an odd sort of friends. Standing at just five feet tall and weighing in at a solid 150 pounds herself, she thought she looked more like the Pillsbury Dough Boy in her white down jacket and matching gloves. Straight, dull, mousy brown hair fell to her shoulders, and even as often as she pushed her glasses back up on her pug nose, she could never seem to keep them there. Wouldn't have mattered to her if they had stayed put, in her opinion they didn't do anything to enhance her boring hazel eyes or cover up her perpetually pasty white skin.

"I just can't stand the thought of missing out on this snow, Andy. It's so beautiful, I'm going to walk home. I'll call you later; we can do Algebra together," Katy called as she slipped her backpack on and skipped toward the sidewalk. "Tell your mom thanks for the ride offer, but it snowed." With a wave, she broke into a full-out run and struck a surfer pose, skidding across the sidewalk.

"Katy, wait." Looking around, she called, "Come ON, that's her coming around the corner. Katy. You'll never get home before dark, it's over a mile." Katy waved in answer and kept going.

Agitated, Andrea slapped her gloves together, sending pellets of snow flying, huffed, then shoved the hair out of her face with the back of her gloved hands. Stomping back up the steps, she scooped up her stuff. As the van stopped, she ran down to the curb and climbed in, knocking the snow off of her boots before swinging her legs in.

"Hi, Mom."

"Hi, kiddo. Where's Katy? Did her mom come pick her up today?"

"No, she said to tell you thanks, but it snowed. She wanted to walk."

Frowning, Denise Parker looked down the street. "How long has she been gone? Maybe we can catch her, instead of letting her walk. It's over a mile."

"I told her that. She started walking just before you pulled up. If she wants to freeze, let her. I told her to wait, she just waved and left."

The tone had Denise glancing at her daughter. Her furrowed brow, narrowed eyes and clenched jaw all said she was irritated with her friend. "Why don't you call her later, make sure she got home safe."

"She said she'd call me." Andrea buckled her seat belt.

Blinking, Denise pushed her glasses up her nose. "Okay, then. You'll talk to her after dinner. We're having lasagna," she said nonchalantly, watching her daughter out of the corner of her eye, knowing that would bring her back around. It did.

Andrea smiled. "Mmmmm, lasagna. Katy should have stuck around; she could have come over. She's gonna be mad at herself when I tell her. Oh, well, her loss."

Denise laughed. "How was your day?" They pulled away from the curb.

"Mrs. Pinch gave us like twenty Algebra problems and she 'wants to see our work,'" Andrea made quotation marks in the air with her fingers and rolled her eyes. "How else do you get to the answer if you don't do the work?" she mimicked in a nasal voice, an almost perfect imitation. Pushing at her backpack with her foot, she continued. "The rest was okay. Practice was pretty good, I guess. We're almost ready for the concert, if Michael can ever get through his solo."

~~*~*~*

Smoke curled lazily from the end of the cigarette, mingling with the lazy drift of the falling snowflakes. The garbage was piled up behind him, by the dumpster in the middle of the alley, but the stink wasn't as bad today as it would have been in the middle of summer. The icy cold more than made up for the lack of smell with its own form of misery by invading Darnell's dirty, worn out tennis shoes and wrapping around his feet like tentacles. The threadbare, ratty, hand-me-down jeans were a size too big, three inches too long and shredded at the bottom, and being held up by a brown leather belt that had seen better days, while the t-shirt and grey hooded sweatshirt that covered it didn't do much to keep the rest of his body warm, either.

There wasn't much wind, barely a breeze, though if he stood just inside the end of the alley as he was doing now, he was blocked from even that little bit. Not that it mattered. He preferred the cold outdoors to the foster parents' shack. At least here he didn't have to listen to her calling out for someone, anyone, to bring her another bottle or a glass of ice or, occasionally when the whiskey ran low, soda to mix with it, so it lasted longer.

"Who are you waiting for?" He startled at the sound, having forgotten that he wasn't alone. The new kid had been around for a few days, looked at the fosters with the same barely-hidden disgust as he did, and kept to himself. He had potential.

Darnell's eyes slid sideways, pinned the new kid with an empty look, took a long last drag on his cigarette, blew out the smoke, and flicked the butt across the sidewalk and into the street. "Karma. Fate. Whoever."

Jerome had been the "new kid" more times than he could count. Didn't matter, he never stayed in one place long enough to bother learning names either. The first time something, anything, went wrong after he'd been placed in a new foster home, he always got the blame and got yanked out and shipped to the next house. Didn't matter that he wasn't to blame, hadn't done whatever it was, he still ended up being moved. Keeping to himself didn't help, maybe trying to make a friend would.

Turning back, Darnell pointed with his chin toward the school. "There."

Jerome looked and saw a girl exiting the school and another one hiding behind the old tree on the lawn. The second girl popped out, and the snowball fight was on. A pang of regret for what he'd never have sliced through him.

"Which one?" Jerome said, stamping his feet and blowing into his cupped hands, trying to warm up, his clothes an almost identical mirror of Darnell's, except the jeans. He'd gotten them at the last house, and those fosters were kind enough to care that the clothes they bought for all of the kids fit them right. He'd still be there if that little prick, Donnie, hadn't lit his mattress on fire and then ran and hid. They said nothing like that had ever happened in their house before, and Donnie had been there for a year. Nobody believed it wasn't Jerome who lit the fire.

When Darnell didn't answer, he tried again. "She do your homework or something?"

Rolling his shoulders, Darnell's face split into a humorless grin. "Wanna... talk." They watched one girl wave and take off running. "Let's go. We'll catch her at the other end."

They turned and jogged down the alley, around the corner and into the next.

The flakes floated to the ground, muffling sound.

####

ABOUT THE AUTHOR

Lindy Spencer currently lives in Oklahoma with Amazing Husband and Super Smart Dog. She has been killing people legally since 2012, and doesn't see it stopping any time soon. When she's not writing she's probably reading, riding motorcycles, or shooting things with a Canon.

She likes to keep in touch with her fans, and can be found on Facebook. Come by, say hello. She'd love to hear from you.

www.facebook.com/LindySpencer.Author

Made in the USA
San Bernardino, CA
17 January 2014